IN THE ABSENCE OF TRUTH

AN EASTERN SHORE MYSTERY

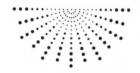

CHERIL THOMAS

D1547767

TRED AVON PRESS

ALSO BY CHERIL THOMAS

In the Absence of Truth
Copyright © 2023
Cheril Thomas
All rights reserved.

This book is a work of fiction. The characters, events, and dialogue are a product of the author's imagination and are not real. Any resemblance to actual events or persons, living or dead, is fictionalized or coincidental.

Thomas, Cheril, In the Absence of Truth, (An Eastern Shore Mystery) 2023.
ISBN: 979-8-9864910-0-4 (Paperback version).
TRED AVON PRESS
Easton, Maryland, USA

Book cover created by MiblArt.

A poem is found in a dead man's pocket.
Is it a promise or a warning?

Don't look back on my life, you won't like what you see.
I've left parting gifts for you and soon I will be free.
When I leave this world, I'll take what you want with me.

Grace Reagan's uncle may be dead, but his plans for revenge are just getting started. Stark Delaney still has one last con to run, and soon the disastrous consequences of his bequests to his family start to unfold. As one mystery unravels, another takes its place and they all come back to Stark's final days. Did he die alone in a run-down apartment, or was he murdered? Is the poem found in his pocket a final insult to his family, or the opening move in his last act of revenge? The search for answers reopens old wounds and the truth Grace finds will change her life.

IN THE ABSENCE OF TRUTH
An Eastern Shore Mystery

CHERIL THOMAS

AN EASTERN SHORE MYSTERY

IN THE ABSENCE OF TRUTH

For my sister,
Clara Seckinger Ellingson

Life can only be understood backwards . . .
Soren Kierkegaard

CHAPTER ONE

"I'm living in an apartment that's smaller than my shoe closet at home. I want my house and I want it now."

Grace Reagan rechecked the calendar app on her phone, but it hadn't changed. There were still three weeks to go before the Fourth of July and a beachfront condo in Ocean City. It would be her first wedding anniversary, too, but she pushed that thought away. Mixing her personal happiness with a divorce case was just asking for trouble.

Reluctantly, she made herself focus on the woman sitting in front of her and said, "You are ridiculous."

Connie Delaney leaned across the desk between them. "Really? How about this–there's also a degenerate in the neighborhood and he's stalking me."

"A stalker. And you're just now mentioning this?"

As she usually did when faced with an unwinnable argument, Connie exploded. "I am your aunt! Don't you dare treat me this way! I'm in danger and it's all your fault. Yours and Niki's. You have to give me my house."

Handling couples going through a breakup could be tricky in the best of times. Although her law firm handled divorce actions, Grace tried to avoid them. Especially the messy ones like *Delaney vs*

Delaney. She said, "You were married to my uncle, and Stark is my client. You have your own representation."

"But the apartment you and Niki stuck me in is a dangerous place! The neighbors are nasty and the stalker—"

Grace, who could do some fine exploding herself when provoked, had heard enough. "I didn't stick you anywhere. I suggested the condo unit to you because it's in a lovely area and it has a short-term lease. Move if you want to. Do whatever you want, but leave me out of it. And don't blame your circumstances on Niki, understand?"

It seemed important to reestablish their boundaries. Connie, Stark and their children, Niki and Winston, were the last members of Grace's mother's family. As far as Grace was concerned, that was three people too many. Her cousin Niki was the only one she willingly claimed.

"Do you think I'd be in here wasting my time if I had any other choice?" Connie whined. "Cyrus said he'd take care of everything and it would be a fair settlement, but he gave our divorce to you to handle! How can he do that? Just throw me off as if I don't matter? He knows how desperate I am. I'm dead broke, and I know Stark has money."

Grace was furious at herself for being in this position. Cyrus Mosley had been the Delaney family's attorney since before any of the current generations had been born, but this action, the severing of Connie's and Stark's marriage, had been too much for him. As his partner, Grace had taken over, but Stark would only deal with Cyrus, which left her doing all the work from the sidelines of an unfolding disaster. Her mother's brother was a bitter and sometimes violent man, and for years he and Connie had been a perfectly meshed toxic duo. Separating them would benefit everyone, but getting to that point was taking its toll.

Connie continued with her litany of complaints. "You and Niki tricked me into giving her my property for your bed-and-breakfast business. You paid a pittance for it, and now you're making a fortune renting my beautiful home to strangers. Well, I won't stand for it. I want my house or I'll, I'll . . ."

"Okay. I hear you," Grace interrupted. "Let's skip the part where I point out that each and everything you've said is a lie. Your daughter bought the house from you at a fair price and you are a poor excuse for a mother." She hoped Connie would make one of her signature dramatic exits, but as usual, the woman wasn't going to be cooperative in any way. "I don't have time for this, so if you leave right now, I'll ask Niki to sign the Queen's Brooke Lane house over to you, no muss, no fuss."

"What?" Connie perked up, all traces of anger gone. "But she said —can you really talk her into it?"

"Of course. She's your *daughter*. And while it's a mystery to me, she still loves you."

Connie looked confused.

"I don't own the house you and Stark sold her, but it's part of Delaney Inns now," Grace continued. "As you know, since you've tried to weasel into the business before, Niki handles all the operations, and I'm an investor, but we both understand which of our properties are profitable and which aren't. The money is all I'm concerned about, something you should understand."

The barb went over Connie's head. "So, you'll give me my house?"

It was like talking to a rock, Grace thought. "Delaney Inns is losing money on the Queen's Brooke Lane rental. I never wanted it in our portfolio in the first place, and I think Niki will agree to sell it back to you."

Connie shifted in her chair and seemed to consider Grace's choice of words. "I suppose I could pay her something, but it wouldn't be much."

Grace shook her head. "Nope. We won't negotiate, but we will be fair. If Niki agrees, I'll start the title transfer when you produce a cashier's check for the full purchase price, plus the cost of improvements we've made."

Having had the prize almost within reach, Connie scrambled to claw it back. "But I'm broke! That's not fair."

"You don't have *any* money?" Grace feigned surprise. "How are you going to pay my bill for today's consultation?"

"Pay you? Don't be ridiculous. We're just talking! And we're family. Besides, Cyrus never charges us for legal services, so you can't, either."

"My partner doesn't charge the Delaney *children* for the significant amount of work he does on their behalf. But Stark wasn't the one who initiated your divorce. You were. Plus, I bill my services separately and you are not a pro bono client of mine."

Connie leapt to her feet. She had always relied on Cyrus Mosley to bail her out of trouble—financial, legal, and every other dip and bump in the rocky road of her life with Stark. That she would lose that security when her marriage ended had clearly never occurred to her. "Cy won't let you do that to me," she insisted.

But Grace knew he already had. "He considers Stark to be family. Stark and Niki. But why don't you run downstairs and ask him if he'll help you cheat your daughter out of the property she paid for."

As persistent as Connie was, she wouldn't get past Marjorie Battsley—a formidable woman who'd been Mosley's secretary/gatekeeper for decades. If Cyrus had shut Connie out, Marjorie would see that she stayed on the far side of his door.

"This isn't over," she insisted as she left.

Grace gave herself a moment to breathe, then clicked the computer monitor on and studied the document on the screen. *In the Matter of Delaney vs. Delaney: Final Decree of Divorce.*

She doubted the legal aid attorney Connie had used would have had time to forward the documents to her. The notice had come in only a few moments before her aunt—ex-aunt—had burst into her office. Despite every rotten thing Stark and his wife had done, Grace felt sad as she read the decree. Forty years of marriage had ended and only bitterness remained in its wake.

Cyrus Mosley rarely climbed the steps to Grace's second floor office suite. The firm's paralegal, Lily Travers, and their part-time investigator and IT wizard, Aidan Banks, were discussing a new software program when the elderly attorney's image appeared on the security camera. Lily alerted Grace, who came out to meet him.

One look at her partner's face told her there was trouble. "Are you okay?" she asked, reaching for his elbow.

"No, m'dear. No, I am not." He batted her hand away, then just as quickly grasped it again. Lily joined them, exchanging worried glances with Grace as they guided Mosley to a chair.

"What's wrong, Cy?" Grace asked gently as she knelt beside him. "We'll get help—"

There was a gleam of perspiration on his bald head and his eyes were moist, but his voice was calm as he said, "I don't need medical help, but I have some bad news. Very bad."

She froze. *Who? What?* Rising panic took her breath away. There were only a handful of people who would rate this reaction from him. "Oh, Cy," she asked, her voice cracking. "Is it Avril?" Her best friend was only a few years younger than Mosley, but Grace considered them both to be immortal and she wasn't ready to be proven wrong.

"No, no." He eased his hand out of hers, pulled a pristine handkerchief from his jacket pocket, and patted his face and head. "It's your uncle."

Grace sighed and rubbed his shoulder. She'd been able to shut Connie out, but whatever her now ex-husband had done would have to be handled.

Mosley reached up and clasped her hand. "Stark died last night and while the circumstances aren't clear, they are suspicious. He may have been murdered."

CHAPTER TWO

G race tried to absorb the news and missed most of what Mosley said next. Lily took over, murmuring instructions to Aiden while she fetched water for the attorneys. "Please drink this," she said gently to Mosley as she handed him a glass. "We'll work everything out."

Grace watched them with a sense of detachment. She'd need more than water to regain her equilibrium. Stark had been a hard, unlikable person, but his death was still a blow. He had often hinted that he knew the identity of her father, but now whatever he'd known—if anything —was gone.

Mosley's next words pulled her back to the present. "There is no easy way to break this to Niki and Connie," he said to Grace. "But you'll think of something before we talk to them, which we have to do right away. Two detectives are on their way to interview them."

She pushed her own conflicting emotions aside and refocused, asking, "Who told you?"

This time she was the one who drew the concerned looks. Apparently, Mosley had already said he'd been contacted by the Ocean City Police Department. "Stark died at home sometime last night," he repeated. Then added, "He has an apartment there, remember?"

She could see she'd worried him and made herself smile reassuringly.

He studied her another moment, then said, "There are signs someone was with him in the apartment, but the details I received are vague. It could be an accidental death, but the local ME is conducting an autopsy, and until there are results, the police will proceed as if the circumstances are suspicious."

That was a logical decision, Grace thought. It was easy to believe someone killed her hot-tempered uncle. He'd relocated to Ocean City six months ago and likely had come to the attention of the local authorities more than once in that time. She thought for a moment, then asked, "Why did the police call you?" Her thoughts were turning to the practical side of Mosley's news and things weren't adding up. "What haven't you told me?"

Since he rarely told her all he knew about anything, an accurate answer would have taken a long time. The look he gave her said as much. "When Stark decided to settle there, I made some calls. A friend of mine on the OCPD agreed to contact me if there was trouble."

When, Grace thought. Not *if,* but *when* there was trouble, Cyrus Mosley would be by Stark's side. And Stark would never wander too far from his only source of income, a trust fund set up by previous generations of Delaneys and administered by the man who'd looked out for him his whole life. She asked, "How many times did this friend have to call you before today?"

She wasn't careful with her tone, and Mosley frowned. "Try to have some compassion, at least for today, Grace. Things are hard enough as it is." He softened his words with a shrug and a what-can-you-do gesture. "A bar fight here, unpaid bills there. The usual. Nothing in the past couple of months, though. In fact, he had a job and seemed to be doing well. A coworker found him when she came to see why he wasn't at work this morning."

Job and *work* weren't words normally associated with her uncle, but Grace kept that thought to herself.

Lily interrupted with the news that Niki had called. "She said you and Mr. Mosley should come to Delaney House as soon as you can. Her mother is there and there's a problem."

"Tell her we're on our way," Grace said. "Did she give you any details?"

"No, but she was crying, and I heard Connie in the background. She sounds upset."

"You may not have to tell them after all, m'dear," Mosley said as he waited for Grace to grab her tote bag and keys. "But we're still going to have our hands full."

And, as usual, he was right.

Mac, of course, already knew.

One of the many benefits of her marriage to Lee "Mac" McNamara, Mallard Bay's chief of police, was access to the latest breaking news. He caught up with Grace and Mosley as they left the office and walked with them to the parking lot.

"Are you all right?" he asked as he hugged her, but she knew the question included Mosley. Losing Stark, as loathsome as he was, would be hard on Mosley, who'd helped raise Grace's mother and her uncle.

"We're about to break the news to Niki and Connie," Grace said. "Are you coming with us?"

There was an uncomfortable hesitation before he answered, and her heart sank as she saw a look pass between the two men.

"We'll handle things at Delaney House," Mosley said. "Perhaps Mac can monitor developments in Ocean City?"

Mac agreed, and after giving Grace another hug, headed back to the police station.

When he was out of earshot, she said, "When were you going to tell me?"

Mosley sighed. "As soon as we were alone. M'dear, this will be tricky. My friend at OCPD implied that Connie, as Stark's spouse, is their first person of interest. And we must assume that Niki will be a close second. We don't have long to get them ready to face their interview. Meanwhile, I don't want Marjorie working herself into a tizzy, and I don't want to ask Lily to keep information from her co-workers if it can be avoided."

Grace nodded. She would have done the same thing if their situations had been reversed. No wonder he didn't want Mac with them. Home was home, and work was work, and at work, Mac was not always their ally.

They took separate cars, and when she arrived at Delaney House, she entered through the kitchen, hoping to find Niki in the private area of the inn. She wanted a quiet conversation with her cousin to warn her about what was coming. Her mind was so fixed on how to handle the uncomfortable situation that it took her a second to comprehend what she saw as she stepped through the doorway.

Just as distracted by what they were doing, Niki and the handsome man she was kissing didn't notice Grace's entrance until she shut the door behind her with a loud click. After that, they wore identical shocked expressions for the moments it took Niki to find her voice and manage a squeaky "hello."

Grace, still in the doorway, said, "Sorry. I thought Lily told you that Cy and I were coming."

"I didn't think you'd get here so soon. Or that you'd come through the kitchen door."

It's my property, was Grace's first thought, but her irritation faded as she took in her cousin's tear-streaked face. "I came as soon as I could," she said. Then, because the mystery man looked so uncomfortable, she offered him her hand. "Grace Reagan. I'm Niki's cousin."

"Dylan Kirwan," he said, taking her hand. "I'm Niki's—"

"Dylan's the long-term guest I told you about," Niki said, cutting him off. "The one who's taken the garden room for two months."

Grace wanted to know more about the very handsome Mr. Kirwan, but tears were running freely down Niki's face and she struggled with her next words.

"Mom's upstairs lying down. The police in Ocean City called her. They dropped the bombshell on her like it was a weather report. She went crazy, of course. If Dylan hadn't been here to help me with her, I'd still be trying to shut her up."

"Let me get you something to drink and we'll sit down." Grace said, sneaking a look at the kitchen clock. Where was Cyrus? He was supposed to be here by now. She'd accepted responsibility for handling the bad news of Stark's death, but they had to present a united front when they discussed the statements all of them would have to give the police.

"I can handle drinks," Dylan said. "Tea for everyone, or something stronger?"

Niki said, "Tea, hell! I think a Bombay Sapphire on the rocks. In fact, make it Bombay all around, we're going to need it when Mom comes downstairs."

"Water for me, please," Grace said to Dylan as she followed Niki to the kitchen table. The last thing they needed was the police to find them all buzzed and crying. She couldn't imagine how Mosley had managed to represent the family for all these years, but at least he wasn't related to them. Grace, however, was breaking the most basic of common-sense rules for the legal profession. She didn't need to add alcohol to her list of handicaps this morning.

From the front hall Mosley called, "Hello?"

Grace rose so fast, she nearly tripped over the chair she'd been sitting on. "I'll get him," she said, hurrying toward the doorway to the long hallway. She and her partner needed to get a few things straight.

CHAPTER THREE

M osley had indeed arrived, and he wasn't alone. He and Mac stood in the front hall, heads together, talking quietly. They broke apart as Grace approached, but not before she heard Mosley say, "As long as we understand each other. We are representing both of them, so no questioning."

Grace stopped, surprised. That they would be Niki's attorneys was a given, but they'd been united in their decision to sever ties with Connie.

"What's up?" she interrupted, not hiding her irritation.

Mac said, "OCPD asked me to make sure Connie will be available when they arrive. I've assured Cy that I won't get in your way, but I will need to keep eyes on her."

Despite her dislike for her former aunt, Grace felt uneasy. "Eyes on her" had an entirely different meaning than "Keep an eye on her." Mac had been asked to watch Stark's ex-wife until he turned her over to the Ocean City officers. The woman had a long history of lying to, and running from, the authorities.

"What the hell is going on?"

As if summoned by their thoughts, Connie appeared on the second-floor landing of the wide cantilevered staircase. Even in such strained circumstances, she didn't miss an opportunity to glide down the steps like a 1930s movie star.

"Mother!" Niki protested as she hurried around the group in the hall and up the steps. "That was a strong sedative you took. Let me help you down."

Never one to miss a cue, Connie channeled her inner Norma Desmond and flung herself over her shorter, slimmer daughter. Mac did a quick trot up to get both women down safely, while Mosley wrung his hands and Grace tried, unsuccessfully, to refrain from rolling her eyes.

Under his breath Mosley muttered, "Foolish girl." He glanced at Grace, then at the clock, his meaning clear. If he'd committed them to representing Connie, down the road, they might need to testify that she was impaired when she was questioned by the OCPD.

"I won't do it, Cy," Grace said, stepping closer to him to make sure he heard her.

"Just for now, m'dear," he said, nodding toward Connie and her entourage. "Please."

"No," she insisted, but he was already moving away.

Anyone who knew Connie could have predicted how the next half hour would go. When she was told she would be questioned in Stark's death, her tears, wails, and non-stop questions made conversation impossible.

In the middle of the uproar, Grace noticed Dylan Kirwan had disappeared. *Smart as well as gorgeous*, she thought.

With Mac monitoring them from the hall, Mosley, Grace, and their clients met in the dining room. Mac had a clear view of the only exit route, so unless her daughter and the lawyers all conspired to shove Connie out of the paint-sealed windows, the chief of police effectively had "eyes on" her.

Which turned out to be unnecessary. Once Connie started yelling, even the neighbors across the street knew exactly where she was.

"I *am* still married to that lying jackass! I haven't signed any papers, and I fired my incompetent lawyer. I'm a widow, dammit! Not a divorcee and certainly not a murder suspect. Now get your judgmental brains together and get me out of this mess."

"Oh, let me, Cy," Grace said sweetly, then stopped when Niki gave her a warning look.

Mosley needed no further encouragement. "As you wish, m'dear. Niki and I will have a word in the front parlor."

When they were alone, Connie said, "I suppose you're going to tell me not to say anything until you can get rid of the cops, right? Do you want me to do anything while they're here?"

"What I want is for you to listen to me," Grace said. "You're Niki's mother, and I'm giving you my best advice, but I'm not your attorney."

"Oh, God." Connie paled and tears pooled in her large brown eyes.

"Your divorce is final. It has been for two days. I received the papers this morning and I know your signature. I'm recommending that you tell the police you need an attorney and won't talk without one."

"Is he really dead, Gracie?" Her words came out as a whisper.

Despite everything she knew about the troubled marriage, Grace's heart broke a little. "I'm so sorry. I know you loved him."

"No." The almost-widow straightened her shoulders and carefully patted her tears away without disturbing her mascara. "Stark killed any affection I had for him years ago. But he was still a big part of my life. The past six months without him should have been wonderful, but they weren't. I don't miss him, but I don't know how to live without him, either."

Three firm knocks on the front door announced the OCPD officers.

Connie grabbed Grace's arm. "You're my attorney. I told you, I fired the other guy, and Cy has Niki, so who am I going to call? I can't handle this on my own."

And that was how, despite her best intentions, Grace once again ended up with Connie for a client. And things went straight downhill from there.

Introductions were made, and OCPD Detective Sergeants Xavier and Greenley greeted Mac warmly. Grace wished she could take that as a positive sign, but she knew little of that camaraderie would extend to her. In their eyes, she would rate only a slightly warmer professional politeness than a suspect. Even that small courtesy evaporated when she asked for five minutes to speak with her partner before allowing the officers to meet Connie and Niki. Mac's assurance that he would stay in the dining room with Connie won the detective's cooperation, but they weren't pleased.

"I need to know exactly what you've promised Connie," Grace hissed when the kitchen door shut behind them. "You can't have forgotten what happened the last time I defended her? I nearly died. And before *that*, she shot me!"

Mosley frowned. "Your behavior isn't becoming, m'dear. Those incidents were years ago. And, if you recall, she didn't shoot you, exactly. She was defending you and Winnie, and one of her shots ricocheted. You said so yourself."

Grace tried to slow her breathing and remember how fond she was of the manipulative old coot. "I can't represent her, Cy. I'm not going through another investigation with us having to split ourselves between murder suspects."

It had happened the year before, with their new firm's first clients. The "Chinese Wall" method of maintaining separate defenses was not only stressful, in this case it would be emotionally impossible. There was no way either of them would sacrifice Niki's welfare for Connie's defense.

"No one is calling it a murder, and you shouldn't either," Mosley said. "It's a suspicious death, and at this time, we don't know why. But let's not get ahead of ourselves. Niki has an iron-clad alibi—she was with Mr. Kirwan, and Connie's is decent, if it pans out."

"How decent?" Grace asked, knowing she'd lost the battle, and probably the war as well.

"She was in Ocean City last night, and she went to see him," Mosley shook his head as he said the words. "But she says he threw her out and neighbors saw her leave and heard him yelling at her. We can't be sure she's in the clear until his time of death is established, but she insists she drove straight home, and a neighbor there saw her dragging her trash can out to the curb around one a.m. They had words about the noise she made."

Grace remembered Connie's "nasty" neighbors. They'd probably be only too happy to testify about her rudeness. "So, if she left Stark no earlier than eleven, and he died after that, then she has an alibi. A weak one, but still."

Mosley said, "Let's get them through this interview and we'll find someone else to take Connie if the police still consider her a suspect."

There was that *if* again, Grace thought.

It felt like Mosley was jinxing them every time he said it.

CHAPTER FOUR

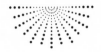

When they were all assembled around the dining room table, the first words Detective Sergeant Greenley said were, "You have our condolences for the loss of your ex-husband, Ms. Delaney." Niki got a nod from the hard-faced detective, but his eyes stayed on her mother.

"I may be his ex-wife, but I didn't understand that until about fifteen minutes ago," Connie snapped.

Grace wondered why she resented being referred to as a divorcee when any sane woman who'd been married to Stark would be celebrating. At least her stubborn client was relatively quiet, even if she was glaring at the police.

"Your lawyer didn't inform you that your divorce was final?" Detective Sergeant Xavier posed the question to Connie, but was looking at Grace with a quizzical expression.

"Her?" Connie snorted. "*She* refused to represent me in the divorce. Her own aunt kicked to the curb. Do you see what I'm dealing with? It's so unfair. Stark was a drunk—"

"Connie!" Grace said sharply, silencing her aunt. "Stop talking." It was a struggle not to say, "shut up."

Tears were always Connie's first line of defense, and her eyes flooded again. "I'm *sorry*. You said to only answer what I'm asked and to tell the truth. But I can't!"

"This is over." Grace stood and pulled Connie up beside her. "My client is obviously distraught with grief over the death of the man she believed was legally her husband. I can't allow this conversation to continue until she's calmer. You have my word that I'll make her available as soon as possible."

Detective Sergeant Greenley reached into his coat pocket, but his partner stood and stepped away from the table. With a withering look at Grace, Greenley joined Xavier on the far said of the room for a hushed, but apparently heated, discussion.

"I don't understand—" Connie started.

Grace tightened her grip. "One more word, and you're on your own."

Connie did as ordered but resorted to whimpering.

"Stop it," Grace hissed.

The Ocean City officers broke apart and returned to the miserable little group at the dining room table.

"I suppose you want to postpone your client's interview as well?" Xavier said to Mosley.

"Yes, please. Mother and daughter are both in a state of shock at the loss of Mr. Delaney. I believe we can provide you with answers to all of your questions without additional trauma to this family if we could have, perhaps twenty-four hours?"

"We'll be back here in ninety minutes," Greenley snapped.

Xavier's previous cordial behavior disappeared. She didn't bother to lower her voice when she turned to Mac and said, "You'll continue surveillance, Chief? We'll leave an officer outside in case you need assistance."

Mac followed the officers out, shutting the door to the dining room behind him.

"I think that went well," Connie said with a laugh. She gave a shocked Niki a hug and said, "There, baby. No worries. They're sure it was me, and I have an airtight alibi. By the time I'm through with them, they'll leave us both alone."

"Mom, what is wrong with you?" Niki said, then turned to Grace and Mosley. "Am I missing something?"

Connie gave an exaggerated sigh. "Baby, your father was murdered and the police think one of us did it. Didn't your attorneys tell you that?"

Niki whirled toward Grace and Mosley. "Is that true?"

"It hasn't been determined yet," Mosley said. "But I'd like to know why you seem so sure of it, Connie."

"W-What do you mean? Isn't that why you thought we needed representation?" Connie's face flushed. "Stark's dead, probably killed by some lowlife he got entangled with, but will the police look in that direction? No! It's too easy to decide the family is guilty."

"Dad isn't associating with lowlifes," Niki protested. "He's gotten himself together, he's sober, and has a job. He even has friends." She stopped, eyes tearing up. "*Had*. He had friends, and a nice apartment, too, which you'd know if you hadn't run out on him."

"How can you say that to me? Your father's a liar and he's always been one. You know what he did to me. He hurt me—"

"Okay, okay," Niki said, losing her steam. "It's just that things are different now. This is," her voice quavered. "This *was* the first time . . . he was trying to be a normal person. He wanted to have a real relationship, a good one."

Connie wasn't buying it. "Not with me. But you were always his favorite."

Grace steeled herself. Niki had never come first with either of her parents, but although she was capable of making a scene to rival her dramatic mother's, she said nothing to this last jab.

"You know I'm right," Connie said. "Well, little girl, I'm not making it easy for the police. Neither one of us is going to be accused of ridding the planet of that man. My alibi is better than yours, of course. I have witnesses who saw me leave your father alive and others who saw me later here in Mallard Bay. If you really were with Dylan, that's good, but he's hardly impartial. Still, you have Grace and Cy, so you'll be fine."

Grace's mind raced. This behavior was too callous, even for

Connie. Unless . . . "I'm not representing you," she said, abruptly. "You'd better call in some favors and find yourself another attorney, and you don't have long to do it."

"You *can't*," Connie's voice rose an octave and ended in a wail. "You can't abandon me!"

"Yes, she can," Mosley said as he took Niki's arm. "M'dear, please come with me. We need to talk."

"What about Mom—" Niki looked over her shoulder, but Mosley kept her moving.

As he hustled her out of the dining room, he said, "Grace will handle things here and I'll explain it all as soon as we're alone."

"What are you doing to me?" Connie yelled after him.

"You did it, didn't you?" Grace said.

Connie didn't answer, but her face hardened. No longer trash-talking and hyperactive, she sat down and let the silence stretch. Finally, she said one word. "No."

Grace wasn't impressed. "You won't take my advice, and your behavior is even more bizarre than usual. Stark's death is suspicious, yes, but you seem sure he was murdered. I won't represent you, and no amount of hysterical bullying is going to change my mind."

"I can't afford a lawyer and you know it. You and Niki have all of my money. Do you really want to back me into this corner? I won't go quietly, I promise you, and you and my loving daughter will be sorry."

Grace had seen her this angry before and that time, there had been a gun in her hand. There was nothing to be gained in arguing now, so instead, she said, "Do you have a phone?"

"Yes. Do you know someone, someone good, who'll represent me? Cy can pay the bill."

Grace hesitated, uncomfortable with what she was about to do and unable to think of another solution to the problems Connie seemed determined to cause. After a second, she picked up her phone and hit the "Recording" icon. She placed it on the table between them and, speaking louder than before, she said, "I'm recording this, Connie. Our firm will not find a lawyer for you, or pay your legal fees. Furthermore, don't threaten me again. I've told you, I'm not your attorney and you shouldn't be talking to me."

There, she thought with satisfaction, let Connie try to prove a breach of confidentiality after that. And in case suing Grace and Mosley for malpractice hadn't been what Connie had in mind, she added, "You were paid fair market value for the property you and Stark sold to Niki. She owns it outright and Delaney Inns leases it from her. Threatening to sue any of us if I don't represent you in the investigation into Stark's death won't do you any good."

"You sanctimonious witch," Connie hissed. "You, of all people, understand what a lying, thieving scumbag Stark was. He stole from his own mother, for God's sake! He took everything I had."

"Connie, stop! Don't say anything else to me, I'm recording—"

"You think I care who hears me?" Connie marched to the door and yanked it open. Yelling into the hallway, she said, "*Everything*. Stark took the money Niki paid for the house and the sale of our cars. He even sold my jewelry! He ruined my beautiful son, turned my daughter against me, then dumped me. You got that on tape, Grace? Your uncle threw me out of that hovel he was renting. He was in a drunken rage and he hurt me. Now the rest of you are abandoning me." She stopped, gasping for air. When she spoke again, her words were cold and clipped. "If I *killed* him, we wouldn't be even."

Mac appeared in the doorway. "Cy and Niki have gone back to your office, Grace. You have another fifteen minutes before Greenley and Xavier return."

"We won't need it," Connie said. "She's not my lawyer." Then, apparently forgetting she couldn't leave, she tried to walk around Mac.

It got ugly after that.

CHAPTER FIVE

As she often did, Grace paused at the bend in the gravel road leading to her home and admired the cottage Mac had remodeled for her. Its front was unchanged, with its peaked roofline and wide porch. Had the first owner, a waterman five generations back in the McNamara line, walked down the drive today, the house would look much the same as it had two hundred years before—until he rounded the corner. A new wing and sunroom with expansive views of the Little Wye River nearly doubled the original footprint.

Left to his own devices, Mac wouldn't have altered his family home, but the redesign had given them a house that fit their family. A family that included a toddler and an infant, and a nanny who was no doubt ready to end her work day. Suddenly desperate to hold her babies, Grace hurried the rest of the way.

Fiona saw her first and squealed with delight, holding up sticky little hands for a lift. Their nanny, Hallie, was feeding baby Sonny, who gave his mother a serious look over the top of his bottle.

"Don't worry, Little Man," Grace laughed as she bent to kiss his wispy dark curls. "I won't interrupt your dinner." Already in twelve-month clothes, her six-month-old son was a perpetually hungry baby with his father's wide brown eyes and placid personality. Mac said

Sonny only resembled Grace when his food was late. She couldn't even pretend to be insulted because it was true.

She listened to the details of their day and, as usual, was torn between regret that she hadn't been with her children, and wonder at how easily Hallie handled Fiona and Sonny. The young nanny had even managed to semi-train their wild canine child, Rocky, who Hallie designated as the day's top troublemaker.

"Don't feed her tonight," Hallie said, as she burped Sonny while balancing on one foot in order to nudge a chew bone toward the Springer spaniel. "She's doing well with *sit* and *stay* but *don't eat Fiona's lunch* is a work in progress."

Grace nodded, but they both knew Rocky would get dinner, and dessert, and whatever treats Fiona could sneak to her. The incorrigible little spaniel and her human twin were inseparable. Rocky even slept at the foot of Fiona's new 'big girl' toddler bed, no doubt dreaming of stray cookies falling out of a pajama pocket.

"So how was your day?" Hallie asked, reminding Grace of the ugly reality she'd left behind her in town.

Before she could answer, the front door opened and an anxious voice called her name. "Well, this saves some time," Grace said as Avril Oxley walked in carrying two canvas bags.

"I thought you'd have other things to deal with tonight, so I brought dinner." Avril's expression said she'd heard about Stark. Dropping the bags on the kitchen table, she went right to Fiona for a cuddle and seemed to lose some of her anxiousness in the child's hug.

Grace had been expecting her best friend and her children's de facto grandmother, and was relieved that she didn't have to tell her about Stark. Avril had known him all his life.

"Liam?" she asked as she relinquished Fiona to Rocky's attentions and reached for the baby.

Hallie handed Sonny over and smiled at Grace. Avril had always called Mac by his first name, Lee, and she was following suit with his son.

Mac had broken his family's tradition of naming the first-born boys Lee Dawson. He'd gone on to outrage Avril by calling baby Liam

"Sonny" after former Washington quarterback Sonny Jurgensen. From the moment the sonogram had confirmed they were having a boy, he'd named the child and Grace had to pull the I'm-the-one-with-labor-pains card to get Dawson as a middle name. He'd eventually given in and she'd agreed to his choice of nicknames.

"Is Lee here?" Avril asked as she rocked the baby.

"No. He's tied up at the station." Then, because she didn't have the heart to dance around the day's events, Grace said, "Let's all go out to the river room. You can tell us what you've heard and I'll fill in the blanks." It was their usual routine. Avril knew everyone and everything that happened in Mallard Bay, and Grace regularly made use of her talent for acquiring information.

While Avril had accurately relayed the broad details of Stark's death and the suspicious circumstances surrounding it, Grace settled Fiona in a playpen with her toys. "Well, the Mallard Bay grapevine is still operating smoothly. That saved us some time." She sat beside Avril and hugged her. "I'm sorry. I know it hurts."

"I wanted you to say I was wrong. I really wanted to hear . . ." Avril's narrow shoulders sagged as her words trailed off.

"What?" Grace asked gently.

"Anything other than he died like that, all alone. Poor Stark. Sometimes I think that boy never stood a chance. He was a sweet little child. I don't believe I've ever told you that."

Grace was sure she'd never heard *sweet* and *Stark* in the same sentence, but said nothing.

Hallie stood, took the baby from Avril, and kissed her cheek. "As soon as this little guy is asleep, I'll head home and take care of the dogs."

"I left your dinner in the fridge," Avril called after her. Not only had she assumed the role of Fiona and Liam's grandmother, for all intents and purposes, she'd also adopted Hallie, who was nineteen and already had an enormous biological family.

Grace called it The Six Degrees of Avril Oxley. Everyone she'd met on the Eastern Shore was connected in one way or another through the tiny, octogenarian dynamo.

Tonight, though, her friend looked smaller and dangerously close to fragile. "I can't wrap my mind around it," Avril said. "Stark has been killing himself by inches for most of his adult life, but he always pulled himself back from the brink. He may have been careless with other people, but he had a strong self-preservation streak and he was doing well for a change."

This was the second time Stark's supposed turnaround had been mentioned. Curious, Grace said, "Had you talked to him lately, or are you quoting Niki?"

"I don't think it was wishful thinking on her part. She'd almost severed ties with him after that business with Winnie."

"Hard to blame her," Grace said, then let the subject drop. It had been nearly three years, but she still felt queasy at the memories of Niki's brother. Besides, Niki's choices were just that—Niki's. "NMP, NMP," she chanted to herself. For a long time, she'd used "Do I Care?" as a calming mantra, but all too often her answer was yes. And chanting the acronym was problematic, too.

"Not My Problem," almost always worked and NMP was easier on the ears.

Unfortunately, there were many ways that Winnie Delaney *was* her problem, so she dropped the whole exercise. Some people were going to cause stress no matter what she did.

Winston Delaney—Winnie—was spoiled, pampered, and amoral. By the time he'd been arrested for drug trafficking and conspiracy to commit murder, the once wealthy and influential Delaney dynasty had been bled dry. Stark, believing he was helping his son, had set him up time and again with cash for schools he didn't attend and business ventures that had never existed. The money he hadn't given Winnie had disappeared into Stark's own addictive vice. A self-proclaimed professional gambler, he had made millions and lost even more.

After a moment, Avril said, "Who's going to tell him?"

Grace didn't ask who she meant. Her own thoughts had been going in the same direction. Winnie was up for parole and according to Mac, he might be released. Grace had petitions for restraining orders ready for herself, her children, and Niki, but the precaution didn't make her feel any better.

The Maryland Parole Commission had its policies, but Grace knew things they couldn't consider. Winnie hated her. He'd tried to kill her once and even if the charges had been dropped in a plea bargain, she would always be a target for him.

Pushing the past out of her mind, she gave her new mantra another shot. "Winnie's not our problem tonight, Granny. Fiona needs her dinner and then a bath and bed. It's time to work your magic."

She got a smile out of Avril, but the peaceful interlude didn't last long.

CHAPTER SIX

When he'd gotten the first call from Bernadette Xavier, Mac had known the Ocean City Police detective was going to ruin his day. And from her first mention of Stark's name, she had. Handling bad news and questioning grieving family members was par for the course in his profession, but he'd been asked to maintain surveillance on his wife and her clients. The only bright spot in his day was when he learned Grace was no longer representing Connie.

He still couldn't believe he'd put his hands on Stark's widow.

The struggle had been brief and ended with Connie sitting on the sofa in the front parlor, trying frantically to reach her divorce attorney. Mac had watched from a few feet away, handcuffs out, feeling like a bully. The look of betrayal on her face poked his conscience. He knew she was no stranger to being physically restrained by a man she'd trusted, but he had no choice. Her performance when the police arrived reinforced that.

When the Ocean City detectives returned, Xavier looked at him sympathetically, while Greenley snickered. Then Connie lit into all three of them and Mac was sorry he hadn't handcuffed *and* gagged her.

Eventually he'd been able to restore peace and Connie answered their questions, waiving her right to counsel, which turned out to be of little consequence because all she talked about was how unfair everyone had been to her. The officers finally got her full attention when Bernadette Xavier said that Stark had been in some kind of physical altercation prior to his death, but may not have died right away. Connie had raced to the bathroom, and Mac had followed her far enough to hear her retching. When she returned to the parlor, she was pale and jittery, her bravado gone.

According to her statement, she'd left Stark alive and ranting in Ocean City at ten o'clock the night before. She'd been seen at a Sunoco service station on Route 13 near Berlin at ten thirty and again at Royal Farms in Easton at eleven-fifteen. Once she was back home in Mallard Bay, she'd angered a neighbor with the trashcan noise at one a.m.

It wasn't a tight timeline, but the eighty-nine miles between Stark's apartment and Connie's rental condo in Mallard Bay made her an unlikely suspect—for now. It would all come down to a final determination from the medical examiner. The critical issues for Connie's defense would be the time and manner of Stark's death, and if he had died during the altercation, or after it.

Mac had followed procedure in everything he'd done that day and yet he felt like a slacker. He'd even been relieved when a three-car pileup on the outskirts of town kept him working late. He didn't know what he'd find when he got home, but he was sure it would be awkward. By ten o'clock, though, things were quiet, and he'd run out of excuses.

Grace had fallen asleep while waiting for him.

He stood at the foot of their bed and watched her for a few, peaceful moments, but he was weary. It was either lie down or fall over. She startled awake when he tried to ease her book out of her hands.

"What?" she mumbled as she turned on the bedside light and pushed herself up against the headboard. "What's happened now?"

He sank down beside her and pulled her close. "Nothing more, honey, except insanity. Promise me you're no blood relation to Connie. Stark was bad enough, but that woman—"

"Hey!" she protested. "I'm sure the McNamara family has a few unsavory characters, too."

"Many. We're a colorful bunch, but to my knowledge, none of us has ever tried to break *into* a prison to tell an incarcerated criminal offspring that his lying, cheating, low-life father was dead."

After a moment of stunned silence, she fell over, laughing with more than a touch of hysteria.

"That's not even my best line," Mac said, warming to his knee-jerk defensive reaction. "At least it wasn't up to me to wrangle her when she got up to Jessup Correctional and tried to get in to see Winnie."

"Don't be coy. What happened?"

"Well, she didn't get arrested, more's the pity, but I had to vouch for her being his mother and identify a photo of her. I also had to verify that Winnie's father had died suddenly." He sighed. "It really isn't a very funny story, after all."

"Did you eat?"

He shrugged. "I had some Cheerios."

"Oh no!" She scooted to his side of the bed and whispered, "I could make popcorn for dessert."

"Pass."

"Or," she kissed his ear. "I could warm up the garlic chicken Avril made. And mashed potatoes and gravy, and I'm pretty sure some chocolate pound cake is left."

"There it is," he said with a sigh. "This is why I married you, my miracle girl." He aimed a kiss in her general direction before grabbing his robe. "Race you to the kitchen."

As he ate, Grace peppered him with questions and by the time he started on the pound cake, she had the gist of what had happened to him after she'd left Delaney House.

"I can't believe that the first thing Connie did when the police finished with her was race over the bridge to Jessup to see Winnie." She sipped her mint tea, hoping it would kill her cake craving.

In an abundance of caution, Mac pulled his plate a little closer and said, "Never underestimate the power of a mother's love."

"Oh, that's not why she did it," Grace scoffed. "We're talking about *Connie*."

"Yeah, well, she insisted she had to tell Winnie the bad news herself. I had no reason to stop her, so I kept tabs on her through a buddy who's on staff at Jessup. He said once they were in the visitation room, they went at each other verbally. Connie didn't give Winnie time to absorb the news before she was demanding to know where Stark had hidden his money. Winnie said she was crazy and he wasn't telling her anything. The correctional officers eventually had to break it up."

Grace frowned. "What was she talking about? What money? Stark was broke."

"Not according to the report that will be sent to the OCPD. Stark's wife and son believe he left a substantial estate for someone to inherit."

"Have you heard from Connie?" Grace asked Niki over coffee the next morning. She was trying to get enough caffeine down to be reasonably coherent. Both children were teething and had taken turns waking each other for most of the night. Somewhere near dawn, Mac had asked if it would be very wrong if he moved out to the garden shed to sleep. She'd assured him it would be the last thing he ever did.

Hallie had received an especially warm welcome when she arrived at eight, and Grace told herself she was still a good mother even as she race-walked out of the house to meet Niki at the office.

It was early by Mosley's standards and he hadn't arrived yet, but Niki had wanted to talk before they were thrown back into yesterday's turmoil. The Ocean City detectives were returning for round two, but this one would take place in the downstairs conference room. There would be no superficial attempt at cordiality by the police after Connie's antics from the day before.

"No. I blocked her calls last night," Niki said. "After her behavior yesterday, I'm not sure I can deal with her. Not for a while, anyway. Dad was horrible, but he was my *father*." She waved her hands as if to shoo away Grace's sympathy. "I'm not grieving, at least, it doesn't feel like it. In fact, I wish I could feel more for him. But the things he did . . . I wish it had all been different." Her voice trailed off, then she seemed to gather herself and cleared her throat. "Dad broke my heart over and over. Winnie's, too. But Win has a streak of whatever poisoned Dad, and he seems to enjoy it. And Mom," she stopped and rolled her eyes. "The only feeling I have for her is my flight-or-fight reflex. Pitiful, huh?" Her weak attempt at a smile failed miserably.

"You pulled yourself through all of their crap and you're an amazing, wonderful person. You feel what you feel, Nik. Or don't feel as the case may be. You don't have to explain your emotions, not now, and not ever with me."

Niki still looked worried. "What am I gonna do, Gracie? Mom's relentless." Grace had filled her in on Connie's wild trip to see Winnie, and Niki had also been mystified by their insistence that Stark had money. "If she thinks Dad cheated her, it explains her ridiculous comment that I was his favorite. She won't get anything out of Winnie, but she'll never leave me alone."

CHAPTER SEVEN

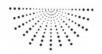

There was little to be done to prepare for the meeting with Xavier and Greenley, but when Grace and Niki joined Mosley in his office, he focused on Niki, warning her not to engage her mother, no matter the provocation.

"Not that it means much, m'dear," he said, "but right now, I believe the officers feel sorry for you. Let's not show them your firebrand temper, agreed?"

Grace laughed until Mosley pointed out that the cousins may as well be twins when it came to anger management. Then he changed the subject. "Niki, I'd like for you to promise me you won't give your mother any money. Not for any reason. If there is a genuine need, I'll handle it."

Niki shook her head. "Don't you think we're past that? Mom and Dad have taken advantage of you for years and it has to stop."

"It has stopped, m'dear. Your mother just doesn't understand the ramifications, yet."

"But . . . How?"

Grace wondered the same thing. Refusing to defend Connie was one thing, but she wasn't sure he'd ever cut the ties with her completely.

"That's a conversation for another time," he said briskly. "We need to keep clear heads for this meeting. And the point I want to stress is that you are not responsible for your mother's actions, no matter what they may have been."

"I know that." Niki straightened up, a little of her usual sassiness restored. "What are you afraid I'll do?"

"Connie claims to need money and she will look to you to pay her bills, perhaps even her bail. I want your assurance you won't give her anything. If she is truly in need, you let me know. She received the lion's share of the assets in the divorce and it will have to sustain her. She has a place to live, a car to drive, and a job if she doesn't lose it during the investigation."

"But—"

"No 'buts'," Mosley said. "I don't say this to protect you from her greed, I'm trying to keep you from being charged as her accomplice."

The last word ended Niki's argument. "I promise, Cy. But what about the trust? Mom will still have that, right?"

"I'm not surprised you think so. I feel sure neither Stark nor Connie ever read a word of the trust documents, but the terms are stated quite clearly. While a Delaney widow is entitled to receive one quarter of her deceased husband's share, a Delaney ex-wife does not. Which is a moot point because the trust closes now with Stark's passing."

"Wow," Niki said. "I guess I never knew that was possible. I thought the investments would keep it running forever."

"Forever isn't feasible, but there's still a substantial amount invested. I think you two girls will be pleased with the balance when all is said and done." The smile that spread across his face lit up his tired blue eyes.

"What's he saying, Gracie?" Niki asked.

"No idea." Grace sighed. What had he kept from her this time? "All right, Cy, let's have it."

Mosley nodded. "In 2014, the executor was your grandmother, Emma. She changed a key component of the trust's provisions."

"Gran?" Niki said. "But we thought you were the executor."

"I am now. The oldest Delaney in each generation is responsible for naming the executor. Before Ford's death, he handed that dubious honor to your grandmother. Emma preferred not to have the responsibility and signed it over to me. In 2014, at her request, I relinquished my authority to her, she made substantive changes to the terms, then returned it to my care."

"My head hurts," Niki said. "Just tell us, Cy, what did Gran change?"

Mosley hesitated. "This was right before your mother died, Grace. Emma knew that more money going to Stark and Connie wouldn't help them, it would make things worse. Imagine for a moment what Stark might have done with executorship."

It wasn't a nice scenario.

"So, I inherited my mother's share," Grace prompted.

"Yes, and that ends now. Under the terms Emma set up, while the trust is dissolved, the remaining funds will be equally divided between you and Niki."

The cousins stared at each other. "Just us?" Niki whispered, then found her voice. "Just Grace and me? What about Winnie? He was always Gran's favorite."

Mosley smiled, but there was no mistaking the emotion behind his next words. "What you saw as favoritism for your brother was something else. Something harder to define. She loved you both fiercely, but in Winnie, she saw her Tony, her firstborn, come back to life. At times, I worried about her attachment to him, but I came to realize I was underestimating her. As a child, Winnie was a balm to her broken heart. But as he grew, she knew perfectly well who, and what, he was. Despite all the love she gave him, all the love she had given Stark, they always wanted more."

Niki and Grace looked at each other. Before this moment, Tony—Winston Stratford Delaney III—had only been a sad story to them.

"I didn't know," Niki finally said.

"There are things I would change, if I could, but now isn't the time for that conversation," Mosley glanced at his watch. "Returning to the trust, or rather, the balance of it. I wanted to give both of you this information now, prior to any new action the police may take regarding

Stark's death. The emotions that will certainly grow in the coming days may tempt you to step in and help Connie, or," he looked directly at Niki, "Winnie."

There was a long silence, then Niki said, "Mom will be relieved that I can pay for the funeral."

"No." Mosley was emphatic. "The trust will cover any kind of funeral you want. You aren't responsible for your parents' expenses."

They had only a few minutes before Connie, her new attorney, and the detectives arrived, but Niki had one more question. "How much?" she asked hesitantly. "I mean for Grace and me. Ballpark, of course."

Mosley smiled. "Only a fraction of what there once was, but Grace, I believe Fiona and Liam can go to college without student loans. And Niki, m'dear, you've said you want to get out of the apartment at Delaney House and buy your first home." He laughed at their expressions. "Use it however you wish, but be the Delaney children who finally make Emma happy."

Ordinarily, the conference room of Reagan and Mosley, Attorneys at Law, could comfortably seat twelve. This morning, it was crowded with four, mostly because Connie wouldn't stop pacing.

"Mom, sit down!"

"My lawyer's late," Connie snapped at Niki. "What will I do if he doesn't show up?"

"Who is it?" Grace asked.

"Not you, that's for sure."

They were interrupted by Lily, who appeared in the doorway and said, "The Ocean City police detectives are here and a Mr. Breedlove followed them in. He says he's Connie's attorney."

Breedlove immediately called a halt to the proceedings, demanding fifteen minutes to confer with his client. Grace, Niki, and Mosley retreated to Mosley's office and shortly afterwards, Lily joined them. Shutting the door behind her, she said, "Connie may have met her match. Her attorney has definitely got her number. The detectives are having coffee in the small waiting room and listening to Connie blab everything she knows at top volume. She's insisting Stark owed her money."

Mosley said, "Well, then. Good thing we aren't out there while she does my job for me. Where is Marjorie?"

All three women gave him the same look. There was no question where the secretary would be. Her nickname—The Bat—had been earned because she heard everything, forgot nothing, and could swoop into any situation without warning.

"Ah, yes." Mosley nodded. "Good, good. She can tell us later if we've missed anything important."

Grace was not amused. "Cy, it's bad enough that Marjorie eavesdrops on *us*, but surely you don't approve of her behavior. She's—"

"An unstoppable force of nature, m'dear. I can't change her, so why waste her talents?"

"But Connie and her attorney are having a confidential conversation!"

"Nonsense. Even I can hear them." Then Mosley seemed to reconsider. "Lily, please ask Marjorie to bring us a fresh pot of coffee. That will distract her for a little while. Niki, I'm sorry if I seem to be callous, but you must know your mother is up to something."

Niki knew. They all knew. The only question was how the *something* pertained to Stark's death.

CHAPTER EIGHT

The OC detectives announced they would question Niki, Connie, Grace, and Mosley at the same time. When all parties met in the conference room, professional politeness only carried them through reintroductions and seating arrangements. After that, Connie's new attorney took over.

Oscar Breedlove, Esquire, from the firm of Breedlove, Breedlove, and Stumpmeyer resembled Harry Potter with a comb over. Grace thought he might be as bright as the boy wizard, too, even if she couldn't imagine how he'd allowed himself to be drafted into representing a penniless woman who seemed to hate him. Connie's animosity fairly glowed, but he'd managed to silence her.

"My client has other commitments, as do I," Breedlove announced. "For one thing, detectives, I shall be lodging a complaint with your chief regarding Mrs. Delaney's treatment."

Detective Sergeant Xavier shrugged and said, "Knock yourself out, counselor." Then turning to Mosley, she asked, "When did you last talk to Stark Delaney?"

"Three weeks ago," Mosley said without hesitation.

This was a surprise to Grace, who made a mental note to follow up on it later. At the moment, she was more concerned about her partner's demeanor. He seemed distant and worried, totally unlike his usual professional persona. She watched him, ready to step in if he needed her.

"Where did the conversation occur?" Xavier asked.

"My home."

"We'll be here all day if you keep this up, Mr. Mosley." Xavier's tone lacked the irritation she'd shown Breedlove, and Mosley gave her a smile.

"I'll be happy to answer you. Would you restate your full question, please?"

"When, where, and under what circumstances did you last speak to Mr. Delaney and what was said in the conversation?"

"On May 18th, he came to my home, unannounced, about seven in the evening. He said little, but he handed me a sealed box and two envelopes, and asked me to sign a receipt for them."

Grace kept a poker face, but just barely. She was hearing this for the first time.

"What was in the box and envelopes?" Greenley said in an irritable tone, earning himself a sharp look from Xavier.

"Stark told me one envelope contained a new will that would override the ones he and Connie had signed in my office several years ago."

There was a squeak from Connie, but it ended sharply, leaving only a charged silence in the room.

After a moment, Mosley added, "He said the box contained messages and gifts for his family members. He said that I was to act as the executor of his estate and told me not to open the box or the will until after he died. The second envelope contained a list of instructions to follow upon his death."

"Well, what does it say?" Greenley demanded, then stopped when he saw Xavier's expression.

"How did Mr. Delaney seem?" Xavier asked, as if Greenley hadn't spoken. "Happy? Sad? Angry?"

Mosley said, "He wasn't talkative and ignored my questions. He left as soon as I agreed to put the will and the box in my safe and leave them there until after his death. He also made me promise to follow his instructions. I did, and he left immediately after that."

Xavier's frown deepened. "Did you hear from him again?"

"No."

"Did you open the box?"

"No."

Xavier asked for the box, the will, and the list of instructions. Mosley refused, then relented and produced the instructions.

Xavier read the document, then returned it to Mosley. "So, you are to hold a formal reading of the will and distribute the contents of the box at that time."

"And that's exactly what I shall do. Until then, both will remain confidential and in my possession."

Grace thought both Connie and Greenley might stroke out, but Xavier seemed unconcerned. "You know that's not how it works, sir. You have to file that will with the Register of Wills, and at that time, it becomes a public document. You notify all relevant parties, give them copies of the will, and proceed from there to settle the estate."

Mosley looked amused. "Thank you, detective. But I assure you, I am aware of, and shall comply with, the law. Directly after filing with the Register, I shall hold the reading my client requested. You may try to secure a court order compelling me to release the will and box now, of course. Or, you can wait and attend the reading."

Breedlove said nothing, but made notes in illegible scrawl on a legal pad.

Xavier took a piece of paper from her jacket. "Have you ever seen this?" she asked, handing it to Mosley.

He studied the paper, then handed it back, saying, "No." His voice had a strained tone that wasn't there earlier. Whatever was on the paper had unnerved him, and he wouldn't meet Grace's gaze.

"When was the last time you saw your ex-husband, Ms. Delaney?"

The change of subjects caught everyone off guard, especially

Connie, who was staring at the paper on the table in front of Detective Sergeant Xavier. With a flourish, Xavier turned it face down and placed her folded hands on top of it. "Ms. Delaney?" she prompted.

Connie actually looked at Breedlove before answering. Whatever he had used to control his manic client, Grace decided she wanted some.

He nodded, and Connie said, "Six months—"

Breedlove whispered in her ear.

Connie glared at him, but continued as if she hadn't been about to lie to the police. "The last time we were together as a *couple*," Breedlove got another nasty look, "was when we split up in Virginia. The last time I *saw* him was Monday."

Greenley seemed pleased, but Xavier only nodded and said, "Where did you see him?"

Over the next half hour, with persistent interruptions from Breedlove, a picture emerged of Stark and Connie's last hours together. Grace wished she were close enough to Niki to hold her hand. Tears slipped down her cousin's face as Connie described her visit to Stark on the night he died.

"I told him I was willing to reconcile and drop the divorce. I said I wanted to try again. But he was drunk, as usual, and I had to leave. I couldn't deal with him." It took another whispered order from Breedlove to push her to the finish. "When he drinks, he . . . hurts me." Blushing, she pushed up her sleeves to show the fading, hand-sized bruises on her forearms.

Grace thought the scene was an accurate display of her aunt's personality. Connie lied easily—about anything—at any time and without hesitation, but admitting the truth, that she'd been abused, embarrassed her.

Xavier snapped photos of the bruises, then said, "Let's revisit the timeline, Ms. Delaney. When did you arrive at your ex-husband's apartment?"

"Sometime in the early evening. I don't remember specifics. I wasn't—"

Breedlove reached out and tapped her hand, and Connie stopped talking.

Grace wondered if he was concealing a mini-taser.

Xavier made a note and continued. "Perhaps your attorney will allow you to tell us what time you left Mr. Delaney's apartment?"

Breedlove nodded, and Connie said, "When I got in the car, the time on the console was about ten."

"Final answer?"

"Move on, Detective," Breedlove said. "My client has answered you."

"You seem to be interested in the paper I showed Mr. Mosley," Xavier said. "So are we. It's a copy—we found the original in the pocket of the pants Mr. Delaney was wearing when he died. There's a message written on it. Perhaps you can tell us what it means?"

Connie snatched the paper from Xavier's hand and for a moment it looked as if she and Breedlove would fight over it, but this time she didn't give in. "It's a poem," she said, looking astonished. "The bastard left me a *poem*?" Hands shaking, she read it out loud.

Don't look back on my life, you won't like what you see.
I've left parting gifts for you and soon I will be free.
When I leave this world, I'll take what you want with me.

"Are you satisfied?" Connie yelled. "This proves he lost his damned mind!" She jerked her arm away from Breedlove's reach. "He was crazy and violent, and I don't know why I need a lawyer to prove it."

Ignoring the histrionics, Xavier said, "So you think the poem was meant for you?"

"Of course—"

"Not your daughter? Or maybe he meant it for your son?"

"These are his last words to *me.*" Connie crumpled the paper and threw it across the table.

"That's enough," Breedlove said. "My client—"

Connie rolled over him. "It's not poetry, it's horrible! Cruel, spiteful, and stupid, just like him. Well, Stark can rot in hell. I want the money he was hiding from me. It's *mine.*"

"Maybe the money is what your *ex*-husband took with him," Xavier said, her voice taunting.

"Don't say—" Breedlove tried again, only to be drowned out.

Pointing at Xavier, Connie said, "That's ridiculous! He's not talking about money, he's talking about love. That's what he *thought* he was taking from me. Love. His ego was enormous, and I'd told him I still loved him. Well, I lied. I hated him. He took everything from me, and he deserved to be murdered."

Greenley didn't bother to hide his smile and even Xavier looked happy.

Breedlove just shook his head.

"Constance Delaney," Xavier said as she stood and motioned Greenley in Connie's direction. "You are under arrest for suspicion of murder in the death of Stark Anders Delaney."

Not even her attorney's impressive skills could stop the inevitable. Connie left the office in handcuffs, sandwiched between the detectives.

"I cautioned your mother not to refer to Mr. Delaney's death as a murder unless the police announced it as such." Breedlove maintained his calm manner as if explosive clients were an everyday occurrence for him, which Grace was beginning to think might be the case.

"But did you tell her not to say he deserved it?" she asked, earning a grin from Mosley and a groan from Niki.

Breedlove ignored her, saying, "Maybe the medical examiner has issued an opinion." He scrolled through messages on his phone. "Nothing new, yet." He retrieved the crumpled note, smoothed it out, and put it in his briefcase. "I have experience with the detectives. Greenley is a hot head, but he's sharp. Xavier's a straight shooter, and smart. And here's a tip—she's the senior officer. They may not be a pleasure to work with, but they're good cops."

"They're cops who think Mom killed my father," Niki said. "Are you going to dump her now? I mean, she can't pay you. And I won't give her any money."

This time it was Niki who got a pat on the hand from her lawyer, but Mosley didn't look concerned.

"I appreciate your candor," Breedlove said solemnly. "You have my condolences on the death of your father. I lost my dad recently and I can't imagine it happening in these circumstances. I'm sorry for what you're going through." He seemed sincere, but he didn't answer Niki's question about his fee. After an awkward pause, he moved on to Mosley and Grace, saying, "Ms. Delaney would like to have a copy of her ex-husband's will as soon as possible."

"Of course," Mosley said. "And if I may be so bold as to compliment you on your skill in managing excitable clients? You were very impressive today."

Grace agreed, but she still wanted to know how Connie had found him and who was paying his bill.

CHAPTER NINE

Mac walked into a scene he wouldn't have believed possible a year earlier. He knew Grace had heard his tires crunching the gravel driveway, as well as the front door that squeaked even after he'd oiled the hinges, but his wife didn't stop what she was doing when he entered the great room. They grinned at each other, and he stepped out of the room without interrupting the story she was reading to the children. He wished he'd had a camera handy.

With one arm around her daughter and a foot tapping the edge of their baby's bouncy swing, she was reading a Berenstain Bears book, and from Fiona's rapt attention, he could tell they were at a good part. He went on into the kitchen to peek in the oven and confirm that the dinner he smelled was lasagna, before grabbing a beer, and the paper, and rejoining his family. If Grace could pull off this level of domesticity, he thought the least he could do was go with the flow. It was too good to last forever.

The big change in his wife had occurred somewhere around the sixth month of her pregnancy with Sonny. Mac thought they were doing fine for a couple of newlyweds preparing for the birth of their first child while dealing with the father of the baby Grace already had, but she'd decided she had to do better. Relieved that she hadn't said *he* had to do better, Mac couldn't imagine what she needed to fix. But in true Grace fashion, once she'd identified a problem, she'd gone to work on a solution.

As usual, she'd gone overboard in the beginning. She devised a schedule that kept their lives on track but required his full compliance. Cleaning routines, chore lists, and details of the children's routines covered the refrigerator's doors. But the hardest change to deal with was the removal of work-related conversations within the children's hearing. And there was precious little time without a child or two around.

He worried about her blood pressure while she struggled not to ask him about rumors she'd picked up during her day.

"I want her to know us as Mama and Poppy, not the worn-out people who show up at night when the fun nanny leaves." Grace had said. "Most of all, I want her to see us happy, not discussing a crime infested world."

So far, the plan—with some refinements—was working. While Fiona was awake, she had their full attention, or at least her mother's. Sometimes her stepfather had to walk the dog, or work in the yard, or just be by himself. Grace never said a word on the evenings when he made his escape, but he thought she looked jealous. He tried to make it up to her by taking on more chores, even doing the laundry once, but after that, they'd both agreed he wouldn't touch her clothes again, unless he was taking them off of her.

The master plan was adjusted from time to time, but Grace seemed to be happy and Fiona and Sonny thrived. Mac had clean clothes and hot meals and tried to appreciate that his headstrong, workaholic wife had morphed into an organized, even-tempered, working mother. Waiting for that miracle to fall apart was making him nervous, though, especially since cracks were appearing in her facade when they had nights like the last one. He hoped whatever was making the children calm now lasted through to six a.m. He was exhausted and he couldn't imagine how she was still awake.

True to the house rules, Grace didn't mention the interview with the OC detectives, or Connie's arrest, or the results of her tumultuous day, until both children were asleep. But as she dished up dinner, she gave him a blow by blow and he filled in the gaps in her narrative with information he'd picked up. It felt like old times as they talked shop between bites of a cheesy-gooey lasagna and a salad.

When she asked him if Winnie could be released for Stark's funeral, he poured her a second glass of wine before answering. "Unless he's done something to screw up his parole, it looks as if he'll be out soon. Possibly even released in time for the funeral."

"We knew it could happen, although it's hard to believe after all the work we did to convince the board he was dangerous," Grace said. "There's nothing I can do about it, I guess, except try not to worry."

"I don't think your 'Not My Problem' mindset is going to work in this case, honey. But remember, he'll be cautioned to stay away from you—"

"He tried to *kill* me, Mac. He won't feel any kinder toward me after three years in prison."

It was true, of course, but agreeing with her wouldn't help the situation. "He wasn't charged with assaulting you, though, was he? And he can't hold you responsible for the distribution charges he was convicted on."

"I have the requests for restraining orders ready to file."

Mac sighed. "We've talked about this, Grace. Winnie wasn't charged with anything related to you. Yes, you might get the orders granted, but if he complains, that's a whole new problem for you. And you'll be dealing with him or his attorney from the get-go. Let's wait and see if we even have to worry about him. He may want to get as far away from here as possible under the terms of his parole. Wouldn't you?"

"You really think so?"

"I really think that you should know that I won't let him hurt my family."

"Do I want to know how—"

"No."

She picked up her fork and stabbed at a piece of romaine. "Well, okay then."

He knew she wasn't happy, and he had more bad news to share.

"Don't look at me that way," she said, softly. "I'm not hiding from hard truths when I do the NMP thing, I'm prioritizing my stressors. Winnie's still in jail, so at this moment he's not my problem." She smiled and added, "Besides, my husband is going to take care of him."

Mac had decided on a course of action long ago, but he said nothing, only leaned over and kissed her. Then pushed her wine glass a little closer to her hand.

"There's more, isn't there?" she asked.

"I heard from Jeff Brixson," he said. "He called to give me a heads up on Stark's autopsy."

Grace frowned. "The state's head medical examiner is handling it?"

"Not personally. But he caught the connection to us and once Bernadette Xavier had been advised, he called to let me know the preliminary findings. He wasn't sure how long the OCPD would take to share the information and the official reports could take weeks. Same old story, too many dead bodies, not enough staff to process them."

She sipped her wine, then said, "Does it look bad for Connie?"

"Looks real bad for someone, honey. Stark died after receiving a blow to the chest, but before that, he was extremely inebriated, and before that . . ." He hesitated and got her raised eyebrow look—the one that meant *spit it out.* "He had end stage pancreatic cancer."

"My God," Grace said. "Niki doesn't know, I'm sure of it."

"I don't know who did, besides Stark. Maybe not even him, although Jeff said the symptoms would almost certainly have driven him to get medical care. He was already dying from the cancer when he suffered the chest injury. But there's no final determination yet on the cause of death. It may be a while."

Grace considered this. "Connie said he was murdered. She could have just been assuming that, of course."

"Spoken like the best defense attorney I know."

"She also said she was glad he'd been killed."

"That'll take some walking back."

She pushed back from the table. "Breedlove's good. I looked him up, just to make sure. . . . I mean, Niki was worried, so I checked him out."

Mac knew her concern was for more than Niki's feelings. She and Mosley may have washed their hands of Connie, but neither of them would let her be convicted for lack of adequate representation.

"Do you think she killed him?" Grace asked, suddenly catching him off guard.

"Based on what little I know right now, she's in the top spot and no one else is a contender. But a lot has to happen before she takes Winnie's cell at Jessup."

"I think that's enough dinner table talk for tonight," she said. "I'll clean up. I can't relax until I work off this nervous energy."

He walked down to the river's edge with Rocky, watching the spaniel bound from shadow to shadow under the sparse light from a quarter moon. The dog would sleep well tonight, but even if the children did, too, he and Grace wouldn't get much rest.

Thoughts of Winnie's release and Stark's mysterious death would be keeping a lot of people awake, but Mac's thoughts were on Connie. He'd known her for years and could see her committing murder in a fit of rage, but what would drive her to it now, *after* their divorce? But then, she claimed to have attempted a reconciliation and that performance gave the prosecution a spurned wife theory to work with. And she kept insisting Stark had hidden money from her.

All in all, Connie looked guilty, but was she?

In the kitchen, Grace scrubbed an already clean lasagna pan, her thoughts miles away. She hoped for Niki's sake that Connie was innocent, but after forty years of marriage, and with a fast approaching death sentence hanging over his head, Stark had changed his will. If Connie knew he'd cut her out—and it would be just like him to tell her —she'd have to get him to change his mind, fast. Assuming, of course, she thought he had anything of value to leave anyone.

Grace thought about Connie demanding the money he'd left, and from there, it was easy to assume Stark had answered her with his dreadful poem.

I'll take what you want with me. If he had money he hadn't disclosed in their divorce settlement, Connie might have been angry enough to kill him to get it.

She loaded the sparkling pan into the dishwasher, then went to talk to Mac. Winnie's release from prison might pose an eventual threat to their family, but right now it was his mother who worried her.

CHAPTER TEN

The office was unusually quiet on Thursday morning. The shocking events of the last two days still hung in the air, making everyone jumpy.

Marjorie was the worst, finding one reason after another to call up to Grace's office and rip into whichever unfortunate person picked up the phone. The downstairs copier was acting up, the front door had an annoying squeak, mail needed to be picked up and couldn't wait. When she called to say Grace had to come downstairs immediately, Aidan didn't bother putting her on hold when he said, "Bat alert, Boss. You are to present yourself to the queen."

The joke did not go over well.

Grace gave him a death glare as she took the receiver and heard Marjorie's icy tone. "Mr. Mosley wants to discuss Mr. Delaney's funeral with you, and if you thought yesterday was bad, wait until you see what happens when all that breaks loose."

The scene on the first floor was a replay of the previous day, minus the police officers and Oscar Breedlove. As soon as she saw

Marjorie sitting at her desk, backbone ramrod straight and face like a prune, Grace knew someone was behaving badly, and that someone's voice came down the hallway clearly. "You two will ruin everything!"

Grace winced. "The police released Connie?"

"Yes," Marjorie snapped.

"Is Niki in there, too?"

"Yes."

Grace sighed. They were all going to pay for Aidan's rudeness, but she wouldn't apologize for him. This was definitely an NMP.

"Quit dawdling," Marjorie said. "Coffee is in the conference room. I put your mug in there, too."

"You did?"

"I said so, didn't I? Given the circumstances, I thought the one that says *Karma Always Wins* was the best choice."

"Oh, my God."

"I don't tolerate fools, Grace."

And neither did Cyrus Mosley. When Grace entered the conference room, she found him squared off against a haggard-looking Connie.

"That's enough," Mosley said, the heat in his voice temporarily halting her stream of complaints.

"But Stark was my—"

"*Ex*-husband," Mosley said.

Connie didn't miss a beat. "He was dying and I'm sure the cancer affected his thinking. Any changes he made to his will are invalid unless I'm still the sole beneficiary. You have to work with me on this."

"No," Mosley said. "I don't have to do anything where you're concerned. Now, we are moving on to the details of Stark's funeral."

"The hell we are! Get that damned will and let me read it. You can't keep it from me."

"I won't keep it from you, but I'm not releasing its contents at this time." Mosley turned to Grace, who still stood near the door. "Come in, m'dear, I've given Niki and Connie the sad news about Stark's cancer and explained that we can't hold a funeral until next week, due to the autopsy requirements, but we can make the arrangements for the service."

Niki looked frozen, and Grace felt a spurt of anger that Mosley had handled things this way. Surely, he had to know she was in a fragile state? Bypassing her Karma cup—it seemed like overkill at this point —she grabbed a mug with the firm's logo, filled it, and added a generous dollop of cream for medicinal purposes. Her nerves needed all the help they could get.

Mosley drew his shaggy eyebrows together and stared Connie down. "What you want is of no consequence. I no longer have any obligations to you and I won't allow you to continue this harassment."

Grace was stunned. She rarely heard her dignified partner speak that way. Then she saw Niki straighten up and lose her deer-in-the-headlights expression.

"Don't say that," Connie pleaded. "I didn't get out of that cell in Ocean City until one a.m. and I'm exhausted, Cy. The police didn't have enough to hold me, but they still think I killed Stark because he changed his will. They're too lazy to look for the real killer!" She swung to Niki. "I could go to prison. Is that what you want for your mother?"

Niki drew a deep breath, then said, "What I want is to arrange Dad's funeral. I can't do anything for you."

"There now," Mosley said. "My client and I are on the same page."

As decisions regarding the service were made, and all of her comments were ignored, Connie's interest waned until Niki said she had everything she needed to make arrangements.

"Well, your daddy's service sounds just lovely, but if you think I'm paying for it, you're mistaken."

Niki looked disgusted. "I'm sure we're all shocked to hear that. You may as well leave now while I handle the details, as usual."

"This isn't over," Connie said.

As the door slammed behind her, Niki looked ready to cry. "Can you release the will now, Cy? For me? She won't stop harassing me until she knows what she's getting."

"I'm sorry. Your father's instructions were clear. And I don't need to remind you how little he had left to give anyone. Your mother won't want to hear that, of course."

"Well, then," Niki said. "I guess I have to wait until tomorrow to give her whatever he left me. It's the only way to get rid of her."

Mosley frowned. "Don't make any rash decisions, please."

Grace thought he should have also pointed out that no one ever really got rid of Connie.

"I'm not being rash," Niki said. "I told you Dad and I had been talking, reconnecting. If I'd known he was sick . . ."

Grace gritted her teeth, but kept silent. She didn't believe for a second that Stark had suddenly become a loving father. Mosley looked sympathetic, but he didn't respond, either. They both knew Niki needed to talk.

"It's hard to explain, but he was different. So different, I wanted to believe his heart had changed, too." Niki said. "He was rocking a beach bum look. You'd have hated it, Cy. He had a scruffy beard, his hair was past his collar, and he'd sold all his good clothes." She hesitated, then pulled a paper out of her purse. "He emailed this to me. I printed it out, but I'm gonna have a better copy made and frame it. It makes me happy to pretend he was always this way."

She handed the picture to Cy, whose face softened as he studied it. When Grace saw it, she understood why they were so moved. The photograph was of a thin man in cutoffs and a plain white tee shirt standing on the deck of a large motor boat. He was holding a swordfish over his head and beaming. She couldn't believe it was her uncle and realized this might be the only time she'd ever seen him looking happy.

"He hadn't given up all of his vices, of course," Niki said. "That's sort of why I believed him when he said things were different. He got a part-time job at a beach bar on the boardwalk and he only did beer and Keno. *Keno.* Can you believe it? He's strictly a high stakes blackjack and poker kind of guy. Or he was, anyway." She sighed. "I can't think about this stuff now, though. I have to find a way to handle Mom and Winnie. I won't let them ruin me."

It was the worried look in Mosley's eyes that bothered Grace.

She'd thought it was his way of processing Stark's death, but what if it was more than that?

As soon as Niki left, she said, "Let's talk. I want to take some of the load off of you, if I can."

To her surprise, Mosley said no, then added, "Unfortunately, it's just not possible."

"Why?"

He shook his head. "This is my responsibility, Grace. But I won't say no to your help tomorrow at the reading. It's going to be a circus."

Later, she would decide "riot" was a better analogy.

The will was pure Stark Delaney—sneaky and manipulative right up to the end.

CHAPTER ELEVEN

Once she learned Winnie would not be released for the reading of the will, Niki asked to have it held at Delaney House. "I like the idea of closing out this last chapter of Dad's life in the home where he was raised," she explained.

Grace had a different opinion, but, as Mac pointed out, she also had a different view of Stark's life than his daughter did.

On Friday, Xavier and Greenly accompanied Mosley to the courthouse, and waited in the hallway outside the Register of Wills office while he went through the formalities of presenting the clerk with Stark's will in its still-sealed envelope. After finally receiving, and reading, her copy, Xavier announced that she and her partner would be attending the reading at Delaney House later that afternoon.

Mosley told Grace that he thought both detectives looked like kids on Christmas morning.

The old grandfather clock in the entry hall at Delaney House chimed two and the small group of people in the front parlor took their seats.

"Where's Agatha Christie?"

The comment came from somewhere behind her, but Grace recognized Detective Greenley's sarcastic voice. She had to admit he had a point, though. If there was ever a setting fit for a 1930s movie, this elegant room was it.

Silence fell as Mosley quickly ran through the preliminaries. He stood in front of the fireplace, under the portrait of Emma Delaney, and Grace thought it was fitting that her grandmother was present, too, if only in spirit. She and Niki shared a love seat facing him, and Connie had been directed to a wing chair beside them.

The most interesting person in attendance was an attractive young woman who arrived at the last minute and introduced herself as Piper Tilden. Mosley had quickly taken charge of her, and she'd been seated behind the family. Mac and Oscar Breedlove sat nearer the doors, and the Ocean City detectives stood behind them.

Connie angled herself so she could see the stranger, and she wasn't the only one who was distracted. When Mosley finished the boilerplate part of his speech, he turned to a box that had been placed on the table beside him.

"As you will learn, Stark Delaney left a rather unusual last will and testament, and asked that it be read aloud to those of you sitting in front of me. Connie Delaney, Niki Delaney Malvern, Grace Reagan McNamara, and Piper Tilden are the named guests." He opened a single page document and began to read.

Niki cried softly at hearing the opening words.

I, Stark Anders Delaney, being of sound mind, if not exactly happy about this whole dying business, declare this to be my official will, replacing any other document my soon to be ex-wife will probably produce. I know I don't have long now, but since I've refused treatment for the cancer that's killing me, my mind is as clear as it's ever been, so anyone who doesn't like how I'm leaving things is SOL. This means you, Connie.

Mosley paused and everyone clearly heard Connie say, "Ass!"

Snickering broke out across the room, and even Mosley's mouth twitched before he started up again.

Well, here we go, folks. The moment you all have been waiting for. Except for certain gifts I will deliver to Cyrus Mosley along with this document, I leave everything I own to Piper Tilden, my co-worker at The Blow Back In Bar. I don't have much, but I want it all to go to the only friend I've ever had who didn't ask me for a damn thing.

My son, Winston Stratford Delaney the Fifth, has already received his inheritance from me, along with a name that probably doomed him from his first breath.

I figure once Cy hands out my gifts, I'm even with everyone else, with one exception. To my daughter, Niki, I leave an apology for dying faster than I could turn myself around and make amends.

I would have settled things with each of you face to face if I had more time, but I'm tired, so I'm leaving it to Cy to deliver my last messages. I may be dead when you get them, but I guarantee you won't forget me. Go chew on that while you open your gifts.

I'm outta here.

"What the hell does he mean?" Connie demanded as Mosley refolded the will and put it in his jacket pocket. "And what is *she* getting?"

Ignoring her outburst and the dirty look she gave Piper Tilden, Mosley said, "I'm going to hand out Stark's gifts now. Each item has a message that he instructed me to read aloud." He opened the box at his side and took out a small white velvet pouch, detached a notecard clipped to it, and passed it to Niki before reading the note.

Your grandmother wanted you to have these earrings, but she made the mistake of giving them to me to keep for you. Your mother's enjoyed them long enough. It's time that you have them in your possession.

Niki held up a pair of glittering diamond and sapphire circlets and shot her mother a furious look. Connie had worn them often.

"Stark told me he'd sold them!" Connie said. Then apparently realizing how that sounded, she added a whiney, "He gave them to me."

"Well, he left a package for you," Mosley said as he handed her a bulky envelope. "Be careful how you open it," he warned as she snatched it from his hands. He could have saved his breath. She ripped off the top of the envelope, and several pieces of paper spilled out.

Connie stared at the contents, then rifled through them. "Bills? He left me his bills?"

Mosley nodded. "According to his note, he left you *all* of his bills. They are unpaid and in both of your names. He also included a copy of the title to his car, showing ownership transferred to Ms. Tilden." He handed her one more sheet of paper. "He signs off saying, 'Keep looking for that prince.'"

They all braced for another round of yelling, but Connie sat motionless and silent, staring at the scrawled note on the paper.

Grace's gift was next.

"A yearbook from Rutgers University?" She opened it, then looked up at Mosley and smiled. Her mother's distinctive signature was neatly written on the first page of the stained and worn book. "Did I get a note?"

The paper he handed her only had two words.

Recognize anyone?

Connie threatened to sue everyone because she had been cheated, but Breedlove eventually got her out the door, earning the admiration and appreciation of everyone else in the parlor. The Ocean City officers ushered Piper Tilden out just as the inn's first guests of the day were arriving to check in.

Dylan Kirwan appeared and went straight to Niki. It was clear from the way she hugged him that she didn't need family support, so Grace left with Mac, the yearbook tucked under her arm. Torn between curiosity and apprehension, she didn't mention it again until they sat on the patio after dinner, watching the sun sink behind the trees on the far side of the river.

"Let's look at my gift," she said, but made no move to get up.

"In a while." He pulled her closer and pushed the glider into a gentle rhythm. "To tell you the truth, I was relieved that an old college yearbook was all Stark gave you."

Grace shook her head. "That wasn't a gift. He hated me, so why would he give me anything sentimental? The note implies I'll recognize someone, and I don't think he meant Mom. I went through it and nothing caught my attention, which isn't surprising, really. She never talked about that year, and dropped out after her freshman class."

They sat in silence until she sighed and kissed his cheek. "Are you waiting for me to state the obvious?"

"No. Just giving you some space."

"I've had forty years of space, Mac. Let's go look at the book together."

He'd known the little bubble of bliss they'd created wouldn't last forever, but he wasn't ready for it to change. Still, he released her as she pulled away, and after a moment, followed her inside. She was afraid, and he didn't blame her. The yearbook was a weapon Stark had chosen for his final attack on his dead sister and her child. Somewhere in those yellowed pages, he felt sure Grace was going to find her father.

***

An hour later, she closed the book with a sigh. "He just wanted to torment me. There's nothing here. Nothing obvious, anyway."

"You didn't think he'd leave you any easy answers, did you?"

"It's nice to see Mom young and happy, but he didn't keep this for a couple of photographs."

"We can do some research—"

She got up and reached for his hand. "Nope. I'm not playing his game. He did this to make me crazy, to send me off on a search for my father, when he knew I'd come up empty handed. Well, I'm not letting him do that to me."

Mac followed her to bed, but he knew the subject wasn't closed. The yearbook and whatever waited inside of it would resurface, the only question was when.

CHAPTER TWELVE

Stark Delaney hadn't wanted a funeral, and everyone knew it. Perhaps he thought he'd made himself clear over the years because he didn't put the directive in his will. Niki wanted a dignified service for a father, and her friends saw to it that she got one. That Stark would have been outraged didn't bother any of them.

Once she learned she'd have no role in the service, Connie lost interest in it. She called Niki and Grace daily to complain that Stark had ruined her, and the police were trying to railroad her into prison. Insisting Stark had a stash of money that hadn't been declared in the divorce settlement, she talked non-stop about being cheated. The possibility that she might be convicted of murder didn't seem to bother her nearly as much, which, at least according to her daughter, was pretty solid proof she wasn't guilty.

"She doesn't have that sneaky look she gets when she's covering something up," Niki said one evening as she and Grace were commiserating. "And she's mad, not scared, so I don't think she killed Dad. She might be the end of me, though. If I have to hear one more time that Dad hid money somewhere and it's all hers, I'll explode."

"It won't be this way forever," Grace tried, but gave up when Niki snorted with laughter.

"She is who she is, Grace, and I need to get the hell away from her for good."

Niki didn't elaborate, and Grace didn't ask what she meant by the comment, but knew she was only delaying an uncomfortable conversation. Her cousin's plans regarding her treacherous mother weren't her problem, exactly, but they were hard to ignore. Repeating "NMP" over was only delaying the inevitable.

The morning of the funeral was sunny and coolish for June on the Eastern Shore. Grace thought it was wasted on a memorial for Stark. Rain and lightning bolts would have been a better analogy for his life than the sunbeams that glimmered through the stained-glass windows and lit up the small sanctuary. She wondered how the man whose ashes sat in a bronze urn in front of the altar rated such a sendoff. Her uncle had always been luckier than he deserved, and it was holding true right down to his last moments among the living.

Niki was pleased, though. "Thanks for helping me do this," she whispered to Grace. "It feels like we're a normal family today, you know?" she whispered.

Grace didn't, but she managed a smile.

The cousins sat alone in the first row of the middle section of pews in St. Mary's Episcopal Church as the small sanctuary slowly filled. Whatever Niki wanted, Grace was all in. It had been a long five days since the will had been read, and they were both feeling battered. As they waited for the service to start, it was hard not to wonder if the other shoe was about to drop, even though they had planned for all the foreseeable problems.

Cyrus, Avril, Marjorie, and Lily filled the row behind them and provided a much needed buffer from the conversations wafting up from pews where Connie sat with a few old friends. Aidan Banks, who had taken on the role of usher and keeper of the peace, stood nearby.

Mac watched the proceedings from the rear of the church, greeting each person who entered. As the service started, Grace looked back, caught his eye, and got a smile and a nod. No known troublemakers—other than Connie—were in the sanctuary.

Enough people showed up to give Niki support without providing an audience her mother couldn't resist. The priest gave a bland eulogy that could have been used for anyone and the organist played extra hymns to eat up time in the brief service. When it was over, Niki greeted people at the front of the church, while Connie held court at the back. Grace was amazed to see that forty-five minutes had gone by, but that only meant that the reception at Delaney House would start soon. She left Niki to mingle with the dwindling crowd, and Mac stayed to see the last attendees out just in case Connie couldn't resist staging a final dramatic breakdown.

The catering crew at Delaney House would have the food and drinks under control, but Grace wanted to be at the reception when the first guests arrived. Piper Tilden had accepted Niki's invitation to attend, and Grace was hoping for a quiet word with the woman who'd charmed Stark in his final days.

"I'm not sure this is a good idea," Piper said as Grace welcomed her into the front hall at Delaney House. Like most people seeing the historic building for the first time, she paused and looked around, taking in the cantilevered staircase that wound its way upward toward the third floor and the domed ceiling above them.

"Where did you park?" Grace asked. The only vehicles on the street belonged to the catering company.

"Uh, a couple of blocks away. I didn't think it was a good idea to drive up in Stark's car, but I didn't have any other way to get here. I was walking to work after my junker died. That's why he gave his car to me. He was such a nice man." She glanced around the hall again. "Before I chicken out and leave, can I have a tour? Old houses are so cool and I've never been in one like this. Did Stark really grow up here?"

"He did," Grace said, smiling at the young woman's excited curiosity.

Piper seemed to relax a little as they walked through the public rooms. "Where is everyone?" she asked.

"They'll be here soon. It's just close friends and family." Then, correctly interpreting the panicked look Piper gave her, she added, "Connie won't be here."

"Good. Oh, sorry. I never know what to say to her when she calls, and I would hate to cause a disturbance."

"Connie's called you?" Grace asked, then answered herself. "Of course, she has. I should have foreseen that and warned you."

"No, it's okay. If I could just get her to believe that Stark and I were friends and nothing else, I think she'd leave me alone. But she insists he gave me money, and she wants it back. But he didn't, so I can't. I loaned him a few bucks a couple of times when he was running short, but he only paid me back. Nothing extra." They had stopped in the dining room where the caterers had set up a bar. Piper's eyes were wide. "Wow. This place is really awesome. I've never been inside a house this fancy unless I was one of the crew. You know, wearing the black and whites and taking drink orders. I take side catering jobs whenever I can."

As if on cue, a server entered, carrying a tray of champagne flutes.

"I know it seems a bit odd for a funeral reception," Grace said as she took one of the glasses. "Stark hated this stuff, but Niki said if we served the cocktails he preferred, everyone would be too drunk to drive home." Then she raised her glass and smiled at Piper. "May he find peace."

Piper touched the rim of her glass to Grace's. "I only knew him a few months, but he talked about his life here from time to time. I've been worried about how much to say to you and his daughter, but if it helps, I'm sure he was happy in OC. At least most of the time, he seemed okay when he was at the bar. I didn't see him much outside of work, but he always had a smile for me, and not even our most obnoxious customers could get a rise out of him. Now, of course, I think that might have been because he knew he was sick."

"You think he's known for a while?" Grace asked. She'd assumed that Stark had only learned about his cancer recently. The old Stark would never have suffered in silence. He'd have come home, demanded everyone drop their lives and attend to him. It felt as if they were discussing two different people, the father and uncle who'd tormented his family for most of his life, and the genial, down on his luck old man who'd made a new life with strangers who had no reason to dislike him.

She realized Piper hadn't answered her, but was watching the doorway. The first guests were arriving, and Niki was with them. Grace knew she and Piper wouldn't have much more time to talk privately.

And as if she'd heard that thought, Connie's voice came through at top volume. "Champagne! Your father hated bubbles in his alcohol. What were you thinking?"

Piper put her glass on the buffet. "That's her, isn't it? I think I should go. Is there a back door?"

"I was telling you the truth," Grace insisted. "She wasn't invited, Piper. I'm sorry. But please don't leave. I know Niki wants to see you."

"I guess you meant well, but I'm not into yelling. I shouldn't have come."

Grace led her through the butler's pantry and out to the back porch, talking all the way, hoping to keep their connection going. "Let's stay in touch. Maybe Niki and I can come down one day soon and take you to lunch."

Piper looked less than enthusiastic at the suggestion, but said, "There is something you can do. According to Mr. Mosley, Stark's apartment has to be cleaned out and all the contents turned over to me. I'd really prefer if Niki could be there when it happens. I'd like her to have anything of her father's that she wants."

"Thank you. I'm sure she'll want to come."

"Good. Oh, and it'll need to be tomorrow. I'm turning the keys over to the landlord on Saturday."

The next moment she was gone and with her went the answers to the questions their conversation had raised. Grace tamped down her frustration, telling herself she wouldn't have long to wait before they could talk again. There was no way Niki was going to Stark's apartment without her.

CHAPTER THIRTEEN

To everyone's surprise, although Connie talked a mile a minute, she dropped her confrontational attitude. Not that Mosley and Avril couldn't have handled her, they'd been doing it for decades, after all. Grace thought that was exactly what had happened while she was seeing Piper off. Avril had a satisfied gleam in her eyes, and Connie's voice was a bit shaky.

Niki stood apart from the three of them, and when she saw Grace, she grabbed her arm and pulled her back into the hall. "I knew she'd show up and ruin everything," she hissed as soon as they were alone.

"Doesn't sound too bad," Grace tried, but they both knew how quickly Connie's "not too bad" could turn volatile.

"Oh, don't you dare make excuses for her!"

"I'm not—"

"One afternoon! One damned afternoon like a real family is all I wanted. We should be telling funny stories and remembering the good things he did, the times we were happy. But no. This is just another episode of the Connie Show."

Grace didn't know whether to start with Niki's unrealistic expectations, or try to distract her with Piper's invitation. But mentioning

Piper would mean explaining why she left, which would make matters worse.

Mac and Aidan arrived, providing a welcome interruption. Niki gave Aidan a brief hug, which ended when Dylan appeared on the second-floor landing, and trotted down the stairs. Niki went to him and held his hand as she led him over.

"It's time you all meet properly instead of running into each other at will readings and funerals," she said as she introduced him to Mac. There was only the briefest of hesitations when she reached out to Aidan, but he stepped into the gap, identifying himself as Niki's oldest friend. With a grateful smile at him, Niki pulled Dylan toward the twin parlors, saying, "They are the easy ones. Let's get the rest over with."

As Dylan was welcomed by Avril and Mosley, they all watched to see what Connie would do. The tone Niki used when she introduced her mother sounded like a warning, but Connie only reacted by taking Dylan's outstretched hand and saying, "I'm so glad my daughter has a friend with her in this difficult time."

For a while, the otherworldly niceness continued while they all waited for the magic dust, or whatever sedative Connie had taken, to wear off. She was quiet, accepting condolences with little reaction until, in a moment of what appeared to be genuine grief, she picked up a photo of Stark that Niki had placed on the mantle under his mother's portrait.

"He was such a handsome man, wasn't he?" she asked Grace, who was standing nearby.

"Uhm, sure." Grace moved closer and looked over Connie's shoulder. She was surprised to see that as a young man, her uncle had, indeed, been very handsome.

"You only knew him a little while," Connie said. "I loved him very much for a long time."

If there was any artifice in her words, Grace couldn't see it, and no one else was close enough to hear them. Before she could respond, though, Connie moved away.

Lunch went well, if slightly boring. Connie was quiet, ate little, and only drank coffee. At one point, Aidan leaned over and whispered to Grace, "I was promised entertainment. What the hell is this?"

"Exactly what Niki wants," Grace replied as she passed him a platter of crab cakes and asked Avril what plans the Mallard Bay Garden Club had for the new landscaping at the library. Everyone else followed suit and for the duration of the meal, not a single voice was raised beyond a socially acceptable level. Conversations were neutral and had nothing to do with the deceased, his death, or the odd bequests in his will. It was all very, very, *nice.*

Eventually, the strangeness of too much civility wore down even Niki's determined smiles and platitudes. When Connie announced she needed to be going, her daughter popped up and ushered her to the door with the speed of someone still holding a hand grenade after the pin had been pulled. She watched out the side windows until Connie's car disappeared from sight.

"Cocktail time!" she announced as she turned back to the room. "Let me have your drink orders. I'm having a dirty martini."

For the next two hours, they gave Stark Delaney a wake. His daughter laughed and cried and seemed to shed some of the anger she'd carried since his death. When the chatter and momentum slowed, a corner had been turned. Whatever came of the medical examiner's final reports, whether Connie was tried for murder, or Winnie moved back to Mallard Bay, and how Niki chose to handle these looming problems, Stark was now in the past.

At least, that's what she told them as they made their final toast.

Grace hoped with all her heart that what her cousin said was true, but Stark's "gifts" were very much in the present. The yearbook waited for her at home, and until she'd determined what—if anything—its contents meant, she wouldn't be able to forget her uncle's last words to her.

Recognize anyone?

She was scared. It was one thing to want something life-changing when you had no way to get it, quite another to risk a peaceful life for the unknown. Wishing for her father to materialize had always been a dream without consequences. Until now.

Maybe.

So why couldn't she make herself look at that book?

Damn Stark Delaney. She wasn't going to let his last spiteful acts affect her family in any way. Suddenly, the thought of the book being in her home with her children was unbearable. She'd destroy it tonight and that would end Stark's presence in her life.

As she trotted down the steps of Delaney House and out to join Mac, she thought, "Bet you didn't see that one coming, did you, Uncle?" and laughed with relief.

After giving Niki a final hug, Mac had gone ahead of Grace to let the cousins have a few moments alone. Aidan walked out with him, and when they were a safe distance from the house, he said, "Well, Chief, what do you make of Nik's new squeeze? Personally, I'm thinking that Kirwan guy is slimy."

Mac gave him a quizzical look. "Why? He's former military and has an impressive resume."

"Ha! I knew you felt it, too. He puts out a vibe, right? The clothes, the Tesla. And *three* security companies? You can't even talk to the guy without getting that smug 'what I do's so secret, I'd have to kill you if I told you' crap. So, what'd you find out about him?"

"I checked on him," Mac admitted. "But I only Googled him and only once. You, however . . . Well, how have you been stalking him without Desi finding out?"

"I don't stalk." Aidan sounded indignant, but his neck flushed. The dig about his current girlfriend had hit its mark. Desi Marbury was a well trained Maryland State Police Detective who kept Aidan on a short leash, but until a year ago, Niki had been the only woman he had ever loved. Dylan Kirwan was the first man she'd dated since their breakup.

Correction, Mac thought—Niki and Dylan weren't just dating anymore. Both Niki and her new boyfriend had filled in details of their whirlwind relationship while everyone had been steering away from controversial issues in the early hours of the reception.

According to Niki, she'd met Dylan through mutual friends in New York and after a brief dating interlude that took place well away from her family, he'd had effectively moved into Delaney House. He'd rented the smallest of the inn's five bedrooms and refitted it as an office where he worked in between trips to New York and Washington. And although Grace had tried to get more information only to meet with blushing evasion from Niki, it was clear that the couple were living together in the small third floor apartment of Delaney House.

Mac wondered if Aidan knew about that development, and decided he did. While his former junior officer may have been oblivious to most of the requirements of police work, anything that caught his attention would be thoroughly and accurately dissected. After which, unfortunately, Aidan's vivid imagination would misconstrue and realign the facts he'd uncovered to fit his opinions. This habit was most annoying when he turned out to be right.

Which, at least as far as Mac could tell, was not the case with Dylan Kirwan, except in Aidan's opinion.

"C'mon, Chief," he said as they reached Mac's truck. "The guy's a tool, which is fine, I guess, if that's what Nik wants, but he's more off than that. He's hiding something."

Mac doubted very much if Aidan thought anything about the situation was "fine." He had been with Niki from grammar school until their early thirties. They'd been on and off so many times, she insisted it wasn't worth packing up every time they needed a break, so they'd been like an old married couple in every way but one—they'd never lived together. With Dylan Kirwan, she'd bypassed all the formalities and gone straight to cohabitation before most people in town knew his name. Aidan had done the same thing with Desi, and he'd done it first, but then he'd always wanted marriage and kids, and if he didn't screw it up with Desi by stalking Niki's new lover, he might get the life he was looking for.

"It's not our business," Mac said. "But I understand how you feel. Let's do this. You back off. I'll take another look at Kirwan, and if anything looks off, I'll make some calls. But we're not spying on our friends, or meddling in their intimate lives."

"Since when?" Aidan demanded. "That's exactly what we do, and you know it."

"*Police officers* have a little latitude when the situation warrants it. You aren't a police officer anymore." Then, softening his tone, Mac added, "As I said, I understand your concerns. I'll look into Kirwan. But you should know by now that Desi isn't big on second chances. Don't ruin it with her, Aidan."

They went their separate ways, each sure he was right and hoping that the other would be reasonable. But Aidan kept hearing the Chief's words. Mac knew Desi well, and everything he'd said was true. Technically. Aidan couldn't risk losing her and backsliding into a relationship with Niki, even if that meant he'd have to let the Chief handle Dylan Kirwan and whatever that bastard was up to.

He drove home to Desi, hoping she wouldn't ask him for any details. He didn't even have a good Connie story to distract her.

CHAPTER FOURTEEN

"What do you mean, we have to go to Ocean City?" Niki said. "Look, you woke me up. Let's talk later."

Grace, who had been awake off and on all night, was juggling a squirming Sonny while trying to feed both children and get a piece of toast down for her own breakfast. Before she could react to her cousin's brush-off, Fiona snatched the phone off the table and threw it at her mother, who caught it with one hand while keeping her grip on the baby.

Her stern, "That's enough, Little Missy!" didn't faze Fiona, but made Rocky bark and Niki apologize for being rude.

Grace didn't bother to say who she'd been scolding, but put the phone—in speaker mode—out of her daughter's reach and let Niki explain she was too busy for a road trip.

"I don't care what he left in that apartment, Grace. Piper can have it all. She seems to be the embodiment of everything the rest of us weren't to him, so let her have at it."

"I promised her, Nik," Grace said over Fiona's demands of 'more duce, Mama!'

Hallie arrived as she was attempting to hold Sonny's bottle steady with her chin while pouring orange juice into Fiona's sippy cup.

"Awesome skills," the nanny said as she picked Fiona up. "But I've got this."

"Are you listening to me?" Niki demanded through the phone.

"You, the children, Hallie, the dog, and Mac singing in the shower where he's been holed up for the last fifteen minutes."

If Niki hadn't laughed, she might have won the argument.

An hour later, they were on the road to Ocean City.

"I apologize for yesterday," Niki said, as she shook Piper's hand. "My mother wasn't supposed to be at the luncheon. I really wanted to talk with you and thank you for being Dad's friend. He didn't have many."

Piper seemed uncomfortable. "No problem. I don't need to be here for you to go inside. It was your father's place, but Mr. Mosley said everything belongs to me. He arranged for the manager to let me in, and I looked around, but I didn't take anything. It's not . . ." she hesitated. "I mean, take whatever you want now. I have cleaners coming in tomorrow and whatever's left in there goes to the dump."

The shy, sympathetic young woman who hadn't wanted to make a scene at Delaney House seemed to have no problem at all provoking one today. They were standing on the sidewalk outside the tiny studio apartment that had been Stark's last home. A cheap remodel of a mid-century motel offered cut-rate rents five miles west of the Ocean City strip. Only the name on the long-burned out neon sign indicated that the *Sand & Sea* had ever housed anyone on vacation.

Grace studied their surroundings and gave the two women some space. She already regretted insisting that Niki accept Piper's invitation. Now that they were here, the ramshackle building jammed up next to a liquor store and vaping bar seemed an unlikely place to find any answers to Stark's death.

"What's the hurry?" Niki asked, frowning. "I thought the rent was paid until the end of the month."

Piper shrugged and pulled her keys out of her back pocket. "I get a refund on the unused days, okay? I know it's pennies to you, but to me it's good money."

"I'm sorry," Niki said, not sounding sorry at all.

Piper didn't let it pass. "Look, neither of you seems to realize what happened to me. I *found* him, remember? I came to check on my friend and I found him dead. It was horrible. *Gross.* Going through his crap is just too much." Unlocking the door, she added, "I can't stay any longer. I have a date."

"Okay, okay," Niki said. "But we didn't know all of that, okay? I'm sorry for what you went through."

"Lock up when you leave," Piper said. "Push the button on the knob and give it a good slam. The door can stick sometimes."

"Wonder how she knows that?" Niki said as they watched the angry woman drive away in Stark's old Camry. "Sounds like she was here a lot, didn't it?"

It did, but Grace only said, "Don't do that, Nik. Let's just check it out and go." She was already sorry she'd insisted on this trip.

Piper was right. There wasn't much of anything that anyone would want in the run-down room. Anything the police hadn't taken in their sweep had a coating of fingerprint powder mixed with dust. There were signs of the fight that occurred on the last night of Stark's life—a shattered mirror, dents on the cheap plasterboard walls of the sitting area, and a broken coffee table with a missing leg. Grace wondered uneasily if it had been used to hit Stark's chest.

"I can't believe the neighbors didn't call the police when all this was going on," Grace said as she gave the mirror shards wide berth and moved into the kitchen area.

"Did you even look at the neighborhood we're in?" Nicki snapped. "Does this seem like a place where anyone calls the cops when they hear a fight?" She half-heartedly poked around in the clothes closet.

Grace thought about the large designer home that Stark and Connie had owned near Mallard Bay. The house, which was now one of the

Delaney Inns vacation rentals, had five ensuite bedrooms, expansive living areas and a gourmet kitchen. The galley kitchenette at the *Sand & Sea* consisted of a dorm size refrigerator, a small microwave, and a four-cup coffee pot. The pool snack bar at the Queen's Brooke house was larger and much better equipped.

"This is all I'm taking of his." Niki held up a dated tweed jacket. "He said he sold all of his good clothes, but I remember this from when I was a kid. It still smells like him." She took a moment, then added, "I hope the police took everything of value, or that Piper did and lied about it, because otherwise he lost his college ring and his great-grandfather's signet ring that Gran gave him on his twenty-first birthday. He wasn't wearing them when the funeral home got him. The rings were the real reason I agreed to come today."

"I'm sorry I talked you into this," Grace said.

Niki shook her head. "Don't be. I'm sorry I gave you a hard time. It would have been awful if I had to worry that I'd missed my only opportunity to look for the rings in here."

"Lost" was the euphemism the family used when Stark pawned something and his gambling winnings weren't large enough to buy it back. Niki seemed resigned, and Grace didn't think another expression of sympathy from her would help. Few people felt sorry for Stark, but so many "thoughts and prayers" sentiments had been heaped on Niki that she'd threatened to scream at the next person who gave her a pitying look.

"One more thing and then we'll go," Grace said as she dragged the lone chair from the kitchen table over to the closet and stepped up on the seat. The only things she found on the high top shelf were bug bodies and dust. Undeterred, she moved on to the bed and stripped back the covers. When she lifted a corner of the mattress, Niki came to give her a hand. "You're crazy, Grace! What are you looking for? The only thing you're gonna find under here is a family of bedbugs."

"You checked all his clothes?"

"Yeah. Maybe Mac can find out what the police took out of here. Although, I guess it doesn't matter since Piper gets all of it."

"It matters," Grace said. She dusted off her hands, then gave up and went to wash them at the kitchen sink. "He hid that yearbook for ages, and I keep thinking he had more information about Mom."

"Why? He never said anything to me, and you saw how he was whenever Aunt Julia's name came up. He shut the conversation down."

"Not every time." Grace said. "Let's go."

Niki waited until they were in the car before she said, "What did Dad do to you?"

Grace said it wasn't a good time and Niki told her to get over herself and spill it. "You're not sparing my feelings," she said. "Just pissing me off."

"Yeah. I can see that." Grace took a minute to let the whole painful memory come back. "When he and Connie came back last winter for that final visit before they broke up—"

"The visit from hell, you mean," Niki said glumly. "Longest week of my life."

"Not a great one for me, either. Sonny was only a few weeks old. I brought him to the office to see Cy and Marjorie, and I ran into Stark on the way in. He was furious because Cy wouldn't release the annual trust fund payment early. Even I thought Cy was being picky about that. It was due to be paid out in three days, but you know what a stickler he is."

She had greeted her uncle civilly and tried to pass him on the porch, but Stark blocked her way. Looking first at her, then Sonny, he said, "So this is the new one. At least you've given your kids their fathers. That's an improvement over your mother's behavior, I suppose. Or maybe that clever mind of yours has figured it all out. Do you know who your daddy is, Grace?"

"Oh, no." Niki shook her head, then stopped. "Wait, did he say anything else? Did he know who Jonathan Reagan was? I mean, your real father. Did Dad know him?"

"I don't know." This was the hardest part to admit. Every time she thought about walking away from Stark without saying a word, she felt the shame of her cowardice. "I got away from him as fast as I could. All I could think of was that I was holding Sonny in front of me in my arms. My baby was between us and I . . ." She stopped, trying to find a kind way to finish her sentence.

Niki did it for her. "You wanted to get your baby away from the nasty man who was always trying to hurt you. You don't have to protect me, Gracie. I know exactly who and what my father was, and I'm not ashamed to say I am glad he can't hurt anyone ever again."

Grace couldn't let her think that. "There's more," she said quietly. "And it's all on me."

CHAPTER FIFTEEN

Who's your daddy, Grace?

"I made a decision when I married Mac. I thought long and hard about my life and I decided to leave everything negative behind me and start over. Not literally, of course, but emotionally. And that meant I closed the door on finding my father. I closed it for good. I forgave Mom for lying to me about his identity, for inventing Jonathan Reagan, and for keeping me away from you and Emma."

"Gran." Niki's correction was automatic. She never let Grace distance herself from their grandmother.

"Mom lied." Grace said miserably. She had adored her mother and had grown up trying to emulate her. Coming to terms with the deception Julia had maintained to her death had been hard, and the wounds they'd caused were proving slow to heal. "But she was trying to protect me, and I'm trying to protect my own children. Mom was never vindictive, and I still trust her instincts. So, I put it all behind me. And I put all the bad things that happened during my first year here behind me, too."

"Then why search this place?" Niki asked with her typical bluntness. "Why are you still looking for hints and information if you don't want to know who your father is?"

Why *was* she? She had made the right decision, and she had to be strong enough to stick with it. Impulsively, she reached over and hugged Niki. "I didn't want to miss any information or evidence that might be important later, especially if Connie's charged in his death. But I fell down the old 'looking for daddy' rabbit hole there for a minute. Stark implied he knew who my father was, but he's lied about that before, so I guess I couldn't help myself. I had to make sure there wasn't more hidden away here. And there isn't."

Niki seemed to be satisfied with that. "I totally get it. It's exactly what I'm doing with my own family. But, Grace, I *know* what I'm walking away from. I know what they've done and what Mom will continue to do if I let her. But you don't know your father's side—"

"He abandoned me." Grace said as she started the car. "He wasn't there. Mom was. And that's the end of it."

Never one to take a hint, Niki said, "But the yearbook! We could just look again, and—"

"No. I'm getting rid of it. I didn't find any information about Mom or my father, and Stark didn't leave any clues. Not in the book, anyway. I'm done. I have a new life."

"Okay. But let's go by the bar where Dad used to work. Maybe he talked to people there about his plan to drive us all crazy with that stupid poem and his will. You said the police didn't make a sweep of that place."

After a moment, Grace relented. They were here for Niki's closure, after all. "Good idea. Maybe the owner or the other employees will have more information about his last days than Piper did."

"You mean maybe they'll be more helpful than Piper was?"

"Well, they could hardly be *less* helpful, could they? And she won't be there to put a damper on the conversation."

But, as it turned out, they found a very interesting development at the Blow Back In Bar. Piper's date was taking place in full view of her boss, co-workers and a half-dozen people who were scattered around the room playing Keno. At the large circular bar that overlooked the boardwalk, Piper sat on the customer side of the counter, smiling up at the handsome, muscular man next to her.

Winston Delaney.

After many discussions on how to avoid Winnie when he was released from prison, Grace and Niki had walked right into him. And neither he nor Piper were happy with the interruption.

Winnie was the first to recover, sliding off the bar stool and grabbing Niki up in a bear hug. "Baby sister! You look great!"

The next few moments were a mash up of Niki freeing herself from his embrace while Grace turned on Piper and said, "Really? Didn't you think we would want to know this?"

"How would I?" Piper snapped. "My friends are hardly your business."

"Friends?" Niki repeated incredulously, looking from her brother to Piper. "*Winnie* is your date?"

Before Piper could answer, Winnie reclaimed his bar stool and slung an arm around her. "Yep. That would be me. Can you believe our old man played matchmaker? He knew Pip and I would hit it off."

Grace noticed Piper didn't look too happy with that characterization of their relationship. She wanted to get the girl away from Winnie and question her, but given the united front the *friends* were projecting, that wasn't a likely option. She realized with a start that the anger she felt was a pretty good equalizer. The fear that always overwhelmed her when she thought about Winnie had disappeared. In the daylight, face to face, she could see the three years of prison life in his once boyish face. His hard, glittering blue eyes were full of malice as he met her gaze, but it only made her want to punch him. Hard.

"Oh, come on, girls," Winnie said. He gave Piper a squeeze and released her. Opening a fat wallet, he extracted a twenty and said, "I've already bought the house a round and we toasted Dad. Let me buy you a drink and maybe you can think of something nice to say about him."

A tall, thin woman who'd been wiping down the bar and openly listening to their conversation, flipped a towel over her shoulder and joined them, saying, "I'm Angela Glass. You can call me Angie. I own this place. Stark worked for me and I'm really sorry for your loss."

"Thank you," Niki said, her eyes suddenly shiny with tears. "Did my father leave anything here? We've been to his apartment, and wanted to check with you, too. "

Winnie said, "Looking for these?" He reached into his front jeans pocket. Without taking his eyes off Niki, he pulled out the two rings Stark had always worn, slipped them on, and held his hand up for them to see. "Let's start over, girls. Angie, let me introduce my sister Niki and our cousin Grace. They've come to welcome me home. Give them whatever they want." He picked up his wallet again and opened it to show them the stack of bills inside. "Dad gave Pip and me pretty much everything, so the least I can do is treat them to a drink."

After a long look at the money, the bar owner said, "You sure don't take after your father, *Winnie*."

"Yeah, I get that a lot." His words were bitter and still aimed at Grace and Niki.

Angie said, "Your father was a nice man, Niki. He told us you were a real success story up there in Kingston County. He was proud of *you*." Winnie got a sideways sneer.

Niki smiled and said, "That means a lot, thank you. And anybody who can slap down my brother is a friend of mine for sure."

"Hey!" Winnie protested.

Ignoring him, Angie said, "So, my new friends, what can I put on Mr. Big Shot's tab for you?"

"Something expensive, please," Niki said as she took a seat next to Piper. "I'm not driving."

"I guess that makes me the DD," Grace said. "How about a Diet Coke?" She took the next stool down from Niki and wondered how she was going to get them out of this uncomfortable scene.

"Think I can do a bit better than that." Angie checked the drink orders that had come in while they'd been talking and went back to work. As soon as she stepped away, all pretense of friendliness evaporated.

"What are you up to?" Niki said to her brother. Her voice was low, but cutting. "I can guess where you got Dad's rings." She glared at Piper, who flushed.

"Winnie said he was supposed to inherit them." After a quick glance around, she added, "I don't care what Angie says, it was Winnie that Stark was proud of. He told me so."

Niki looked crushed, but Grace could practically feel the deceit in the taunt. She ignored the entire exchange and said, "Where'd you get that money, Winnie? You went to prison without a cent to your name and just got out yesterday morning. How did you get all that in less than a day? Or are those bills all ones?"

With a sly grin that Grace remembered all too well, Winnie pulled random bills from his wallet. When the counter was littered with twenties and fifties, he scooped it all up. "You know where I got this, Cousin. Dad told you himself, in his will, remember? I got a copy of it, too, you know. He said he'd already given me what he wanted me to have. Niki got earrings, and I got a nice bank account he's been feeding for me since I had to go away. By the way, thanks for the long vacation, Cousin Grace, but next time you want me to leave town, just ask nicely, and I'll go without a fuss."

Niki flushed with anger and leaned in to block his view of Grace. "Dad would *not* have given you any money. He hated what you'd done and besides, he was broke."

"That's where you're wrong," Winnie said. "I guess poor old Pop loved me enough to hide a little bit away for me. And not only the money to start over, but he set me up with a job with his friend Frankie's business. Who better to work in a pawn shop than the son of his best customer? Frankie even found me a place to live. He was real torn up over Dad."

"Frankie Elmer is a loan shark, you imbecile!" Niki shouted, all restraint gone.

"Hey!" Angie said sharply, walking over to address Winnie as if he'd been the one making noise. "Keep it civil, man, or get out. Piper, your shift started ten minutes ago and table nine needs another round."

Piper quickly did as she was told, pausing only to give Winnie a kiss.

CHAPTER SIXTEEN

Niki eyed the pinkish cocktail the bar owner handed her, then took a long sip. Her eyes bulged as the alcohol hit the back of her mouth.

"Slow it down, girlfriend," Angie said. "That's the OC version of anesthesia. All alcohol with a hint of pineapple." She handed Grace a lookalike drink with a green straw. "Yours is non-alcoholic, but the fresh juice is nice." To Winnie she added, "That'll be sixty bucks and another ten for the server."

"The hell you say." Winnie stood and leaned across the counter. "You're full of—"

They never learned what Winnie thought Angie might be full of because in the next moment he was dangling two inches off the ground, his feet scrabbling for the floor as a massive man held him up by the collar of his shirt. "Whatcha want me to do with this fool, Angie?"

"Put him down so he can pay me, Billy. And get yourself another beer. I appreciate the help."

Angie's smile for her bouncer was warm. The look she gave Winnie, not so much. His feet hit the floor so hard his knees buckled.

"Aw, hell," the big man complained. "You coulda took him just fine, Ange. Them muscles he's showing off are from weight lifting. Got 'em while you was inside, ain't that right, *Winnie*? You ladies okay, now?"

"Yes, thanks," Niki said, and gave the giant a grateful smile before turning on her brother. "Stay away from us. I never want to see you again."

Before Winnie could answer, Billy thumped Winnie's shoulder and said, "You heard her. Now pay your bill."

Angie smiled her approval.

After another round of thanks to Billy, Niki took another gulp of her drink, shuddered, and said, "This is excellent, but—"

"Yeah," the bar owner grinned. "You want to live through the day, huh?"

When a sullen Winnie had paid their tab, Billy did a monster-sized version of an up and down glare and shambled off. Niki wasted no time in saying goodbye to Angie and heading for the door, but as Grace rose to follow her, Winnie caught her elbow.

"Gonna run home and tell on me, Cousin? Send your husband after me? He can't touch me. Those lies you told can't hurt me anymore."

Grace wanted to echo Niki's order for him to stay away, but she knew it would only encourage him. He would probably follow them home out of spite. Plus, his touch was nauseating.

"Grace!" Niki called from the doorway. "Let's go."

"Bye, girls," Winnie said, waving. "Oh, Nik! Better check those earrings of yours. Dad said to tell you he was sorry." His laughter followed them out onto the boardwalk.

"I hope the Hulk beats his brains out," Niki muttered.

Grace agreed, but she didn't think they'd get rid of Winnie that easily.

They were nearly to Ocean Pines when Niki realized the silver link bracelet she'd been wearing was missing. Her emotions already in turmoil, she burst into tears. "I have to get it back," she wailed. "Dad gave it to me for my sixteenth birthday. God knows it isn't expensive, but I don't have much from him and I wear it all the time."

There was no appeasing her and Grace's suggestion that she call Angie was met with scorn. When she stopped at the iconic Pop's Market just outside of Trappe, she got a scathing, "What now?" from her still sniffling cousin.

"Look, Mac's got both kids today, and I promised him a pie, okay?" She was also going to get tomatoes, squash, and late season peas, but the look on Niki's face stopped her from saying so. "Why don't you call Angie while I shop? I'm sure you had the bracelet on when we left the apartment, and you've crawled all over this car, so it has to be in the Blow Back In or on the boardwalk."

"Great," Niki said. "You go ahead and get pie while I reinsert myself into Winnie's and Piper's world and give him a reason to contact me again."

"I'll call," Grace said, pulling out her phone.

She got a chilly, "forget it," for her trouble. The fragrant peaches she bought as a peace offering barely rated a smile, but by the time they drove through Cambridge, Niki loosened up a bit, muttering, "Sorry," as they crossed the Choptank River and entered Talbot County. Then, as if some barrier had been broken, she began to talk, sounding angrier with each word.

"Dad did a lot of despicable things, but getting Winnie a job and an apartment and giving him *more* money? Hooking him up with a *woman*? That's just gross! He probably gave Piper his car as a bribe." She lowered her voice to a gravelly imitation of Stark's. "'Here, sweet thang, if you'll date my ex-con son who tried to kill my niece, you can have an eight-year-old Toyota with four bald tires.' Yeah. What girl wouldn't jump at that?"

Grace laughed, even though the comment about Winnie's attack made her wince. "You know Winnie would say anything to upset you."

Niki sighed. "I called Angie while you were debating pie options. She said she'd look for the bracelet, but with my luck, Winnie will find it first and give it to Piper. She has everything else, why not that, too?"

"That's not going to happen. Angie will find it, and Winnie'll be lucky if Billy lets him live to see his next beer."

This seemed to cheer Niki a little, but she said, "No more jokes, okay? And for heaven's sake, don't say everything will be all right, because it won't be."

"I'm sorry." Grace dropped it after that. This time, the silence wasn't charged with anger, but it still wasn't a pleasant ride. She tried again as they entered Mallard Bay. "Remember, Mac and I are taking the kids and Hallie and Avril to Ocean City in a couple of weeks? We've got a suite at the Princess Royale and have no intention of going anywhere near the boardwalk. Why don't you come, too? We'll have a blast." She knew as she said the words that Niki would refuse. While she loved Grace's children, she got nervous after an hour of baby-centric activity. "Get a room of your own if you don't want to bunk in with us. Please come. To get away will do you good."

"I do need to get away," Niki admitted. "But a few miles of beach won't be enough of a barrier between my brother and me."

"It *will* be okay," Grace said as Niki got out of the car at Delaney House. "The worst is over now. We have some rough times ahead, but nothing like the last few weeks. You'll see."

Niki sighed and said, "I love you, Gracie, but you're a terrible liar."

CHAPTER SEVENTEEN

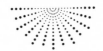

Avril, Mosley, and Mac seemed to feel the same way that evening when Grace gave them the details of the fiasco at the Blow Back In. Mac had organized dinner to surprise her and save her the trouble of filling everyone in separately. And, as tired as she was after wrangling the children into bed, Grace was happy to unload on the three people who would understand all the nuances of the day's events.

They ate on the patio, enjoying the evening breeze off the river, and for a while, Grace almost believed the platitudes she'd spouted to Niki. But even the fried chicken from Baldy's Market and Avril's lemon artichoke potato salad couldn't lessen the gloom that fell over the table when she described finding Winnie with Piper Tilden at the Blow Back In.

"Stark, Connie, and Winnie," Avril said as she finished the last forkful of buttery sautéed squash that had been Mac's contribution to the meal. "That trio is like an incurable fungus. I'm convinced the hospital switched babies when Niki was born. Somewhere a perfectly lovely couple can't figure out how they spawned a narcissistic sociopath."

No one argued with her, but the comment gave Grace an idea. "You told me Stark was a sweet child. What changed him, do you think?"

Avril and Mosley looked at each other, but said nothing.

Mac looked interested, though, so Grace pushed a bit more. "Maybe if we knew why he was so warped, we could make some sense of that poem. You know, the part about how he's taken what we really want?"

More silence.

Under the table, Mac bumped her leg, then said, "I think some things are lost to time, honey. What's important is that we're all here to help Niki get through whatever comes next from Winnie and Connie."

Looking relieved, Mosley quickly agreed.

But Avril understood what Grace had been asking. "Some things are hard to talk about," she said slowly. "Especially if you don't know the whole story."

Grace hesitated, but there were no more nudges from Mac, so she asked her question. "Do you know why Stark was always so angry?"

"No," Avril said. "Not for sure. I can guess, but I don't want to drag up old pain and make things worse."

In a rare display of affection to his lifelong friend, Mosley reached out and patted Avril's shoulder. "It's okay," he said, softly. "I'll tell her."

Mac refilled the wine glasses as they waited for the old lawyer to arrange his thoughts. When Mosley finally spoke, though, it wasn't about Stark. Not at first. Tucking his thumbs in his waistband and rocking his chair back, he settled into the story by saying, "As you know, I loved Emma."

Grace nearly choked on the wine she'd just sipped. She knew how he'd felt about her grandmother, but he never spoke about their long, often one-sided love affair. So why now?

"What you don't know," he said, "is that I loved her from the day I met her and Ford knew it. Unfortunately, young Stark knew, too."

From everything Grace had heard about her grandfather, she couldn't imagine how the men had remained friends. She noticed Avril didn't look shocked, even though Mosley had been engaged to her sister during the same time period.

"We were gentlemen," Mosley went on, as if acknowledging her thoughts. "I never acted on my feelings while Ford was alive, and he didn't challenge me on them. Only once, about a week before he died, out of the blue he said, 'You'll take care of Em and the children when I'm gone.' We'd just updated the family trust and his will, so I thought he was referring to that. But then he said, 'It shouldn't be a hardship since you love her.' We were interrupted and never finished the conversation. In fact, we never spoke privately again."

There was an uncomfortable silence, but Mosley didn't seem to notice as he studied the fading sunset, lost in his thoughts.

Avril finally broke the silence. "Those were awful, tragic days for everyone, but especially for Emma and the children. And you, Cy."

He nodded, still gazing past them. "I opened my front door the morning after Ford shot himself and saw old Chief McNulty coming up the walk. He'd come to take me to Emma. She'd found Ford right after he died, and called for help, but didn't cooperate after that. She wouldn't leave the children and told him I would handle everything. Later, she told me it was because of Stark."

Avril shook her head. "Let's not, Cy. It's over, don't dwell on it."

He ignored her and continued. "Stark never spoke of it, but Emma was sure he'd seen his father's death. He was so young, and he was almost catatonic for a while. Then one day he walked in when I was holding Emma. He started screaming and after that, he talked non-stop for hours. He seemed to know everything about Ford's death. Or, he thought he did, and he blamed me. He wasn't in that shell any longer, but after that, he was always angry when I was around. If Emma and I ever had any chance together, Stark killed it."

"Now, that really is enough," Avril sputtered. "Even if he saw Ford die, he was too little to have known what happened." Turning to Grace and Mac, she added, "We've argued about this for years. Stark has always blamed others for his misfortunes. Yes, he had a terrible childhood and for ages we made excuses for him." She gave Mosley a pitying look. "Eventually, I started holding him responsible for his actions, but Mr. Pushover here always covered for the boy when he could."

"I promised Ford." Mosley's tone said the subject was closed.

"I'm sorry I brought it all up and made you relive it," Grace said. "It's such a sad story, and it doesn't seem to have anything to do with the poem's meaning."

"Maybe we should look at the yearbook together," Mac suggested. "Cy and Avril might see something you missed."

Neither of their guests seemed enthusiastic and Grace said, "No," more sharply than she intended, earning her surprised looks. "I'm sorry. I didn't mean it to sound that way."

"You're tired," Mac said soothingly. "But you'll eventually want to know what's in it."

She tried to tamp down the frustration she felt at yet one more person, *her* person, trying to tell her what she wanted. "It's 'no' tonight, Mac, and 'no' for good. I'm happy. Really happy right now with what I have and I don't want to screw it up. Mom thought she was protecting me, and I think Stark knew why. He'd never have given me that book unless it would hurt me." Then, in fits and starts, she told them about her last meeting with her uncle and his taunts about her father.

Mac was livid and Avril ranted non-stop until she ran out of breath. But Mosley was the one Grace watched.

When he realized she was looking at him, he said, "I remember that day. He made some threats when I refused to release his annual trust fund payment early—mostly that he could make everyone sorry if he was cheated, again. I wasn't concerned. That was his usual reaction when he didn't get what he wanted. When he showed up at my door unannounced a few weeks ago, I thought he'd returned for round two, but that evening he was actually calm. That was when he gave me the new will and the box of gifts. Now, of course, I know he was dying and tying up loose ends."

"Loose ends, my foot," Avril snapped. "He was planting little bombs to detonate after he died."

"It doesn't matter," Grace said. "He's gone, so let's forget him, at least for tonight." She was sick of the whole topic, but forced a smile and got up to hug each of them, making Mosley blush by planting a kiss on his bald head. "I have blackberry pie from Pop's Market and ice cream."

Later, as they walked their guests out to Avril's car, Mac told them to call right away if they saw Winnie or heard from him. "I don't expect any trouble, especially since he's down in Ocean City."

"We'll handle Winnie if he shows up," Grace added, smiling at her husband. "We outnumber him, especially in brain cells. It will all be fine."

Mosley and Avril laughed, but their bravado was only a polite wrap up to the evening's conversation. Winnie always caused problems and all they could do was wait and see what he did next.

CHAPTER EIGHTEEN

The weekend was an abrupt change from the emotional stress of the past week, but instead of providing her with a much-needed rest, Grace felt overwhelmed on Saturday morning. Her system for compartmentalizing tasks and problems and being present in the moment with her children evaporated, and she wondered how she'd ever managed the routine that kept everything on track.

Her mind wouldn't stay put, but floated like an untethered balloon. By noon, her house was a wreck, her children were dirty, and they were all still wearing pajamas. When Mac's phone rang and he stepped out of the room to talk, she wanted to cry with frustration at being left alone.

Then he announced he had to go out of town.

To Miami.

Somehow, she held her tongue as he explained about a big break in a human trafficking case he'd worked on last year and the need for his testimony in front of a federal grand jury.

"I wasn't expecting this to happen, honey, and I'm so sorry. Yesterday, all they needed from me was the report and my sworn statement, but the panel had questions that weren't addressed and I have to be there when they reconvene on Monday." He started picking up toys and baby detritus. "Maybe Hallie can stay over? I'll only be gone until Tuesday."

Grace decided that honesty in a marriage was overrated—right now she could use a big fat lie from her husband. Something along the lines of "I'll retire and take over all the housework and child care. Why don't you go to the spa?"

A shriek from the nursery ended the conversation and saved her dignity. She knew Mac would be useless on the home front while he prepared for Monday, and in theory, she understood why. "You need to go to your office and get ready," she called over her shoulder as she left to sort out her cranky baby. "Give me time to shower and dress and I've got it from here, okay?"

There was silence from the den, and she knew he was trying to decide if she was serious.

"I'm serious, Mac. You need to go, and it's okay."

It *was* okay, she told herself. But he needed to get out of the house before she broke down and begged him to stay.

She was able to keep a smile on her face and amuse Fiona with silly versions of *Old MacDonald* while Sonny had his bottle. By the time Mac had arranged his flight and left for his office in the police station, the baby was down for his nap and she and Fiona were sharing a lunch of chicken strips and carrot sticks. They walked him to the door, waved goodbye, then Grace promised her daughter ice cream for dinner if she'd take a nap now with Mommy.

"We'll be fine, Sweet Pea," she said, then kissed the top of Fiona's head as they snuggled on the sofa.

She only had an hour's reprieve, but it got her through to bedtime. The house was destroyed, but Fiona accepted a side order of macaroni and cheese with her cup of vanilla ice cream and Grace did two loads of laundry with the help of *Sesame Street*. All in all, it was a win, she decided when she was finally in bed.

Now, all she had to do was let Mac actually leave tomorrow morning and stay sane until it was Monday and she could go to the office and relax. She was so tired that the irony of that last thought was totally lost.

She had just turned the children over to Hallie on Monday morning and was in the living room loading up her briefcase when she caught sight of her mother's yearbook. It lay half buried under the Sunday paper and a novel Mac had been reading. She picked it up, running her fingertips over *1980*. She had so many questions about that time in her mother's life.

It had always seemed unlikely that Julia, with her never-back-down-from-anything personality, would have let a surprise pregnancy keep her from school, but she had no other explanation. Her mother had never discussed that period in her life and Stark's lies were all Grace had ever heard about the year before she was born. Again, guilt poked at her. Was she really going to let her uncle's hateful rhetoric stand unchallenged?

Stark's taunts had varied depending on his mood. Sometimes he said Julia lied about Jonathan Reagan because she didn't know who Grace's father was. Then he'd say she knew and dropped out of college to get away from the boy who'd impregnated her. Whenever he talked about his sister, a new, uglier twist on one of the two stories would spew out.

"It's behind me," Grace said, picking up the book and shoving it into her briefcase. She didn't know what she would do with it, but it didn't belong in her house.

"So, what are you going to do?"

"I don't know. She seems so fragile now, I hate to say anything at all."

Grace stopped at the turn in the staircase leading to her second-floor office. Ordinarily she wouldn't eavesdrop on her employees, but

Aidan sounded frustrated and Lily—who was never without a solution to any problem—was clearly stumped by whatever they were discussing. Who was the "she" who was so fragile?

"I get it," Aidan said. "Two little kids and a whacked-out family. It's a wonder she gets here at all in the morning, but we can't keep covering for her. For one thing, I'm crap at that and for another, it's not fair to her."

Grace stopped. They were talking about *her*.

Her happy anticipation of being a functioning professional in clean clothes vanished, and she felt overheated with embarrassment. Her watch said nine-thirty. How had it gotten to be so late?

"I'll talk to her today," Lily said. "But I hope she's had a good weekend."

She had to move before one of them saw her on the security camera that sat on Lily's desk. Abruptly, Aidan asked Lily if she'd tried the new Indian carryout in Easton, and Grace knew she'd been spotted. She trotted up the rest of the steps and pretended not to notice how uncomfortable her staff looked when she appeared on the landing. Ordinarily, she'd stop for coffee and a chat, but the awkward silence made that impossible. She went straight through to her office, embarrassed and in desperate need of caffeine, and tried to decide what to do.

"I guess you heard us."

She looked up to find Lily in the doorway holding two cups of coffee. Reaching out for her Wonder Woman mug, she said, "Did Aidan run off and leave you to mend fences?"

"At the speed of light. But it's probably for the best. He's not likely to make it better, is he?" Lily sat down across from her without waiting for an invitation. "I'm sorry that we hurt your feelings, but we're worried."

"You were discussing me with *Aidan*."

"I guess it would look bad if I said he started it."

"Did he?"

"No." Lily sighed and sipped her coffee. "He's a team player, Grace. I know you and Mac have had other experiences with him, but he's changed. He thinks the world of you, no matter what he says."

Not in the mood to be placated or redirected, Grace said, "Want to explain why my team players were discussing how to handle me and my apparently many shortcomings?" She crossed her arms, now more angry than hurt. They were supposed to be her team, her support. Critiquing her performance was not in their job descriptions. Then she remembered what Aidan had said. "What kind of covering up have you and Mr. Wonderful been doing for me behind my back?"

Lily blinked, but otherwise didn't react to the barb. "He used a poor choice of words, but we have had to scramble to cover a few things lately."

A sinking feeling told her she would regret asking, but it was too late to stop now. "Such as?"

"The meetings you had me reschedule last week. Everyone under-stood about Stark's funeral and you needing time off, but it came on the heels of the two near misses on the Murphy's application deadlines for their rezoning requests. And the Rotary meeting you missed the week before is still a sore point for Mr. Mosley."

"I'm not a member of—"

"You were the guest speaker."

"That was ages ago!"

"Week before last," Lily said, not giving her an inch. "This morning you had an eight-thirty teleconference with Ellender York."

Grace picked up her now lukewarm coffee and drank half the cup, willing the caffeine to go straight to her tired brain. Lily did her usual Lily thing of waiting with a neutral expression and who-knew-what kind of thoughts.

"I'm sorry," Grace finally said. "I'm doing the best I can, so an apology is all I have. But I'm likely to be in this phase for a while, so we'd better figure out how to handle it." She flipped to a clean page on the nearest legal pad, picked up a pen and looked at Lily. "I don't suppose you have any ideas?"

"Only if you can stand for me to micromanage your days."

"You'd have to fight Hallie for that privilege."

"Already done. She's on board."

"You've discussed me with my nanny, too?" Grace wanted to be insulted, but she was the one responsible for the embarrassing situation. In fact, this was almost a replay of the morning Hallie sold her on hiring a nanny for Fiona, or, as Hallie referred to herself, a maternal engineer. "All right," she groused. "Since it apparently takes a village to raise me, how do you, Aidan, and Hallie think we should handle my life?"

CHAPTER NINETEEN

L ily said, "You know there's a reason Mr. Mosley has The Bat, and he doesn't have two babies and an overload of work to deal with. Not to mention your current family crisis."

Grace winced. "I think you mean cris*es*."

Lily nodded. "That's true for Stark's murder, and that riddle he left. But Winnie's return is part of your personal life that you have to deal with. I wouldn't interfere unless you asked for help."

"How about the yearbook? My mysterious father?"

"Your business. Unless—"

"I ask for help," Grace finished for her.

"Either of those topics could consume all of your attention. That would just be natural, Grace. Listen, I love Mr. Mosley, too, but you have to admit that you have three times his workload, plus the other complications I listed."

She was right, and as much as Grace wanted to say she wasn't, there was a feeling of relief at hearing the truth spoken out loud, even if guilt came on its heels. "Cyrus is older than God," she protested. "*And* he's supposed to be retired!"

"I know all of that. I'm still saying you need help, maybe your own Bat and optimally, more staff, too."

Grace stared at her. "Why? You're not leaving, are you?" It had been a worry since Lily had agreed to take the paralegal job while she decided whether or not to return to law school. "I mean, you would be a fantastic attorney, and if you have to leave . . ." Her voice trailed off, mainly because no words came to mind that were even remotely encouraging.

"That depends," Lily said. "I wasn't going to bring this up now, but you asked if I had solutions, and I do. I'd like to finish my law degree —piecemeal—one online or evening class at a time. But to do that, I need a steady job, and more money, and some kind of control over my day. All of which—"

"Could solve my problems with productivity?"

"Exactly."

"You'd be my Marjorie," Grace said with a twinge of apprehension. Did she want her very own Bat?

Lily didn't flinch at the comparison. "I could be your executive assistant and paralegal and take over the boilerplate work that comes in. I'd manage your schedule electronically and drive you crazy with reminders. I'd have authority to rearrange your appointments when necessary and take some of the basic meetings off your plate when we're busy. I can also screen and prioritize potential new clients and weed out the ones that would be a drain on the practice."

Grace's head was swimming at the scene Lily was describing. "You're into crazy land, girl."

Lily grinned. "I figured I'd keep going until you stopped me."

"What was next?"

"Catered lunches."

"Crazy. Land." She studied the woman who sat across the desk from her. Lily was ten years her junior, but had extensive life and work experience that Grace would never acquire. Her military training showed in her posture and demeanor, and Grace had seen her move from passive bystander to police-style action without hesitation.

But how would the firm pay for it? What would Cy say?

Lily had an answer for that, too. "More work would get done, which means more money coming in. It would be a while before you and Mr. Mosley would see any of it because of my increased compensation, but we'd continue to scale up and eventually everyone will be better off financially. And in the meantime . . ." she hesitated.

"Go on," Grace said. "Tell me the rest."

"Well, right now, you also need help with the issues surrounding Stark's death, plus whatever Winnie and Connie get up to. I have resources I can call on if we run into something we can't handle."

"*We* can't handle?"

"Yes. We. As in, *we* are a team, and you can trust me."

What Grace couldn't trust was her voice. She had worried they might never fully mend the rift that had driven Lily out of the firm two years ago. After a moment, she cleared her throat and said, "I'll talk to Cy, and we'll find the money. Twenty percent raise?"

Lily smiled. "Twenty-five, with a review in six months. Salaried position, four weeks paid leave, full benefits."

It would be money well spent and the relief Grace felt was amazing. "Well, here's your first executive assignment. Update your resume and create a new job description. Redraft our operating budget to cover the expense and we'll go over it. Try to find enough to hire a receptionist, too, and think about how we can reconfigure the floor plan to give you an office. Now where's this prenup I've supposedly written for Alma Bailey?"

The hours flew by. High protein salads were delivered at noon, and more work was accomplished in one day than Grace had managed in the past two weeks. At four-thirty, she glanced at her reflection in the restroom mirror, saw a neatly dressed, smiling woman, and realized she'd gone seven hours without wringing her hands or searching for a lost file.

As she reentered the office, she said, "I need to get home." The last few hours had been wonderful, but if she could push a button and be transported to the nursery at home, she'd be gone. How did other mothers manage this pull from both ends of their lives? "One day at a time."

It took a second for her to realize she'd spoken the words to Lily.

"That's right, boss. We're getting there. I've emailed you a calendar for the rest of the week and notes on your appointments. Nothing else has to be done today, and your first client meeting tomorrow isn't until ten. You'll need to review and edit some correspondence before that, but it shouldn't take long."

Grace looked at the stack of folders in the center of her new assistant's desk. The top of her own was nearly bare. "Are you sure about this arrangement? It's a big change."

"It's all going to work out, you'll see," Lily said. "But if it would make you feel better, we could continue discussing the amount of my raise."

Grace tried to look irritated, but couldn't suppress a grin. For the first time in ages, she was able to leave without taking work home. She paused on her way out, opened her briefcase, and handed the single item inside to her new executive assistant. "Can you put this somewhere safe but out of sight? Don't tell me where. It's a long story." The yearbook looked ancient in the bright office light. "Those resources you mentioned, they're still available?"

"Absolutely," Lily said. "I do, or I *did,* freelance work for a couple of people I served with in Afghanistan. Security issues mainly, insurance investigations, some missing person cases. My friends will be happy to return the favor."

Grace was tempted, but didn't feel right. "Maybe down the road if a client needs that kind of help, but I'm good."

She stopped just short of adding, *for now.* She didn't know if she was avoiding the inevitable or locking the door on her past, but either way, she was going home to her family with a guilt-free mind, and that was all that mattered.

CHAPTER TWENTY

H er newfound Zen lasted exactly twelve hours.
"I need help!"

"Damn." Grace didn't disconnect the call, but she did pull the bedcovers over her head. She wasn't completely awake, but the children would be if they heard her talking. "Slow down, Connie," she whispered into the phone. "And tell me what's happened." Seconds later, she scrambled out of bed and slipped down the hallway, gently closing doors behind her as she went. In her ear, she listened to Connie's disjointed account of walking into her kitchen for a glass of water and finding the creepy neighbor looking through the window. He'd smiled at her.

Grace checked her own kitchen windows as the recital wrapped up with another plea for help. In typical Connie fashion, she'd called Mosley, then Niki, and when neither answered, Grace was next on auto-dial. Calling the police hadn't occurred to her.

"I'll call 911," Grace said. "But right now, lock the doors and get into the bathroom. Don't come out until you hear the police. I'll have to hang up to call them, but I'll call you right back."

Connie didn't argue. Somehow that worried Grace more than anything. Sunrise was less than an hour away, but outside it was still dark. She called 911, explained the situation and asked for a Sheriff's deputy to be dispatched to Connie's address. Then since there were only two deputies on night duty for the entire county, she followed up with a call to Tremaine Harper. Mac's only officer on Mallard Bay's police force wasn't due to start his shift for another three hours, but he promised to meet up with the deputy and call with details when everything was handled.

She hoped they were only dealing with a creep with a sick sense of humor, but the prickling at the back of her neck said otherwise.

"I couldn't stay there another minute," Connie said. "After the police left, I packed a bag and got out, but now I don't know what to do. Niki's out of town, and that housekeeper at Delaney House won't tell me where she is. My daughter has blocked my calls, and she's changed the locks at the Victory Manor Inn. She even changed the ones at my old house, so I checked into The Egret and got cleaned up so I could go to work, but now what?"

What, indeed, Grace thought, resisting the urge to ask if the less expensive chain hotels on Route 50 were all booked. A night at The Egret would cost more than Connie would make today at her job as an office manager at Wye Realty.

"Tremaine said there wasn't anything else he could do, Grace. And that sheriff's deputy acted like I was making a big deal out of nothing." Connie's eyes were bloodshot and her hands trembled. "Please. I know we're in a bad place, but please help me."

Grace repeated Tremaine Harper's report that there was no evidence of a peeping tom, and none of Connie's neighbors had seen anything, but she was still upset.

Lily appeared in the doorway. "Sorry to interrupt, but your next client has arrived downstairs."

Connie stood obediently and picked up her purse. "I have to leave, anyway. If I'm late from lunch again, it will be a problem."

The unusual experience of seeing Connie act responsibly made

Grace hesitate. "Leave your keys here and I'll go check things out." She glanced at Lily, then added, "*We'll* go. Lily has special training for that sort of thing and if we should see anything suspicious, I'll call the police again. I'll also get your window measurements and text them to you so you can pick up some of those stick-up temporary blinds. Aidan can install a doorbell alarm with a camera, too. You should feel safe at home after that."

The old Connie would have scoffed at these cheap, temporary solutions. The scared woman who used to be her aunt whispered, "Thank you," and hugged her.

When she was gone, Lily said, "You're booked straight through the rest of the day. I'll call Aidan and get him going on the alarm."

Grace fished her American Express out of her wallet and handed it over. "This is a family thing, so my expense."

"But Connie's not your family anymore."

"I can't explain it," Grace said with a sigh. "But their divorce didn't set the rest of us free."

"Give me Connie's keys. I'll go look around and measure any uncovered windows and get some blinds up. Otherwise, you'll be over there tonight doing it. I'll also check out the neighborhood perv list if I get a chance. Did Tremaine talk to any neighbors that might fit the description? Never mind. I'll talk to him, too."

Grace gave Lily the key and thought about protesting, but she knew the former Marine didn't need help from an out of shape lawyer. She settled for saying, "Perv list? We have a list of *local* perverts?"

Lily nodded. "Tremaine will have already checked it, but I want to take a look, see if anyone matches Connie's description."

Grace struggled with feeling both sick and grateful that Lily knew these things. "Be careful," she said, mainly because she couldn't think of anything else.

Lily gave her a mock salute and left her to the normal workday issues that didn't involve Delaneys, murder, or perverts.

"Nothing," Lily said as she returned Grace's credit card at the end of the day. "A few footprints, but you know how that unit Connie's renting fronts right on the sidewalk. Anyone could have left the prints for an innocent reason. Nothing seemed out of place outside, and the inside appears to be undisturbed. I picked up a couple of those paper blinds on my way over and stuck them up over the two uncovered windows and closed all the other curtains. While I was there, Aidan came by and installed the doorbell camera and wired the windows for an alarm. None of it will actually do much, but we put up alarm warning signs around the building, so it's obvious that she's taking action regarding security and that's usually enough to scare off the average peeper."

"Is that what you and Aidan think we're dealing with?" Grace asked hopefully. 'Peeper' sounded much better than the 'P' word they'd been using earlier.

Lily shrugged. "Who knows? Maybe the thrill of the police showing up and security measures being installed is enough excitement for this guy. Or not. It all depends on what he wants."

It hadn't occurred to Grace that the peeper wanted anything other than to frighten a woman living alone. Her brief hopes for an easy answer dashed, she said, "We'll know soon enough, I guess. Connie doesn't suffer alone."

"The old Connie didn't, for sure," Lily agreed, "but I think something has changed."

CHAPTER TWENTY-ONE

"What do you mean?" Grace asked. "How long has the guy been bothering Connie?"

"Apparently, she's been having problems for several weeks," Lily said. "Aidan told me he talked to her on the day of Stark's funeral. She said the creepy man has never actually spoken to her, but she's afraid of him because he hangs around outside her house and is always smoking. She told him to stop, and I think we can accurately guess how she phrased her request that he not smoke near her house. Afterward he made a point to light up whenever she saw him. She swears it's the same guy that was at her window, but Tremaine said no one fitting his description lives within two blocks of her place."

The more Lily talked, the worse Grace felt. "How did you leave it with her?"

"She came home while I was there, so I returned her keys, described the security measures we'd taken, and told her Aidan said to call him if she got nervous. She was ringing him as I left. She said she couldn't go back to The Egret because they wanted cash in advance for tonight. Thanks to Stark, all of her credit cards were declined."

Grace hadn't given any thought to the ramifications of Stark's final 'gift' to his ex-wife. "You mean those unpaid bills he gave her were in both their names?"

"Well, she didn't exactly share all the details, but I'm guessing she never took herself off of their joint accounts because she couldn't pay off the balances."

"And Stark maxed them out and let them go into default."

Lily nodded. "She said while they still had credit scores in the lowest range of acceptability, he opened new accounts in both of their names, forging her signature. He maxed those out and never made the first payment."

"And she's just now finding out about it? How's that possible?"

This time Lily said nothing, but waited for the obvious answer to sink in.

"Oh no. How long has she known?"

"A while. I'm surprised OCPD hasn't recharged her for his murder."

Grace had to agree. "It's an odd sensation, feeling sorry for Connie, but imagine someone hated you that much." Even as she spoke those words, she remembered Stark had hated her, too.

"Yeah," Lily agreed. "And imagine you were *married* to him."

"Well, that street went two ways, you know. They were both horrible, as a couple and on their own. And the problem with helping Connie is, you don't know when she's lying. She may know this peeper, or at least know why he's stalking her. *If* he's stalking her. This whole thing could be a sham."

"I don't know what purpose it would serve," Lily said. "She said she was going to go through the envelope Stark gave her tonight and make a list of all the bills and then bring them in to show Mr. Mosley. She thinks if he sees that Stark really did run up all the debt, he'll pay them."

"Of course, she thinks that. It's what he always did for Stark, but she'll be disappointed this time, I think." Exasperated by her conflicting emotions, Grace moved on to something she could actually handle. "Check in with Aidan, please, and tell him not to stay too long. And make sure to mark these extra hours as work for Connie. I'm not sure which account Cyrus will pay him out of, but it's definitely over-time. If we had hazard pay, he'd get that, too."

"You know, I don't think he looks at it that way," Lily said. "Did you notice how kind he was to her on the day of the funeral? And today, he said he didn't mind the extra hours for a friend."

"He didn't mean *Connie* was his friend," Grace scoffed.

"Actually, he did. And he said Mac was the one who'd told him that some people are part of our lives because that's the way it's supposed to be." She smiled at Grace's surprise. "Aidan also said you'll owe him some morning carbs tomorrow. Want me to stop by the bakery on the way in?"

"No. I can pay my own debts," Grace said, determined to hold on to at least some control of her own business. She'd been managed enough for one day and was ready to go home to the two people who still believed she was in charge of the universe.

Lily's watch erupted with Big Ben-type gongs. "That's our reminder for you to wrap things up. Gets your attention, doesn't it?" She held out Grace's briefcase.

"And jump starts my heart. Any requests for breakfast?"

Her assistant insisted she was all Keto, but it turned out to be a moot point. When the next morning rolled around, they didn't have the time—or appetite—for anything.

When Aidan Banks was in law enforcement, he'd never been any supervisor's first choice for a nighttime stakeout. He couldn't say what woke him from his nap, but he was grateful something had, otherwise he might have missed seeing the peeper.

His eyes were barely focused when he saw someone moving across the backyard of a house several doors away from Connie's condo. As it was, he only got a quick look at the shadowy form before it disappeared from view.

"I still suck at this," he muttered as he straightened up and rubbed his face.

Until today, he hadn't really believed Connie was in any danger. His short career in community policing had taught him that some people would go to extraordinary lengths to harass neighbors who irritated them, and Connie could irritate a saint. But most of the people living around her were locals he and Lily recognized, and the remainder were easily located on social media. The stalker Connie described wasn't a neighbor.

Lily had also learned that Connie's loud and often rude behavior routinely rated negative posts on the neighborhood's Facebook page. A woman who lived next to her posted about people cutting across their yards from the public walking trail. Was that what he'd just seen? Some random person taking a shortcut to Main Street?

He took out his phone. He really should call 911.

Then he thought about what a rush it would be to deliver the peeper to his former colleagues, handcuffed and limping from unregulated arrest methods.

He slipped out of the car and crossed the street to stand in the shadow of a large tree. His breathing had barely settled when he heard rustling sounds and a small beam of light appeared from the rear corner of the house in front of him, followed by a bulky shadow. In seconds, both disappeared behind Connie's building.

Aidan took out his pepper spray and removed the cap before he started running, flying on the burst of energy he got from knowing that he wouldn't have to read the peeper his rights before he beat the crap out of him.

Connie handed him a towel to dry his face and patted his shoulder. Aidan didn't know which was worse, being lectured by a sheriff's deputy who looked like he was in junior high, or being nursed by a woman who wouldn't stop talking or crying.

"Do you think you landed any punches before you sprayed yourself?" Connie asked.

"I didn't spray myself," he said for what had to be the tenth time.

"And yes, I hit him square on the jaw, but he's a tall dude, so I had to swing high to make contact. He went down but grabbed my left hand as he fell, and he sprayed both of us." This was his story, and he was sticking to it. For all he knew, the only tears in the peeper's eyes right now were from laughter.

Connie, who'd heard—and told—many a tall tale in her time, just sighed. "Well, maybe it was enough to keep him away."

The easy thing to do would be to let her think that. To walk around the house and lock the doors and windows and tell her she'd be fine now because the real police officer with his gun and legal authority had checked the surrounding yards and declared the area to be free of bad guys.

But despite his watering eyes, Aidan could see how she watched him. Connie expected him to lie. Maybe even wanted him to. But he was going to do at least one thing right tonight. He wiped his face and told her everything he knew.

CHAPTER TWENTY-TWO

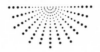

"You got in a fight, got pepper sprayed, and then slept with my mother?" Niki looked ready to fly at Aidan with all ten of her salon-hardened nails aimed at his red eyes.

Grace debated letting nature take its course. She had made it through the two day single-parent marathon without incident, but Mac's absence was wearing on her and she was in no mood to referee this fight. Or to fire Aidan, which had been her first thought when he'd called her late last night. Or was is early that morning? She was too tired to remember.

They were squared off in the small conference room in Grace's second floor office. Niki and Aidan faced each other across the table, which wouldn't be large enough to keep them separated if Grace couldn't calm her cousin down. "Come on, Niki," she said. "Connie's accounts of a man looking in her window are apparently true, after all."

"She's never lied about that," Aidan said, his face now as red as his eyes.

Grace thought he resembled a sunburned Bart Simpson, but kept the observation to herself as she talked over his grumbling. "Lily searched Connie's house and the grounds and Aidan installed some basic security equipment, hoping to make her feel safe enough to stay there." Giving him an *I can't believe you* look, she added, "Then he decided on his own to watch her place last night to see if anything happened. That's why he was there to stop the, uhm, peeper. You should thank him."

Niki didn't thank her former lover. "You've never been that concerned about Mom before. So, some poor guy is outside at night and you tackle him because she says he's after her? She lies about everything, she may have killed my father, and yet suddenly, you're her new best friend. Why is that?"

Coming half out of his chair, Aidan yelled, "The man who's been stalking—yes, *stalking*—your mother isn't her neighbor."

"Aidan!" Grace said, but it was too late.

"He comes down the walking trail from Memorial Park to spy on Connie. Who, by the way, isn't the only person he's creeped out. Another neighbor thought something was off with him, too, and she snapped a photo of him with her phone. She brought it over to me yesterday when I was outside installing the alarm signs." He stabbed his own phone's screen and said, "I gave Lily and Grace a copy and now you have one, too. Connie says she's sure this is the peeper." He sat back and crossed his arms with a grunt that sounded a lot like "so there."

"Gracie?" Niki asked. "What's he talking about?"

"The police and Lily—independently, of course—have been canvassing the neighbors and checking social media looking for the man Connie described."

"They're helping Mom stalk this guy? That's just great. Why are you doing any of this, Aidan?" Nicki demanded. "You aren't a cop and you aren't a bodyguard. What's in this for you?"

"Don't do this, Niki," Grace tried, knowing she was wasting her breath.

"You haven't changed a bit," Aidan said. "If you could, for one damn minute, stop thinking about what you want and what you need and what you've been cheated out of, you might spare a thought for your mother."

"That's enough," Grace snapped.

"No, it isn't," he said, looking at her as if she'd betrayed him. "How could you do it, Grace? You're the one Connie came to for help. How could you let her go back to that house? You've got a spare room, don't you? Hell, between you and Niki, you've got two inns. Were both of them full? No? I didn't think so. Neither of you took her fears seriously. She asked me to promise that I'd scared the peeper off for good. She wanted me to say that she was safe. I couldn't lie to her, so I did your job for you."

"You didn't tell her—"

"I told her everything. That you and Cy and the police think she's lying about the stalker because she murdered Stark and is trying to shift the blame to some fantasy bad guy. That no one is looking out for her safety and she needs to do it herself. And I told her I was sure I felt a gun in the peeper's pocket when I tackled him. What's the point of secrets when she could get killed?"

Grace stared at him, her mind racing as she assessed the damage that he'd done.

And he wasn't finished. "I don't know what else she's told you," he said to Niki as he gave Grace another injured look. "But in addition to stopping an attack on your mother, I spent three miserable hours on her incredibly uncomfortable sofa, listening to her crying in the next room. The only thing I could do for her was keep her safe until this morning. As soon as it was light, I made coffee and waited until she packed up and left. I don't know where she went, but she said she wasn't coming back except to move out."

Grace had to admit that Niki's suspicions were understandable. When, and why, had Aidan taken on the role of champion for a woman he'd tried his best to avoid for the past twenty years? He wasn't a sentimental man and 'suspicious' was his middle name, but something had changed his mind about Connie. Changed it enough that he'd purposefully given confidential information to someone who wouldn't hesitate to weaponize it.

When she hired Aidan as an IT specialist/investigator/jack-of-all-trades for the firm, he'd made her a promise to maintain confidentiality with any information he picked up while working for Reagan and

Mosley. Their handshake agreement was a professional equivalent of a pinky swear, but she'd trusted him. Despite his personality quirks, Aidan was her friend, a kind but hot-tempered, loner who always did what he thought was right, no matter what rule—or law—he had to break. When he perceived an injustice, nothing stopped him from going Don Quixote on it.

She should have known better.

"Back up and tell me everything," Niki demanded. "Because I *do* know where Mom went. She's at the Queen's Brooke property, which at the moment is leased to the Ahmed family for a week-long reunion. Apparently, she's moved into Dad's old office over the garage. Mr. Ahmed called me just before I got here to ask why people were moving boxes into the third bay and blocking his boat trailer. "

Grace's heart sank. The Ahmeds' rental fee was substantial, and it was the first time the house had been rented out in a month. Not sure she really wanted to know, she asked how Niki had handled the call.

"I took care of it, and that's not the point. I want to know what's going on with Mom, and I want to know now. Is what Aidan's saying true?"

The door opened, and Lily appeared with a coffee pot. "Five minute break?" she asked. "We have a thing that needs your attention."

"Excellent timing," Grace said as they went to her office.

"I have my ways," Lily said. "Must not be too bad, they're both still alive."

"If they weren't, would you handle that, too?"

"Yep."

Grace sank onto one of the matching arm chairs that flanked her desk and waited for the punchline, but Lily didn't look up from the laptop she'd picked up. She said, "Aidan went rogue and told Connie everything we told him. Now Niki knows, too, which is nothing compared to Connie's ability to spread the word that we are railroading her."

Still nothing from Lily except the *snick snick* of the computer keys as she typed.

"For heaven's sake," Grace snapped. "Will you listen to me? I have to decide how to handle the mess he's made."

"It's a no matter," Lily finally said. "Other than, you know, the personnel problem we knew we'd have with Aidan eventually. We have a more serious issue to discuss with Niki and her mother."

Then she turned the laptop so Grace could see the screen.

CHAPTER TWENTY-THREE

"I'm pretty sure this is the guy he tackled last night. Dennis Mays. He's got a rap sheet a mile long, and it includes assault with a deadly weapon." Lily tapped the screen, and the mug shot changed to a nighttime photo of what appeared to be the Ocean City boardwalk. "Mays's parole officer has been looking for him since he was caught on one of the city's news camera tourism feeds. There's a warrant out for him, so they visited surrounding businesses, checking their security videos and caught this." She gave the screen another tap and zoomed in on the same man, this time standing at the front entrance to the Blow Back In Bar.

"Oh, no." Grace said. It was too much of a coincidence.

"The OCPD and the MSP have a joint task force to shut down unlicensed gambling, and the Blow Back is under surveillance," Lily said.

"For unlicensed gambling? That seems a bit odd."

Lily shrugged. "That's what they're investigating. Remember, it's not only the licensing fees the state's losing, it's the tax on winnings over $5,000. Several high-stakes poker players are frequent customers of the Blow Back. They arrive, disappear into the rear of the building, and don't return. The investigation is at a standstill, I'm guessing, because I can't find anything recent on it. I only know what I learned from my source."

"Who is this source?"

"A friend of mine has a small private security service over in Rehoboth. One of his clients was a regular at this bar until he had a visit from the OCPD on behalf of the gambling task force. My friend followed up on his client's concerns and confirmed the task force's findings. This morning, when I asked him to check out Connie's peeper, he recognized Mays."

"You think someone connected to the bar Stark worked in is also here stalking Connie? That's a real stretch."

Lily produced more photographs of Dennis Mays. "When Connie started bugging her neighbors about the peeper, a few of them went on the hunt for him with their cameras. In addition to the woman who gave Aidan a photo, two other citizens snapped him with their phones and gave their shots to the deputy who canvassed the area this morning. The sheriff's deputy sent copies to Tremaine, who forwarded them to us—with Mac's permission, of course."

Grace rubbed her aching head. Mac had been another complication in her morning. Having him beside her in person was wonderful, being peppered with incessant questions over a static-y phone connection while she had her hands full was not. He'd be home in a few hours and she'd have to smooth over her short-tempered responses.

She focused on the photos. One could have been any tall, thin man walking across a lawn at twilight. The other was a full-face close up of Dennis Mays. She asked Lily for another look at the security video from the alley behind the Blow Back In, then said, "Do I want to know how you got these?"

"It's all good," Lily assured her. "My friend got them from the company that owns this building." She pointed at the property across the alley from the Blow Back. "These shots are from their security feed, and the OCPD already has them, plus a lot more."

Grace studied the grainy photographs. "Good thing you have such helpful friends."

"A girl's gotta make a living," Lily said. "I've been doing research for him on a freelance basis, and I knew about the surveillance. I didn't call in a favor, I just asked him if I could see this footage again because I thought I'd recognized someone on it. I shared our photos the neighbors took, and he was grateful for the verification."

At least she hadn't directly disobeyed instructions, Grace thought, even though it felt like it.

A glance at the clock told her Niki and Aidan had been left to their own devices for too long. Pointing again to the screen, she said, "Okay. Give me a quick assessment on all this—the Mallard Bay connection to OC, Connie's connection to this Mays guy, Mays' connection to Stark —whatever's running through your head, proof, or no proof."

Lily didn't hesitate. "I think Stark worked at the Blow Back to be close to the illegal activities. I also think he talked about Connie ripping him off in the divorce. If Stark won big in the illegal games, Mays might want to see if Connie had any of his winnings."

"And Mays might want to frighten her enough to give it to him?" Grace asked. Lily's theory certainly sounded like a Stark and Connie type of disaster.

"I'm not sure what the end game is. We don't have enough information, yet. But it sounds plausible, doesn't it?"

It did. Grace said, "I think we have to assume the police haven't put it together yet, and we certainly don't want to be the ones sitting on the information. Email me everything you found. I'll get it to Mac and call Detective Sergeant Xavier."

"What about Mr. Mosley?" Lily asked.

"I'll tell him everything as soon as I handle our problems in the conference room. This time I'm going by the book. No more improvising."

"Before you do anything, look at these," Lily said, tapping the laptop keys again and bringing up two surveillance videos. Dennis Mays was not only connected to the Blow Back In and Connie's home. The first video was dated three weeks earlier and showed him in the alley behind the bar, talking to Stark Delaney.

The second was only two days old. It showed Mays with Winnie and Piper.

Aidan thought Niki had a lot of nerve to act offended when Grace
came to get him and asked her cousin to wait a few more minutes. He
was the one who was going to get canned. Niki was only here because.
. . Why *was* Grace asking Niki to wait? It wasn't as if she hadn't
already heard everything. *Everything you know*, said the voice in his
head that always spoke up when it was too late to be helpful. As usual,
the consequences of what he'd done last night and what he'd told
Connie and Niki were becoming clear much too late to save him.

"I won't be long," Grace was saying. "But there's a complication.
Give me a few more minutes, Nik, okay?"

Aidan, silent and sullen but not nearly as cocky as he had been,
followed her to her office. As soon as the door closed, he said, "You
don't have to fire me, I quit."

Lily rolled her eyes, and Grace said, "Oh, stop acting like a child. I
don't need a third one on my hands. You made a royal mess and you're
going to help me fix it."

This is what always pushed him over the edge—these women
never listened to him. Enunciating slowly, he said, "I fixed it. I quit.
Done."

Again, with the eye rolls. Lily added a snort for good measure.

"Okay," Grace said agreeably. "But before you make your big exit,
I need to debrief you. Sit down." She spoke to him as if he were
already on the outside of their circle, even adding "please" in a polite
tone. But it was the way Lily looked at him that made him sit.

Grace gave the date, noted that the conversation was being
recorded for the purpose of being used in court, and stated that Aidan
had been in her employ when the events he was about to recount had
occurred.

Oh, no. Even in his agitated state, he realized she was trying to give
him some protection. "I quit," he said in the direction of the phone. It
was all he'd offer by way of an apology.

Grace ignored him as usual, then told him to describe everything
that had occurred while he was with Connie Delaney during the last

thirty-six hours. "Specifically," she said, "I want to know word for word, as accurately as you can remember, everything you told Ms. Delaney and anything she may have said about the individual who she claims has been stalking her. Also, everything she said about Stark Delaney."

CHAPTER TWENTY-FOUR

It took a minute for Aidan to process the implication of those instructions. Then some of his police training kicked in and he gave the accounting in chronological order. When he finished, Grace and Lily exchanged relieved looks.

Grace said, "Did Ms. Delaney say anything about seeing her now ex-husband in Ocean City, or anywhere else for that matter, in the last three months?"

"No."

Again, the women looked at each other. Then Grace thanked him in that impersonal tone that angered him more than being ignored. "Did you leave anything out?" she said after Lily had stopped recording.

He wished he had, but he didn't even have that satisfaction. "No."

Not seeming to appreciate his truthfulness, she kept pushing. "The only confidential information you gave Connie was that we thought she was lying about the peeper and that we suspected her of killing Stark?"

"Yeah. I told her she was being investigated and that no one believed her and she had to stop doing stupid stuff and be careful because she was in danger." Why was he repeating everything? He was in the wrong and should just shut up. Yet his mouth kept on in overdrive. "Connie believed Mac and Tremaine were looking into the peeper. It was only fair to tell her things were worse than she thought."

Lily looked like she was considering where to hide his body, but Grace gave him a sad smile. This was why he wasn't a cop. Not because he couldn't do the work, but because he couldn't do it the way the rules said he should. He knew it, Mac had always known it, and if Grace had been blind to his shortcomings up until now, it wasn't his fault and he was furious at her for thinking it was. "So, am I fired, or what?"

"You quit."

Damn her, he was getting twisted up again. "I won't apologize. You two didn't see Connie last night. Or that guy who was headed for her back door."

Grace said, "It doesn't matter that I understand and sympathize with your decision to tell Connie she was in danger. But you could have called 911 like any other citizen. Instead, you might have wrecked a long-running police task force investigation and insured that a dangerous criminal stays out on the street. Only time will tell."

"Time and Connie," Lily added.

Now he really was done, Aidan thought. There was more at stake than Stark's murder. And of course, no one had told him, so he'd assumed they were all being unfair to Connie. "Right, I quit."

Grace nodded and stood up. "If I can't trust you to do the job I hired you for, then it's probably for the best. We'll talk at some point tomorrow. Right now," her voice softened, "I don't have the heart for it."

As he left the large white Victorian building that housed Reagan and Mosley, Attorneys at Law, Aidan wondered if this was how Connie felt when she hit rock bottom. He should be an expert at handling "How could you?" scenes by now, but it felt like he was running away from home. And that wasn't the worst of it.

He could handle women who screamed and threw handy objects, but Grace had hugged him and promised to always be his friend.

She couldn't have hurt him more if she'd tried.

To her relief, Grace saw Niki hadn't waited. Not that she'd get a reprieve from the grief her cousin would give her when they did talk. And now she had no excuse to delay telling Cyrus and Mac about the escalating situation. She didn't know which she dreaded more, but Cy was in the building, so she headed downstairs.

And, as usual, he already knew what had transpired last night. She no longer had any pride as far as these things went, so she just asked outright who'd told him.

"The correct question is, who told me *first*, m'dear." His tone was wry, but she could tell from the frown under his wrinkles that the stress was getting to him. "Marjorie's grandnephew was the responding deputy from the Sheriff's Office. Then Connie cried in my ear at the uncivilized hour of seven a.m., and after that, I ran into Aidan in the parking lot. He provided details in line with Marjorie's nephew's account, so I believe I'm up to date."

Grace glanced at the empty hallway. Then, knowing that it meant nothing as far as the Bat was concerned, she shut the door. It wouldn't do any good, but it was their routine. "Afraid not, partner," she said as she took her usual place, sitting on the elegant upholstered chair at the far side of his massive desk. She handed him the photos from the surveillance camera at the Blow Back In.

When she finished updating him, his wrinkles had spawned wrinkles, but behind them, she could see the sharp instincts and decades of experience calculating the impact of the new information. She said, "How do you want to handle it?"

For a moment, she thought this might be the day he finally said, "Screw the whole crazy bunch of them, let's have a drink and see how they do on their own." It wasn't, but he also hadn't forgotten that they only represented Niki. He said, "Kind of you to ask for my opinion, m'dear, but I believe we both know who's in charge of this calamity. However you handle this, I'll back you up."

Despite everything, she grinned at him. Then remembered there was more. "Aidan's gone. He quit before I could fire him."

Mosley didn't look surprised and he didn't object. With the exception of Marjorie, and anyone he might hire, the staff was also Grace's responsibility. But he looked sad when he said it was for the best. "I'm not sure what the boy's cut out for, but it isn't working for us. Shame, though. How did you leave it with Niki?"

"As far as she knows, Connie's just being Connie, and she's made some creep mad. I need to go talk to her. But first, I have to turn everything we know over to Mac and Detective Xavier."

They agreed she would handle Mac and Xavier, and he would talk to Niki. Grace would join him when she got free, but both conversations needed to happen sooner rather than later.

She caught Mac at the Miami airport, waiting in a slow-moving TSA line. She was prepared for a what-did-you-expect lecture, but his first response when she finished describing what had taken place was, "Poor Connie. I'm glad Aidan was with her."

"But doesn't this put the OC investigation at risk? According to Aidan, Connie only thinks some pervy guy has a thing for her, but it won't be long before she learns about his record and his connection to Stark and Winnie. I need to get the information over to Xavier and Greenley. It's all going to unravel, and in the meantime, I'm really worried about Connie. She knows just enough to be dangerous—to herself and God knows who else."

"You didn't tell Aidan what Lily found?" Mac asked.

"No. Only that he may have screwed up a task force investigation. I didn't see any other way to keep him quiet."

"You sure? No details about the investigation?"

She gritted her teeth and made herself answer calmly. "None."

The noise from his end increased and he raised his voice. "Send the photos and anything else Lily's got to my phone. I've got an hour here before boarding. I'll find a place to talk and call Bernadette. You're Niki's attorney, you've reported what you've just learned to me, now I'll turn it over to the OCPD. I'll also tell her that while you'll do everything you can to protect the investigation, you're keeping your client up to date, particularly in light of the disturbing information linking her father and brother to Dennis Mays, and Mays' potential threat to her mother."

Grace felt lighter. She could handle Cy and Niki without the OCPD on her back. Which only left their home-grown troublemaker. "What about Connie?"

She heard a grunt of irritation from a thousand miles away. Then he said, "If she's holed up out in that dead end subdivision surrounded by nosy neighbors and a large family reunion, she should be safe enough until either Bernadette's team or ours picks Mays up for questioning. What are you going to do about Aidan?"

"He crossed the line, Mac."

"That he did. Gotta go, honey. We're finally moving. I'll call when I know something."

Reluctantly, Grace disconnected, checked in with Lily, then left the office, hoping the ten-minute walk to Delaney House would clear her head. But as with everything else on the fractured day, the plan didn't work out the way she wanted, either. Mac called back with an update from Bernadette Xavier and it wasn't good. There was more to the Blow Back's illegal enterprises than unlicensed gambling.

And there was nothing she could do, including warning Connie.

CHAPTER TWENTY-FIVE

The first thing she saw when she turned the corner onto Barclay Street was Mosley's gold Lexus parked in front of Delaney House. Seconds later, she found him inside with Niki and Dylan Kirwan.

They were sitting in the front parlor and Grace was struck again by the irony of all of this playing out under her grandmother's watchful gaze. Everyone turned around when she came in, but only Mosley seemed glad to see her. His smile, however, looked like a plea for help.

"There now, m'dear," he said to Niki. "I told you she would be here. I'm sure we can ease your mind and put everything back on track."

"I'm going to run along," Dylan said, and got to his feet. "I've got a stack of calls to return." He went upstairs, giving Grace a sympathetic smile as he passed.

"I'm worried about Mom," Niki said angrily. "Aidan freaked me out this morning, and you shut him up when I know he had more to tell me. And Cy won't tell me anything. He said I had to wait for you."

Grace sat in one of the large tapestry-covered wing-back chairs facing her cousin who, without Dylan beside her, looked even more petite and fragile than usual. She knew it was a mistake to judge Niki by her delicate appearance, but it was hard not to. She said, "This is all such a mess, and I'm sorry that I didn't handle it better. When Aidan blew up at me, I wasn't sure what he was going to say next, and I wanted to make sure that whatever it was couldn't hurt you."

"Hurt me? *Aidan*?"

Grace nodded. "You and Connie are still suspects in your father's murder, but there is more to the OCPD case than they previously shared with us. You shouldn't repeat this, not even to Dylan, not now, anyway. There's a multi-jurisdictional undercover investigation into something taking place at the Blow Back In." Mac hadn't given her details, but there was no mistaking the concern in his voice as he told her they were in over their heads. What had started as a small-time gambling ring had grown into something much more dangerous. She chose her next words carefully. "I've just gotten some of these details from Mac, so Cy's hearing them for the first time, too. The OCPD was moving in to arrest Stark on the morning Piper found his body. That's why they reacted so aggressively in the early days. Then we got Stark's gifts and the strange poem, and they started looking at all of us as suspects."

Niki's eyes were enormous. "You mean Mom really could get hurt?"

"We all should be careful." Grace pulled a folder from her tote and took out the photographs Lily had printed. "First Winnie arrived, flashing money he didn't have when he went to prison, and hooking up with Piper Tilden, and then this happened." She handed the photos to Niki.

After studying them for a minute, Niki said, "Okay, I give up. Who's the guy they're talking to?"

"His name is Dennis Mays. He has a record for assault and voyeurism. Aidan wasn't wrong, Nik. Connie was in danger last night and she may still be. I've notified Mac, and he's passed everything we have on to the task force, which includes the state police, and although I'm guessing here, probably the feds. Maybe the FBI."

Niki's focus was on the photos. "But Dad's with him! Why would he have anything to do with a guy like that? I mean, I can see Winnie getting right back into something illegal, but Dad? And Piper? What's she doing there?"

"I don't know, but the police are on it now," Grace said.

After a moment, Niki looked up and said, "Aidan doesn't know all of this, does he?"

"No," Grace said gently. "Yesterday, all we knew was that the guy Connie said was bothering her probably wasn't a neighbor. At that point, I'm afraid Aidan was the only one who didn't think she was lying to get attention and sympathy. She wanted the Queen's Brooke house back and seemed to think we'd hand it over to her if she couldn't stay at her place."

"That sounds about right."

"There's more," Grace said. "Remember the morning your father died? The first time you and Connie talked to the police? She acted squirrelly and told us she'd tried to implicate herself to draw attention away from you?"

"Yeah, that was strange," Niki said, but Grace could tell it wasn't connecting.

"Later she threatened me. She said if we backed her into a corner, you and I would be sorry. She insisted we'd cheated her in the Queen's Brooke house purchase."

"But that's a lie!" Niki protested.

Mosley spoke up, startling both women. "Lying seems to be a hallmark in this family. Frankly, I'm finding it exhausting. I can't criticize the methods you use to cope with your family, Niki, but your father's gone now, and I can't imagine Winnie will stay out of prison for long." He stopped as his voice cracked.

Niki looked startled. Grace felt guilty about all of it.

Mosley bowed his head for a moment then regaining his composure, said, "Niki, you and I loved Stark and Winnie. And Emma loved them most of all, but I'm not sure anyone else ever did. Stark was broken as a child and he married a kindred soul. And as for Winnie, well, I don't know that anything could have saved him. The only truth I know about this situation we're in right now is that none of it is our fault, and it's time we acted like it. No lying. No deceit.

Not between us. You have Grace and me, and we'll have to be enough."

He stood, kissed each of them on the cheek, and left. In his wake, the grandfather clock chimed three, the notes lingering in the silent room.

CHAPTER TWENTY-SIX

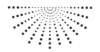

"You think Mom killed him, don't you?" Niki's words were barely a whisper.

"In my heart?" Grace asked, remembering Connie's expression as she looked at the young Stark's photograph on the day of his funeral. "I think she and Stark were killing each other without knowing it for a very long time. But did she cause him to die two weeks ago? Maybe. I believed she was lying about the peeper, and I was wrong. I just don't know anything for sure."

"I'm sorry." Niki wiped her face with the sleeve of her silk blouse, leaving damp patches on the pale pink material.

"You don't have anything to be sorry about," Grace protested, but even as she said the words, she knew Niki wasn't apologizing for her parents.

"I need to leave, Gracie. I've been trying to talk myself out of it for ages, before I ever met Dylan, actually. Now that he's a part of my life, though, it seems like a sign. I wanted to prove everyone wrong, to prove I'm smart and strong, and that I could make a successful business out of our properties, and I've done it. Funny thing is, no one really cares. Those accomplishments were only important to me."

"That's not true," Grace protested. "I'm really proud of you and I appreciate what you've done here. I renovated the house, but you returned it to its original beauty."

Niki waved the praise away impatiently. "We're a good team, I agree, but we've finished the challenge of creating Delaney Inns, don't you see? From here on it's just maintaining the business, there's no more creating to be done and we're limited in how much money we can bring in. It's a healthy enterprise, and we have a way to go before the potential is maxed out, but that day will come."

Grace felt numb. What did Niki expect her to do? She couldn't run the inns and the vacation rental, and most of her assets were tied up in them. Anger poked at the edges of her panic, and they'd had enough of that in the past few days. Finally, she said, "What exactly do you mean by 'leaving' and when are you planning on going?"

Niki seemed to weigh her next words more carefully. "You believed in me and I won't let you down. I'll figure it all out, but I can't stay here in Mallard Bay." She stood and glanced over her shoulder toward the hall and the staircase that led to Dylan. "Please don't worry about any of it. Like I said, I've been thinking about this for a while and I've got a plan in place. When Cy told us about the trust and said he was sure I'd like to have a real home, he was right. I just don't want one here, where Mom can pop in and out wrecking things at will. It was like my prayers had been answered that day. I won't do anything rash, and I'll consult with you every step of the way. You won't lose your money. I promise you."

After she left, Grace sat and studied their grandmother's portrait. When the clock's chimes reminded her the children were expecting their mother, she said, "You're going to get your wish, Gran. All the Delaneys will be out of this house."

As always, Emma's eyes seemed to look right at her, and Grace thought she was happy.

———

"Maybe we should fold up our tent here and move into Delaney House," Mac said that night as they lay in bed, holding hands and waiting to see if the fifth bedtime story had been the magic that would keep Fiona asleep until her brother woke them all up again.

Grace smiled and rolled over into his arms. She knew nothing short of a tsunami would move them from their home. "Don't even joke about it. I think Gran was right. No one with Delaney DNA will ever be happy there."

"I've never heard you call her Gran, you know, off the cuff like that."

"I spent some time with her today, at least that's how it felt. That portrait in the front parlor looks so real, you know? Like she and the dog are just hanging out up there over the fireplace. I think she was about my age when it was painted."

"She was almost as beautiful as you are, but not quite," he said, and kissed her.

But Grace wasn't ready to be distracted. "That's not how you knew her, was it? I mean, by the time you were an adult, her life had fallen apart, hadn't it?"

"She was in decline, yes, but that woman in the portrait was still very much present in the eccentric old lady who drove the neighbors crazy."

Grace was so surprised it took her a minute to process what he'd said.

She'd thought of her grandmother as two people. Emma had been a beautiful bride when she arrived in Mallard Bay. But Grace had a box of receipts, tax returns, and bank statements that revealed the life of the broken old woman who'd lived in squalor, depriving herself of everything but the bare necessities.

She knew there was a third Emma, too, and maybe more. The Emmas who, with increasing determination, had allowed decay and isolation to creep in and take over, while the young bride slipped away.

"You and the children would have made her happy," Mac said.

She wondered if that was true. "When Cy told Niki and me about the trust dissolution, he said we should be the ones who made Emma happy by using the money for its intended purpose."

"Which was?"

"Don't know. But she was emphatic that the money wasn't to be spent on Delaney House, which, of course, is exactly what I've done until now."

"You had to, or it would have fallen down."

Grace looked at the clock. Midnight. "It's over, Mac."

He sincerely hoped she meant their conversation. He'd drifted off twice already, only to be reawakened by her random thoughts and worries.

"That part of my life is over," she said.

His hopes dashed, he pushed another pillow behind his head and tried to focus on what his wife was saying.

"I thought I'd already done it," Grace said, "but I didn't realize what it meant to actually let the past go and move on. Gran hung onto it. She stayed in Delaney House with those letters and kept everyone out. Then Mom ran away and started over, also shutting everyone out." The image was so clear to her that she stared into the dark, waiting to see if anything else materialized. "Oh, Mac!"

She sat up so abruptly, she woke him. Again.

Clicking on the bedside lamp, she turned to him, hair wild and eyes huge with surprise. "Niki is Mom, all over again. And I've been acting like Emma. I've hidden the yearbook away, so no one will ever have the answers that are inside it.

He'd given up tracking the conversation two dozes ago, but tried to look like he understood. "Okay. I'll support you however you decide to handle this epiphany, but could we do it all in the morning?"

The smile she gave him almost changed his mind about going to sleep, but he'd been awake for over twenty hours and wasn't sure he had both eyes open.

"There's nothing to decide, Mac. It's all good."

She snuggled down next to him and listened to his heartbeat slow into sleep and knew that she was right.

She would make Emma happy, but she would do it for herself. And when she moved forward in her life, she'd take everyone she loved with her.

The yearbook still weighed on her mind, but now she knew what to do with it. If she learned her father's identity, it didn't mean she had to contact him. It only meant she would have information she should have known all along. The more she considered that, the better she felt. She'd get a DNA test. If it turned up anything related to a genetic problem, she'd be able to contact him if she needed to. And if there were no problems, she didn't need him. Whoever Jonathan Reagan turned out to be, he never had to know she'd looked for him.

CHAPTER TWENTY-SEVEN

Despite Niki's life altering decision and Grace's epiphany, the drama unfolding around them continued the next morning.

"I'm going to arrest myself and go sleep in jail," Mac said as they watched the old Mercury Marquis come down the driveway and listened to Fiona shriek in excitement from the family room as The Count sang his way to the number of the day on *Sesame Street*.

Grace handed him a fresh mug of coffee and said, "Sorry, Poppy. Avril's blocked the driveway with her tank. But if you hurry, you can hole up in the bedroom and watch the news while I try to clear an escape path for both of us."

She didn't have to tell him twice.

"What's going on with Connie, and I don't mean the stalker or the police investigation," Avril demanded as she and Hallie came into the kitchen.

"Good morning, Hallie," Grace said. "I can't tell you how happy we are to see *you*."

"I'll bet," the nanny laughed as she went to calm the bedlam on the other side of the room. In seconds the TV went off and giggles filled the air.

"It's the strangest feeling, this mixture of failure and gratitude," Grace said as she watched the transformation.

"Nothing you couldn't do if you were eighteen and had fifteen years of baby whispering experience." Avril said. "Now, answer my question. And tell me why I had to hear the news at the market."

"I would say tell me what you know and I'll fill in the rest," Grace said as she poured a cup of coffee for her interrogator. "But it sounds like I don't know much more than you do. Let's sit on the patio."

And, of course, Avril had almost all the details that were supposed to be under wraps.

"Did any of this come from Aidan?" Grace asked.

"No." Avril looked genuinely surprised. "He would never. Well, maybe he would, now, since you fired him, but I heard it at Baldy's Market late yesterday from the new butcher."

"The butcher."

"Yes. He got it from his brother, the deputy." Seeing Grace's blank expression, she snapped, "Oh, keep up with your community, will you? Marjorie's ex-husband's sister has two boys. The youngest one is the new butcher at Baldy's. His brother, the deputy—"

"Marjorie had a husband?" Grace asked, not wanting to hear a retelling of Aidan's and Connie's big night.

"Not a legal one, and we don't talk about it. Quit trying to redirect me. What's Connie doing out at the Queen's Brooke rental? And how long will Niki be gone? Surely, she's not leaving you with Connie and Delaney Inns?"

"That didn't come from the butcher," Grace said. She set her coffee down and got up to examine a climbing rose bush that kept trying to inch down the trellis instead of up. When she'd readjusted the new stalks and gotten a painful prick for her trouble, she rejoined Avril, who silently handed her a tissue for her punctured thumb. "I don't know for sure what Nik's doing, but she's leaving. Connie's return was hard enough, but Stark's death, and now Winnie . . . I don't know how it will shake out, Avril, but it's too much for her. And then there's Dylan. She says we won't lose her, but she has to go."

"The inns have bookings through to next year," Avril said, but she sounded thoughtful, the agitation gone. "And Niki has a good staff in place. There's just the issue with Connie being at the rental house. Assuming the assassin doesn't pick her off, that is."

"Let it all land for a while," Grace said, not bothering to correct the hyperbole or point out that Connie wasn't Avril's problem.

They went inside, Grace to get dressed for the day, and Avril to play with the children. Both women had long lists of tasks and worries and were determined to set everything right.

"Well, that didn't last long," Lily said when Grace asked her for Julia's yearbook. "Want to close your eyes so you won't know my secret hiding place?"

"Very funny. So, what's happening here?"

Lily handed her a folder. "I've prepared a summary of everything we know about Stark's final days, including the background on the Blow Back In and its operations. There are few new details in there if you'd like a recap?"

"I have to do something first," Grace said. An hour later, she emerged from her office and returned the yearbook with a handwritten list. "You have a new client. Me. Freelance, off the payroll. I'll expect a bill for your going rate and you can hire whoever you need to help you."

"I can pull some favors—"

"No. We may need your friends' generosity later for the firm. This is all on my bill. I . . . I need to pay for it."

"Your father?"

Grace nodded, recalling her plan from the night before. "Don't contact him, though. I'll decide what to do with the information once you find him. Everything I could deduce or guess from my study of the book is on that list, along with Mom's history and everything she told me about my father that might be useful. And don't forget, this book may only be a last jab from Stark. It might have nothing useful in it at all, so don't try to make something fit that's unrealistic."

As she left the office on her way to Delaney House, she thought about her poor choice of words. Whatever Lily found was bound to be unrealistic—this whole situation was. She was involved in an unsolved suspicious death and the hunt for an ex-con stalker. Niki was bugging out on her, and she was running a law firm with only one cooperative employee. Starting a search for a man who'd stayed hidden for forty years and who probably didn't want to be found wasn't smart, let alone realistic.

But she was going to do it, anyway.

CHAPTER TWENTY-EIGHT

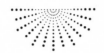

Once again, she found Niki in the kitchen at Delaney House, alone with a man, but this time, she was with their accountant. The last time they'd talked with Barton Gilmer was to incorporate Delaney Inns. "Niki's Empire," as Grace had dubbed the new venture, was the culmination of her cousin's dreams and the solution to Grace's problem of what to do with Delaney House. Now most of her assets were in their business and her partner was having a solo meeting with their accountant.

Gilmer seemed unaware of the flood of emotion that filled the room with Grace's arrival. He stood to greet her, saying, "Good to see you. Niki said she was meeting with you later today, but I'm glad to have the chance to hear how your family is doing."

The pleasantries took ten excruciating minutes, during which Niki made room for Grace at the long kitchen table and passed her several sheets of paper with the accounting firm's logo. One glance confirmed it was a balance sheet for Delaney Inns' assets and debt.

"I've explained to Barton that I'm moving and trying to determine the best way to structure things financially to protect your investment," Niki said. "I wanted to consider the options before I talked to you."

This was Niki, Grace reminded herself as she studied the papers.

Her cousin would never hurt her, but apparently she would keep secrets. Or try to. "It looks like we're in decent shape," she said lightly. "So, what's the plan?"

Barton looked surprised. "Well, as I told Niki, a week's notice wasn't enough to do a thorough study, but I was able to put together some options for discussion. We can at least do some brainstorming today."

Grace didn't respond, but her mind raced through the implications, and as it did, her heart sank.

Niki had called Barton a week ago—before they went to Ocean City and found Winnie, before they knew the truth about Connie's peeper. She'd set things in motion after learning about the money she would get from the dissolution of the trust, and she hadn't said a word.

Grace took the slim portfolio Barton held out to her and said, "Thank you. It was kind of you to do all of this on short notice."

When they'd heard all of the accountant's proposals, Niki finally spoke, but it was only to ask Grace for her opinion.

Calm, calm, calm. This is Niki. "I think Barton is right. Delaney Inns has been unusually successful for such a young business, which is entirely due to your efforts. It would be a shame to see it fall apart now, which is what will happen without professional management." She stopped and finally looked at her cousin and saw what she'd known would be there. Niki was leaving no matter what happened today. She would go with Grace's blessing or without it. "I want to think about it for a day or so, and talk to Mac, but in my opinion, Option Three is out."

Niki nodded. "Agreed," she said, as if they'd just decided on ham sandwiches for lunch. "We won't sell the business. I'd also want to cross out Option One."

Grace looked at Barton's report again. "You don't want to keep the inns running with the current staff?"

"No. I'd like to sell the Queen's Brooke house and use the assets to pay for a General Manager for the Victory Manor Inn and Delaney House."

Grace double checked Barton's report. Selling Queen's Brooke, which Niki owned outright, wasn't one of his options.

The accountant frowned and said, "That will change the financial structure of the corporation. Perhaps we should review the implications?"

"I also want to give the Victory Manor Inn to Grace."

"Clearly, I'm missing something," Barton said, raising his voice over Grace's surprised protests.

"I'm sorry. I don't mean to be secretive," Niki said. "But that's why I wanted to meet with Barton before we talked, Grace. I wanted to see if he came up with any ideas I hadn't considered, and I wanted him to do it without your input because I knew—or I thought, anyway, that you'd try to stop me. We need to talk."

Grace waited silently as Barton gathered his papers and left. When she and Niki were alone, they sat across from each other at the old pine table, in the same places where they always seemed to end up when there was a crisis at hand and a decision to be made.

"I need to do this," Niki said, "Will you let me?"

Grace asked the only safe question she could think of. "Why?"

"I'm not floundering around looking for a new antidote for my screwed up life, I promise. I've known for a long time that things would probably come to this point, and oddly enough, Mom and Winnie have cleared the path for me. And, no, I'm not running away. I'm removing myself for a while, that's all. I can't control them, and I can't see the future, but I've learned from the past."

"But to let them drive you away—"

"They *aren't.*"

"But you said they've cleared your path." Grace was confused and exasperated. "Don't give in to their manipulation. You don't have to leave. I'll have them barred from coming into any of the inns. We'll set up security, and keep both of them away from us."

Niki smiled and shook her head. "I've given in so often, it's a wonder I have any backbone left."

"Then you'll give it a try? We can—"

"No. I meant I won't give in to *you.* I have to leave. Know what the breaking point was?" Niki got up, crossed the kitchen to the Hoosier cabinet that sat against the far wall, and retrieved a small jeweler's box from the long-unused flour sifter. Handing it to Grace, she took her seat again, saying, "Remember these?"

Inside the box were Niki's sapphire and diamond earrings that Stark and Connie had kept for themselves. Grace held them up to catch the light. "They're beautiful."

"They're fakes. Dad's message to me? He lied, imagine that. He sold the originals God knows how long ago, had copies made and gave them to Mom, who never suspected a thing."

"She knew they were yours, though, right?"

"Oh, that didn't matter at all. She wanted them, so she took them. You should have been with her in the days after the will was read. First, she said the earrings had always been hers and asked for them back. When I refused, she didn't argue, but the next day I found her upstairs, in the apartment, going through my dresser. She was sure they were real. Then after what Winnie said as we were leaving the Blow Back In, I had them appraised. Nice quality simulated stones. The jeweler said the originals would have cost a fortune. Dad cheated both Mom and me with these fakes."

Unable to think of anything comforting to say, Grace returned the earrings. "You think leaving will stop Connie from hurting you?"

"I know it will. In their own way, Mom and Winnie love me. They aren't trying to hurt me, they just want what I have. Anything I have. Any happiness, anything tangible. They either take it, or they try to ruin it, but only when it doesn't require too much effort on their part. I'd go months without a word from her when she and Dad were in Virginia."

"Maybe, but the properties. Why can't you keep them?"

"I want to go through my numbers and check a few things again before we discuss this, okay?"

Not okay, Grace decided. "But—"

Niki threw her hands up. "I told you. I have a buyer for Queen's Brooke. If I can make the deal work, it will be sold before my loving family knows what's happened. There will be a small profit for me, which will go to you to pay for the general manager for maybe as long as a year. We'll keep the basic premise of our partnership, but flip roles. I'll be the silent partner with a percentage of the net profit based on the current assessment value of Victory Manor. You'll take the lion's share for the inconvenience of being the go-to owner. And you'll own both inns. Mom and Winnie may find a way around me, but you can handle them. The Victory Manor is mortgage free at the moment and I want it to stay that way. It will if you hold the deed."

"That's crazy unfair to you."

Niki shrugged. "Take it for a year, Gracie. If you don't want the business this time next year, we'll sell it or dissolve it equitably. Either way, you get all your original investment back plus a minimum twenty-five percent profit. Plus, you'll still have Delaney House. I promised you would make money, and you will."

"Any other alternatives?" Grace asked wearily.

"I can't stay. I'm drowning. You will always be my family, but please, *please,* let me go."

Since neither of them ever relinquished control easily, it took a while, but when Grace left, they had an agreement. Glad she'd walked over from the office so she could pull her thoughts together before she went back, she detoured to Memorial Park and found an empty bench near the water's edge. Niki had given a reasonable answer for most of the questions that came up and promised to work out the rest of Grace's concerns. "Give me until Monday and I'll be ready with the final details, all right?" she'd asked.

And Grace had said yes because it was the only answer she had.

CHAPTER TWENTY-NINE

M ac took the news better than she expected. Ordinarily, she would have waited until the children were asleep to discuss something this big, but she wanted to give him time to think through everything before they discussed the details. Plus, he gave her the perfect opening.

"I called the office this afternoon and Lily said you were at Delaney House with Niki. How's she handling the latest developments?"

"Well . . ." Grace tried to condense Niki's plans into a bullet list, then told him that on Monday, she would have more details. Throughout the recital, he alternately spooned dollops of strained bananas into Sonny's mouth and wiped the excess off his son's face.

"So, what do you think?" she asked, suddenly desperate to get past this hurdle and into that blessed space where they would be a team for whatever came next.

"Niki's sure about this?" he asked, holding out a paper towel full of rejected banana.

She took it, gave him a fresh one and said, "We agreed to let it rest over the weekend, but I saw the stress leaving her as we talked."

"Is it jumping over to you?" he asked as he dodged the small, sticky hands trying to grab his hair.

"I love you," Grace said as she helped him clean the baby and wrangle him out of the highchair.

"Because I'm a champion baby wrestler?"

"Because you walked in the door, locked up your gun, washed your hands, and took over Sonny-man, and now you've got mashed fruit on your badge and your tie and it's adorable. You're a hunk."

He gave her a long, speculative look. "And?"

"I don't think she's changing her mind. But you're still—"

"A hunk. I know." He took off his tie and badge and cleaned them, then took both children out to the garden where Sonny could practice his ear-splitting squeals of excitement over just about everything and Fiona could practice walking—and falling down—on the soft grass.

And Grace knew that while he was being Dad, everything she'd told him would percolate in the background. She could have watched them all day, but when her phone rang, the peaceful moment was over, at least for her.

It was Niki.

Queen's Brooke Estates Quality Waterfront Homes consisted of one dead-end street lined with ten early twenty-first century bloated, upscale houses. That they sat in a cornfield and their "waterfront view" was a quarter mile away always made Grace wonder why the current residents didn't remove the long-gone developer's sign. Maybe they hoped if they were patient, he'd return and give them the parks, club-house, and riverside beach they'd paid for. But despite its many fail-ings, the little neighborhood looked well kept and peaceful. And once Stark and Connie's former home had been updated, the modern Bohemian style mini-mansion had plenty of room for large families who wanted a "rural life" vacation without actually setting foot in the countryside.

Grace thought Niki was crazy for wanting to dump the property just to keep her mother from trying to take it back. But she changed her opinion when she arrived at Queen's Brooke to find Niki squared off against Connie and Winnie. The neighbors had long ago given up any pretense of minding their own business and several were out in their yards watching the show.

Grace wished Aidan was still on her payroll. Maybe it wouldn't be too wrong to call him. He'd have a blast knocking Winnie into the next county and then he could charm Connie into leaving. She pulled up behind Niki's car, careful to leave plenty of room for a quick departure.

"Great!" Winnie called out as Grace approached them. "The gang's all here. Or are you playing the part of *consigliere* today? Got any cops on the way to back you up?"

"You have to go, Winnie," Connie said. Her tear-filled eyes made her look pitiful, but Grace knew better than to buy that. "Please don't provoke the girls. This isn't my home anymore. Niki bought it and is graciously allowing me to stay here—"

"I am doing no such thing," Niki snapped. Turning to Grace, she said, "When Mr. Ahmed called to say they were cutting the reunion short, he didn't mention it was because Winnie had arrived and was taking over the pool house. I think that sweet, normal family felt sorry for me, but they left in a hurry and I need to get in there and clean up. Unfortunately, the Dynamic Duo won't leave."

"I don't have anywhere to go," Connie wailed.

"Since your stuff is all over the garage, you can leave it here tonight," Niki said. "But you and your favorite child need to move your party to his place."

Connie switched to her "How could you" expression.

"*Now!*" Niki said, rounding on Winnie. "Get. Out. Now." She pulled her phone from her pocket, stabbed the side button, and held a finger over the *911 Emergency* icon.

Winnie shrugged and said, "I'll be back to get you in the morning, Mom."

"No, you won't," Niki said. "She's going with you. Both of you stay away from me and my property. If you don't, Winnie, I'll call your parole officer and tell him you're dealing again."

"You're crazy!" he protested. "That's not true!"

"Sure, it is," Niki said, not giving an inch. "Saw it with my own eyes."

"That's a lie!"

"I've learned from the best, big brother. Get off my property." She turned to her mother. "Follow him out, Mom."

Connie had been pale before, but now she looked ready to pass out. "Tomorrow, baby. Please." Without waiting for an answer, she turned and ran back into the garage.

When Winnie was in his car, Niki said, "Actually, this worked out for the best. On the way over here, I got a call from the buyer I told you about. She's in the area and wants to see the place today. At least something good is coming from this debacle. Watch him until he's out of sight, please. I'll get started in the house."

While Grace watched Winnie leave, she tried to push the scene that had just taken place into the NMP corner of her mind, but it wouldn't fit. She wasn't responsible for any of this, but it was her problem all the same.

CHAPTER THIRTY

The buyer, who turned out to be a real estate broker, ran a half hour late, and since the Ahmeds had been tidy as well as kind, Niki and Grace were able to show her a presentable property. Crystal Ribbe was from Calvert County, and didn't offer a reason for her client's interest in a McMansion in an Eastern Shore cornfield.

"I'm listing it with an agent tomorrow," Niki said. "If you want to make an offer today, I can give you a discount."

When Niki named her price, Ribbe's only response was to ask for a tour. As they walked through and around the property, she was silent, making occasional notes on her phone and taking a few photos. They wrapped up in the garage.

"There's a nice two-room apartment upstairs," Niki said. "I can't show it because my mother's staying there for a few days, and she isn't feeling well."

Ribbe shrugged and tapped something into her phone, then shut it down. "I have a non-negotiable offer. If you accept it, our title company will handle everything at no cost to you. A ten percent earnest money deposit will transfer to escrow tomorrow and settlement will take place a week from today. All transactions will occur electronically, and aside from removing whatever you want to take from the property, no other responsibilities will fall to you."

The offer was ridiculously low, but Niki took it.

When they were alone, the cousins sat by the pool and watched the sky darken in the east over the lush green of the corn field. Light spilled from the garage apartment and cast odd shadows, and Connie would occasionally appear at the window, turning away quickly when she saw them.

Niki broke the silence with a sigh that ended in a moan of relief. "Thank you for not saying I could get more if I waited."

Grace had been grinding her teeth for the past hour and now her jaw hurt from all the warnings, cautions, and arguments she'd held in. "I'm thinking you got exactly what you wanted, the money is just a bonus, right?"

"Right." Niki looked relieved until she saw Grace's expression. "Please don't worry. It's not like this place was ever going to be a money maker for us. I'll get enough from the sale to repay your investment in the upgrades and cover the new manager for Delaney Inns for a few months."

A few months. Grace let it go. "What about you? You'll lose almost everything you put into this place."

"It's worth it. You saw Mom. She'll never give up. This house is her last link to Dad. And where she goes, Winnie goes, but in a week, wherever they are, it won't be here."

"Would you really lie to the parole officer about Winnie dealing?"

"No," Niki said, her voice sharp again. "But I will tell him that Winnie's in with Frankie Elmer and spends his days in a bar, which violates his parole."

Grace remembered how upset Niki had been at the Blow Back In when Winnie bragged about the deal Stark had made with the man Niki had called a loan shark. "How did Stark connect with Elmer?" she asked. "I mean, I assume he borrowed money from him, but what made them such good friends?"

Niki frowned. "Dad sold things through Frankie's pawn shops. They'd been in school together as kids and Dad always used Frankie as a bad example lecture. Obviously, he left a lot out of the versions he gave me since he trusted his old friend enough to set Winnie up with him."

"Maybe," Grace said, but she wondered if Stark's opinion of Frankie had improved, or if his anger at Winnie had grown.

Niki said, "Frankie and being arrested for dealing again were the only things I could threaten Winnie with that would carry any weight. But I don't want Frankie to turn his attention to me, unless I can't get rid of Winnie any other way."

Get rid of Winnie. Grace knew that wasn't possible unless he wanted to go

"I have you and Mac and the children," Niki continued, as if she hadn't just mentioned eliminating her brother. "And Cy and Avril. I'll never let any of you go, but I'm also not going to keep the people and things that are broken in my life. Mallard Bay is Mom's home as much as it is mine and I'm the one who wants the break, so I'm moving to New York."

"With Dylan?"

Niki hesitated, then said, "You found your best life, Grace, and I'm happy for you. I thought I had mine here, but this is just my transition phase. I've told Dylan all of it. All about Mom and Winnie and Dad. He knows the worst. He'll stick with me or he won't. We'll see how it shakes out. He's back in New York now. I told him I had to do this break on my own."

Resigned and exhausted, Grace asked what the next steps were.

"I'm subleasing a studio on the upper west side. I'm going to sort things out and readjust and see where I am, but while I do that, I'm going to plays and the symphony and I'll hit every museum in the city. I don't think it's the home Cy had in mind for me to spend the trust money on, but I'll get him up there for a visit, Avril, too, and we'll get to know each other all over again. I'm thinking you and Mac and the kids have to come every weekend, and we'll talk every day."

"I know," Grace said. She put an arm around Niki and hugged her. "We'll be a long-distance Thelma and Louise, just you know, without the convertible and the scarves."

Niki giggled. It was a sound Grace hadn't heard in a long time, and on this warm summer night on the edge of a cornfield, it was enough to make everything seem possible.

Returning to her beautiful home, a man she loved, and her babies felt almost awkward after the unsettling experience at Queen's Brooke. Just being a witness to the dissolution of Niki's family made her want to shower and put on clean clothes, as if pain and heartbreak could be washed away and happiness donned like a warm shirt from the dryer.

"I brought Chinese," she told Mac when she found him in the nursery rocking a sleepy Sonny while Fiona "read" an upside-down Richard Scarry book. It was well past both children's bedtimes, but everyone seemed happy. Even Mac, who Grace guessed was listening to a continuous loop of Fiona's favorite pages in the counting book.

When they finally made it to their dinner and had traded the highlights of their time apart, both were back on an even keel, one happier than she had been and the other less cheerful about rejoining the world of adults.

"So, to summarize," Mac said as he pulled a pint of Cherries Garcia from the freezer, "Winnie's back in town and after tomorrow morning, Connie will be homeless unless she lives with him in an apartment that a loan shark is letting him use until his parole officer hears about it. Meanwhile, Niki's going off to find herself in New York, and you will be operating a business neither of us knows anything about."

Grace said, "Well, put that way, it sounds bad." She took the spoon he offered her and said, "Fiona can read."

"Fiona has her mother's memory and imagination."

Grace wished she'd imagined the events at Queen's Brooke, but had to settle for ice cream and hope that the next day brought more answers than problems for her to solve.

CHAPTER THIRTY-ONE

A last-minute rearrangement of her schedule dashed Grace's hope for a peaceful end to her work week. Bernadette Xavier and Cyrus Mosley came up to her office together, and neither one of them looked happy. The unannounced visit took a bad tone from the outset when her partner deferred to the OCPD detective instead of taking charge of the conversation.

It didn't take Grace long to figure out why.

"What do you mean, Dennis Mays works for Frankie Elmer?" she asked Xavier. "Why would a pawn shop owner send a thug to terrorize Connie?" She stopped short of adding, "And why does this involve us?" Lily had removed much of the backlogged work from Grace's desk, but she still had a full day, and that was without this interruption.

Detective Xavier didn't seem to recognize non-verbal messages. "We don't know for sure, but I believe your uncle had something Elmer wanted. Elmer didn't get it before Mr. Delaney died, and for whatever reason, he thinks that Ms. Delaney has it now."

"So, he sends a peeping tom . . ." Grace started, then hit a blank. It was ludicrous.

"I don't think that's what Elmer had in mind," Xavier said. "If I'm right, he sent Mays, who is experienced in threatening people, to scare

Ms. Delaney while also checking to see if she's showing any signs of having newfound wealth."

"Again—a pawn broker with thugs on his payroll? Doesn't that make him something else?" She wanted to hear the detective say, 'loan shark.'

"A loan shark," Mosley said wearily. "Elmer is a loan shark who runs informal card games and who also has pawn shops that Stark has used for decades. Stark was in debt to Elmer more often than not. What else, Detective Xavier?" He gave Grace a disapproving look and got an incredulous one in return.

"If by informal, you mean illegal, you are correct in your description of Mr. Elmer's enterprises," Xavier said.

"Wait a minute," Grace said abruptly. "Are newly paroled felons who were convicted of distributing controlled narcotics allowed to hang out in bars?"

"It depends," Xavier's face gave away nothing.

"We know there's an illegal gambling operation going on at the Blow Back In!" Grace said angrily. "And we know that you're investigating it and you have videos from neighboring security cameras showing Winnie and Stark and Piper with Mays."

Xavier nodded, but didn't comment.

And suddenly, Grace knew why. "Winnie's not bright, but he's cunning," she said slowly, watching Xavier's face. "He would think he was smart enough to play along with the authorities, who needed someone of his ilk hanging around the bar, acting as their eyes and ears."

"That certainly fits the boy's character," Mosley said, looking as angry as Grace felt.

"Was Stark working for you, too?" Grace demanded.

"You give us too much credit," the detective said. "But if you ever want to turn that Machiavellian mind of yours to the side of right and might, call me."

It was the final straw. Furious, Grace said, "I think Winnie is an informant for you. Stark provided the plausible reason for him to be at the bar, and you had the great idea to let Winnie out on parole, right?"

She felt like throwing up. "He wouldn't have been released if he hadn't taken the deal you offered him, would he? He couldn't stay out of trouble for ten minutes, let alone three years. He never earned good behavior time off his sentence, did he?" Her voice was shaking and it made her even madder.

"I can explain," Bernadette Xavier started, but Grace cut her off.

"What was it worth to you to put a degenerate drug dealer who almost killed me back on the street so he could get to my family?" Mosley tried to interject, then stopped as she recounted Winnie's crimes and cruelties. She was disgusted and heartsick that the legal system she'd worked in for fifteen years had betrayed her. "He's out of prison, and thanks to you, he's strutting around with an even greater sense of invincibility. Nothing bad ever sticks to him for long, because everyone finds it easier to just give him what he wants. And you're getting what you want, too."

"What are you going to do?" Xavier asked.

"You mean, will I jeopardize the task force?" Grace took a moment to consider her answer. "Fortunately, I have a few more resources than I did the last time the authorities asked me to look the other way so their case against Winnie would be easier to prosecute. My husband and I will decide how to handle things going forward. If you need to know what our decision entails, we'll be in touch."

"I need to know now, Grace. A lot is at stake here."

"The decisions I was referring to involve our children and whether to take them and leave the area until you finish playing with Winnie, his friend the peeper, and the Blow Back In." As she said the words, she realized she'd missed something. "How does Frankie Elmer fit in? And don't try to tell me it's a coincidence that he's helping Winnie."

Xavier looked confused. "I can't comment on that, but since Elmer and Glass are partners . . .you know that, don't you? Elmer is the majority owner of the Blow Back. He's Angela Glass's business partner."

Mosley cleared his throat. "I assumed you knew that, m'dear?"

"How would I?" Grace snapped, off balance again.

"It was in the report Lily prepared for us," he said quietly.

His tone softened the rebuke, but Grace felt her cheeks get hot. The report was in her briefcase, unread and forgotten.

Xavier broke the awkward pause. "I'm sorry for the impact all of this is having on your life. And as much as I hate to make a bad situation worse, the reason I'm here is to ask a favor."

Grace couldn't summon a polite response. The 'impact' would linger long after Xavier and Greenley had moved on. How could she have ever thought this woman was a decent human being?

"Please explain, detective," Mosley said. "Although I must tell you, I am appalled at the actions you and your task force have taken so far, and your lack of regard for our safety."

"I understand," Xavier said. "But I need to ask you about Piper Tilden."

"Lovely girl with crappy taste in men." Grace snapped. "Not what you meant? Haven't you already paid Winnie for that information? He could ask Mays or Elmer for the scoop on her, couldn't he? Why are you dancing around with us when everything you want to know is tied up with those three?"

"We don't want to give Mays any reason to run before we have enough evidence to arrest him," Xavier said, sidestepping the rest of Grace's question. "He's pivotal in more than one investigation."

Grace decided there was no point in wasting the leverage she had at the moment. "Frankie Elmer. What do you think Stark stole from him?"

"Money."

"And?" Mosley said. "Details, please, or my partner and I will need to return to work."

Grace didn't wait for another evasive answer from Xavier. "She thinks Elmer killed Stark. We were thinking of Winnie's release, Connie's peeper, and Stark's death as personal to us. She doesn't care about any of that except as side events to the task force's goal of taking down Elmer and Glass. Which, now that I think of it, is a pretty extreme reaction to a small unlicensed gambling operation."

"Is that correct, detective?" Mosley asked. "Did Frankie Elmer kill Stark?"

Xavier wiggled her hand in a maybe, maybe not gesture. "If he did, it wasn't on purpose. He hadn't recovered his money yet. What I am sure of is that when Mays got up here to Mallard Bay, on his own and without a handler, he reverted to his favorite methods of intimidation instead of following Elmer's orders to assess Connie Delaney's life-style. And as usual, he got caught. That led us to Elmer, then to Elmer's relationship with Stark, which closed the circle. Or will, as soon as I have some evidence. I hope you can see the reasoning behind the actions we've taken."

"You think Piper Tilden has that evidence?" Mosley asked.

"We've hit a dead end everywhere else," Xavier admitted. "Ms. Tilden might have heard unguarded comments from Stark, or seen him steal from the bar."

"Or she might have information from Winnie," Grace said. "I can assure you he isn't telling you anything useful or remotely related to the truth."

Mosley spoke up again. "All of which means Connie is still in danger."

"We've already warned her to be careful," Grace said, not caring if she had to explain Aidan's big mouth, they were well past that now. "But I guess someone," she glared at Xavier, "someone in authority, should tell Connie that the next emissary from Frankie Elmer might not be so obvious."

"On the contrary," Xavier said. "Elmer's man is right under his mother's nose."

Winnie. Grace forced herself not to react and waited for Xavier to finish.

"The transponder we've got on the car Winston Delaney is driving —which, by the way, belongs to Elmer—shows that he's made multiple trips from Ms. Delaney's home to the apartment Elmer is letting him use in Salisbury. Winston is probably helping her move and has decided by now that his father didn't give her anything except a hard time."

"Is Piper helping them?" Grace asked, wondering what Winnie's new girlfriend had to do with Xavier's visit.

"We'll ask her when we find her," Xavier said. "No one's seen her for two days. We think she ran when she figured out how Stark Delaney died, or that Winston Delaney is working with us, and is also taking money from Elmer, or that the games in the back room are more than a few friends getting together for some fun. Maybe all of it, but something spooked her. She got scared, and I don't blame her."

"Well, you're really off base if you think she'll talk to me," Grace said, remembering the last contentious scene with Piper.

Xavier stood and said, "You don't have to talk to her, just let me know if you get a lead on her. But if you do talk to her, please ask her to call me. Assure her she isn't in trouble."

"And if she refuses?"

"Then ask her if she knows Stark Delaney stole $25,000 from the unlicensed operation running in the back of the bar. If she's still listening after that, ask her if she thinks Frankie Elmer knows about it and believes she had a part in the theft. Tell her I'll protect her if she comes in."

CHAPTER THIRTY-TWO

W hen Xavier was finally gone, Grace remembered she needed to fill Mosley in on the events of the night before. It felt cruel to upset him further, but neither of them could afford to operate in a vacuum. Not any longer. Keeping bad news from each other was counter-productive—a point she made as nicely as possible before getting into the wild scene at the Queen's Brooke house.

"I'm glad you've realized that," he said, nodding in agreement. "I know you try to protect me, m'dear, but there's no need."

He thought she was apologizing. The morning had to end soon or she would explode from all the words she was swallowing. "It would have been nice if I'd known about Stark's connection to a crime syndicate well before any of this happened, Cy."

He looked surprised, then confused. "I'd hardly call Frankie Elmer a syndicate. He's just Frankie. He ran around with Stark in school, and while I was dismayed at the path he chose in life—the paths both boys chose—"

"Stark was sixty-one!" Grace said, unable to stay quiet any longer. "And if Elmer's business model rates a police investigation, he's a damn sight closer to being a crime syndicate than 'just Frankie,' isn't he?"

Mosley shrugged. "I'll admit I'm dismayed to learn that Winnie didn't earn his parole and is double-crossing the police by working with Frankie."

Grace gave up and moved on to describe Niki throwing Winnie and Connie out of the Queen's Brooke house and her intentions to leave Mallard Bay.

"Everything comes at a price, doesn't it? We get rid of Connie and Winnie and lose Niki." Mosley slapped his hands on the arms of his chair and pushed himself up. "We've done the best we could with what we had to work with. It's out of our hands, now."

"But, Cy, what about Connie?" Grace stopped, loathe to bring the woman back into their lives, but also not willing to leave her ignorant and under Winnie's thumb.

Mosley's face hardened. "Winnie will abandon his mother once he's sure she's penniless. She will then come home, and we'll deal with whatever her arrival entails. And if Stark gave her some of the stolen money, which I doubt, she'll either give it to Winnie, or to Frankie Elmer, because $25,000 isn't enough to make Connie Delaney risk messing up her hair, let alone get herself killed. You underestimate her, Grace. I, however, do not."

She checked her watch. If he left now without getting into a 'back in the day' story, she might salvage her schedule if she skipped lunch. "I propose a compromise," she said. "Let's put it all aside for a while. You bring Avril over for dinner and the four of us will brainstorm everything and see what we can come up with."

"Should we include Niki?" Mosley asked.

Grace didn't hesitate before saying no. She had enough to handle.

Mac was delayed at the police station and Grace ended up in charge of dinner, a situation Avril didn't even pretend to like.

"I could have made manicotti," she said when she saw the selection of salads. "I'd have brought something nourishing if I'd known you were cooking."

Grace grinned and opened the oven to release the delectable scent of a roasting pork loin. "Doesn't that smell good?"

"You bought that prepackaged in a marinade, didn't you?" Avril snapped. "This is what comes from removing shop classes and home economics from the schools. You can't change a tire or cook properly, and your poor children will grow up thinking hamburgers magically appear at McDonalds."

Grace laughed, partly because it was true. Also, she was determined to keep her friend entertained until they had to get down to the business of murder and motives. "Mac thought he would have time to do pasta, but this is better, anyway. It seems as if he and Cy have a lot to discuss."

The men were on the patio, the drone of their voices inaudible, but constant. She handed Avril a plate with cheese and crackers and said, "Want to take this out to them while I finish getting everything ready?"

"No. I'll be eating all of it myself." Avril selected the two largest cheese cubes and a fist full of Triscuits. "But I'll tell them to get their butts in here and fill us in."

So much for easing into unpleasant topics after a nice dinner. Grace's plan to discuss Stark, Winnie, and the illegal operations at the Blow Back In went awry as well.

"Not tonight, m'dear," Mosley had said firmly. "We have a plethora of problems to discuss. I told Mac about our conversation with Detective Xavier, only to learn she visited him, too. I also told Avril everything on the way over here. Both conversations clarified my thinking, and I really believe we should stay away from the investigation into Stark's death. That boy," Grace got a nod and a sad smile, "*Stark* did what he's always done—the wrong thing. What happened with Winnie's release is beyond our control, as is whatever transpires between him and his mother. You'll tell Niki all of it, and she'll go to New York with her new love, and life will go on."

It was a long speech for Mosley.

"I, for one, agree wholeheartedly with Cy," Avril said as she critically examined a floret of cheese-covered broccoli from the only dish Grace had made from scratch. "But only about discussing other things tonight. Now, let's figure out that bizarre poem of Stark's. I certainly would have liked to have gotten a gift from him. The little thief stole twenty dollars from my purse fifty years ago and never paid it back."

Since she didn't have any choice, Grace gave in to the change of subject. "I don't think you'd want a gift like the ones we got," she said.

The discussion of Stark's poem took them through most of dinner without turning up any new insights. Grace changed the subject each time the yearbook was mentioned.

With the exception of the broccoli, Mosley finished his dinner and leaned back in his chair with a satisfied sigh. Hooking his thumbs under his waistband, he fixed Grace with a stern look. "Connie's gift of his unpaid bills is an easy call. He ruined her financially for the immediate future. Niki's gift of jewelry and the knowledge that Connie had kept the earrings from her for years was the final blow to her relationship with her mother."

Avril agreed. "I believe he meant to ruin any possibility for reconciliation between them. Probably his revenge because Niki wouldn't cut Connie out of her life."

Mosley continued as if she hadn't interrupted him. "Winnie's gift did triple duty. Connie and Niki were both hurt by it, and far from benefitting his son, Stark ensured he'd get involved with criminals as soon as he was released from prison. I don't see any way the boy isn't a recidivism statistic in the near future."

Grace wondered if Winnie had been the subject of Mosley's earlier conversation with Mac. "What about Piper Tilden?" she asked. "She got his car, and his rings, plus who knows what she took from the apartment before Niki and I arrived."

Mosley nodded. "His gift to Miss Tilden seems to be simple generosity, except it would be the first time Stark has been generous to anyone, in my knowledge at least. And now the young lady has disappeared."

"They were beautiful children," Avril said, causing them all to look at her in surprise. "Stark and Winnie," she added in exasperation. "If you're expecting the wizened old crone to say she could always see the evil behind those little faces, you're out of luck. I'm not a cliche, you know."

"Nobody thinks—" Mac started.

"What?" Avril snapped. "Nobody thinks I'm a wizened crone, or nobody thinks I should let loose with a heart wrenching memory of poor, warped children?"

"Is there a third option?" Mac asked, then scooted his chair away from her as she shook a bony finger at him.

"They were beautiful," she repeated, then drained her glass of wine. "Rambunctious, yes, but for a while they were innocents. Nobody stays that way, though. Stark was ruined early and Winnie . . . Good Lord, he has Stark's DNA *and* Connie's, and he was spoiled to a ridiculous degree by Emma, and he embraced all of it. The boy's a kind of bad that nothing will fix." She glared at each of them, saving her fiercest stink-eye for Grace. "Now see what you've done. You've irritated me until I sound like a country western song."

"Me? Mac started it. And anyway, the next stanza in your song is about my gift, right? Go ahead. What about the yearbook?"

Avril shoved her glass at Mac and said, "If you've run out of wine, there's going to be trouble."

He filled her glass and Grace's, giving his wife a "God's Will Be Done" look.

Avril ignored him, staying focused on Grace. "Since you insist on discussing your mother's yearbook, let me say that I think you should burn it now. Why let your uncle win with you, too? It's all in the past, you said so yourself."

"There's nothing to win," Grace said, her voice gentle. She was sensing an unfamiliar emotion behind Avril's bluster.

Don't look too closely at my life, you won't like what you see.
I've left a parting gift for you, and now I will be free.
And the one thing that you really want is what I'll take with me.

Avril recited the words, her gaze never leaving Grace. "Know what's odd about that little ditty? We've explained away all of Starks' bequests but one, and I'm sure the poem is only written to one person. Connie can insist all she wants that he wrote it to her, but I believe he was warning you, Grace. *You* won't like what you see and it's your happiness that he'll take with him, because he knows you'll never stop until you unravel whatever it is in that book. You're going to be hurt if you don't get rid of it now."

CHAPTER THIRTY-THREE

Niki didn't call, Connie and Winnie stayed gone, and both children slept for six straight hours on Saturday night, and repeated the miracle on Sunday. Everything was calm, homey, and happy right up until Monday morning. Grace's nine o'clock appointment rescheduled, but she didn't have a chance to decide how to use her unexpected free hour before Lily appeared with a somber look on her face and the yearbook in her hands.

"Is it a good time to brief you on what we've found?"

Grace pointed to the conference table and got up to join her. "What you found," she repeated as they took their seats. "Not who you found?"

The yearbook had sprouted several sticky notes and tabs and Lily handed her a report. "I've emailed a copy to you, too," she said. "It details the steps I took in analyzing the book and the reasoning behind my conclusions. I couldn't pin down one man with any certainty, but I feel there are three possible candidates who could be your father. If, of course, your father is someone who was at Rutgers during the 1979-80 term and is in this book. I also used a contact in New Jersey who specializes in this sort of thing to look at everything we have about your mother and her activities during that time. Neither of us found a

Jonathan Reagan in the age range of 15 to 50 living within fifty miles of the campus. Both of us found connections between the men in my report and your mother."

Grace took the paper Lily held out and read, "Roy Bascombe, Abel Finney, Marcus Valenti."

Lily opened the yearbook, selected a sticky with Roy's name and flipped to a shot of a handsome young man in running shorts who stood in front of a judging stand. His wide smile and the trophy he held over his head didn't need the photo's caption to confirm that he'd won a race.

Abel Finney didn't have Roy's good looks, but he also had a trophy of sorts. The headline of the newspaper he was holding up read, *Rutgers Senior Wins Rhodes Scholarship*.

"I suppose you're going to tell me that the third guy is an astronaut?" Grace said, surprising herself with the irritation in her voice. She apologized quickly.

"It's okay," Lily said. "I thought the same thing, but Abel and Roy are the leading contenders based on all the information we found. Marcus isn't a student, he's an assistant professor, and he's a long shot. In fact, he's in the also-ran group of fifteen males that we could connect to your mother. And by that, I mean they appear in a photo with her, or they've written a message in the book, or they're in the same classes and are referred to in some way that connects them to Julia. Also, we found school records, newspaper clippings and random postings on the internet. We also talked to a few people."

Grace didn't know what to ask first. "I guess you'd better start at the beginning."

Lily smiled. "I'm confident in the results, but we need to leave room for new information and for the possibility that your mother had other friends off campus who didn't make the yearbook, or the newspapers, or otherwise draw attention to themselves. You told me she preferred tall men, even though she was petite, and she disliked smokers and heavy drinkers, but all of those opinions could have been formed as a result of her college experience. Besides, who among us hasn't lowered our standards from time to time?"

Grace smiled. She wasn't going to argue that point. "Okay, explain why you narrowed it down to Roy, Abel, and Marcus."

"Roy Bascombe was, according to everything we could find, an all-around nice guy. He was on the yearbook committee, which is how he met Julia. She was the freshman apprentice to the editorial staff. They met during the summer before classes started, though. They had jobs at an ice cream shop near campus. He's our number one pick because of that and because of this." She turned to a page near the front of the book and pointed to a message written in a bold, vertical script.

I will never forget you was printed across a shot of Julia and Bascombe, who appeared to be listening to a speaker at an outdoor rally. Abel Finney was nearby, wearing a sour expression.

"Bascombe is also number one," Lily continued, "because just like Julia, he dropped out of school and went back home to a small town in Texas. Only he didn't do it until the next year, and he took his girl-friend with him. They're still married and have five children and eigh-teen grandchildren. I have his address in Austin if you want it."

"Well, Bascombe makes sense in one way," Grace said, studying his photograph. "My birthday is April 4th, which means Mom got preg-nant in July. The only thing she ever told me was she met my father when she was away at college. I tried to get more details over the years, but we'd only end up arguing."

Lily looked thoughtful. "That adds a point to Bascombe's column, but you could have been premature—"

"No. Or at least, not by much. Mom also mentioned once or twice that I was the size of a boulder."

Lily winced. "Okay, so not premature." She made a note on her report. "But the summer conception date doesn't really knock the other two men out of the running. Finney lived in the area and Valenti gave a series of lectures during the summer semester, as well as during the fall term."

"What about Abel Finney?" Grace asked, pushing the timeline puzzle aside for the moment.

"From what we could learn, Abel and Julia dated a few times. We know this and other random details about all three men because we found Julia's dorm mate, Regina Waller. I have her name and number, too, if you want it. We told her the truth, that Julia had passed away, and you were trying to find out more about her time at college. I believe she knew about the pregnancy, about you, because she didn't question me about your age. She talked freely, even offering information I hadn't asked for. I think she'd love to talk with you. She sent this for you."

Grace looked at the photograph of two laughing girls, standing in front of a poster for the movie *Alien*. Both were short blondes, but Regina had long straight hair.

Lily said, "Finney was very popular because, according to Regina, he was rich, smart, and good looking. He and Julia had instant chemistry, and Regina hung out with them as often as they'd let her. It didn't last too long. Julia didn't pine over him, and it was months before she dropped out of school. He went on to do graduate work at Oxford, married a girl from the UK, moved to Spain, got a divorce, and died about fifteen years ago in an auto accident. No children."

Grace's immediate reaction was to root for poor Abel, who wasn't alive to complicate her life.

"What?" Lily asked. "You seem upset."

"I'm a horrible person and I hate being reminded of it," Grace said, shaking her head. "Okay, well, Abel Finney is possible, but I look more like Roy Bascombe, and we know she knew him early on. What about the professor?"

"Assistant Professor. He's the speaker at the rally." Lily returned to the photo of Julia and Roy Bascombe. "This shot includes all three men. Valenti was only at Rutgers at intervals on exchange agreements with Columbia University for visiting lecturers. He taught political science. Regina said he looked like a tall Dustin Hoffman with aviator glasses. She said all their friends were gaga over him, and your mom was no exception."

"Gaga?"

"Gaga," Lily insisted. "But despite that, Valenti is only on my list because he took your mother out for coffee after one of his lectures."

"That's all?"

"All that Regina knew, but as you pointed out, your mother could keep secrets. She might have been with him all along and not told anyone. Instructors dating students was a no-no in those days, too. He returned to New York and eventually moved to the New Jersey suburbs. His wife died five years ago, and he's currently in an assisted care facility, condition unknown."

Grace sat for a moment, thinking about the three young men and her teenaged mother. "So that's it?" she finally said. "No bombs? Nothing shocking about any of them? No connection to Stark or the family in any way?"

"Nope," Lily said. "No scandal at all, at least not that we turned up. Only young people whose lives intersected over a ten-month period between June 1979 and February 1980 when your mother left school for the last time. If you want to know more, I can make it happen."

Grace didn't have to think about the offer. "No. Thanks anyway, the book is what Stark thought would hurt me, and that's the only reason I had you check it out. But it looks like he was just jerking me around. I'll put this in the cedar chest with the rest of Mom's things and let it all go."

She meant the words as she said them, but after Lily left, she wondered if she could do it. It had been one thing to forget about her father when she had no hope of finding him. But quite another to ignore the names, locations, and photographs of likely candidates.

"Damn you, Stark," she thought. She walked out to Lily's desk and said, "I'll take Bascombe's address. And the care facility where Valenti is living. May as well keep all the information together."

CHAPTER THIRTY-FOUR

The yearbook seemed to double in size and weight while the paper Lily had given her was crumpled and worn from handling. It was impossible to ignore either of them. It was also impossible to decide what to do with them. Shoving them in the cedar chest was out of the question.

So was thinking about anything else.

"Let me do it," Mac said after watching her fumble with the zipper on Fiona's sleeper. "Those things are hard to work with only one hand."

Grace hastily pulled her left hand out of the pocket that held the crumpled paper with its potentially life changing words. She'd been fidgeting with it since she got home, but still hadn't looked at it again. "I've got it," she said, unsticking the zipper and trading him a clean toddler for a smelly infant.

"You going to tell me what's making you so nervous?"

"I don't think I mentioned that Lily sometimes does freelance work as an investigator for some friends she made when she was on active duty."

"No, you didn't. But I knew that. I've had requests for background checks on her. Not lately, though. A couple of insurance agencies and a private investigation firm out of Wilmington, if I recall correctly. Did you ask her to do that kind of work for you?"

She didn't answer right away. The warm sudsy water in the baby's yellow ducky bathtub was soothing, and this was always one of the best moments of her day. When Sonny was rinsed and wrapped up, she said, "Let's wait until later, okay?" Then before he could agree, the words flew out of her mouth. "I think she found my father, and I didn't want her to. I wanted her to prove that the yearbook was another worthless gift of Stark's. I thought it was like Niki's fake earrings—something to make me happy, then disappoint me. I was sure nothing important was in there."

"What's in your pocket?" he asked gently.

"Names."

They put the children to bed and took glasses of wine out to the patio swing. When she saw Mac had brought the bottle along, too, she laughed. "I'm not upset, promise. But you read the signals right. I may need a refill before dinner's over."

"Is there dinner?" he asked in mock surprise.

It was her turn to cook, and she hadn't even thought about food, but she managed an indignant tone as she assured him there was a lovely cauliflower crust pizza in the freezer.

"We ate that night before last," he said. "I'll make sandwiches later. Let me see the paper, honey, and tell me what Lily found." When she'd finished, he said, "I think you were right in your first assessment. Stark planned a nasty surprise for each of you, and now you've got your hopes up."

"That's just it, Mac. It's not hope, it's more like dread. My life is settled and I love it. I don't want the pain of finding my father. Whoever he is, he'll be a disappointment because he left me, but having the possibility hanging out there is nerve-racking."

He kissed her and said, "Sweetheart, I hate to break it to you, but you've always had a father and wishing him away won't change that. He is, or once was, a real, live person. His name might not be Jonathan Reagan, but he existed, and maybe still does. It's hard for people like us to live with a hole in our lives. But finding out the truth doesn't have to mean you establish a relationship with him."

"What do you mean, people like us?"

"Fixers. Problem solvers. We know what happens when there's an unanswered question. Something untrue will fill the hole in the narrative and change the course of that tiny thread in history. Most of the time, it's an insignificant alteration." He hugged her a little tighter.

"But sometimes it isn't," she finished for him, and reached into her pocket. "There are the three men." She smoothed out the wrinkled paper and handed it to him. And then she told him their stories.

If Avril was surprised to find Grace at her front door at eight a.m., she didn't show it, and Grace didn't give her a chance to leap to the wrong conclusions. "Everyone's fine," she said, before adding, "Good morning."

"Took you long enough," Avril groused, then waved her inside. "I knew you'd get around to picking my brain eventually, but I have to be caffeinated and, you know, *awake*, for the big tell-all." She turned and stomped away in the direction of the kitchen.

"How do you do that?" Grace called after her cranky friend. "I didn't say what I wanted."

"Oh, please." The words floated back in Avril's wake. "Get in here if you want coffee."

The retro kitchen with its outdated appliances was one of Grace's favorite places and she took her customary seat at the 50s style chrome and red enamel table. "Seriously," she insisted. "What do you think I came here for?" No way was she planting any new ideas in that calculating mind.

Avril made a rude noise. "You want me to talk about Stark's murder, Niki's love life, or what you've found in that damned yearbook. You'll get around to asking me about all of it, but Stark won't get any deader, Niki's as stubborn as a mule so what's the point in worrying about her, and that leaves the book. Did you bring it with you?"

Grace took the book, her notes—which had a new page with Mac's thoughts, and Lily's list out of her briefcase and laid it all on the table. "Do any of these names mean anything?" she said, pointing to the list.

Maybe it was the early hour, or that Avril's grey helmet of hair was sleep-matted and her eyes were encased by more wrinkles than usual, but she looked vulnerable, and Grace considered packing everything up and putting the uncomfortable conversation off.

We know what happens when people don't know the truth. Mac's words stopped her. Then she realized Avril looked relieved.

"No," she snapped and handed the paper back. "Never heard of any of them. But why would I?"

"Because Mom had to talk to someone, and she was always fighting with her mother, and she didn't tell Cy, and God knows she wouldn't have told Stark."

"A girlfriend."

"That's what I think, too. And I'm looking at that girlfriend right now."

CHAPTER THIRTY-FIVE

"Nonsense. Let me see their pictures," Avril said, and fumbled in the pocket of her robe for her reading glasses.

Grace opened the yearbook to the page where Roy Bascombe held his trophy, and was surprised to feel a pang of regret when Avril shook her head.

"That would be nice, wouldn't it? All that beautiful hair and athletic ability. Probably a good dancer and a smooth talker, too." Avril sipped her coffee, then said, "But no. He's too show-offy."

Grace knew she was on the right track. Avril knew something. Why she'd kept it a secret for so long was an issue for another conversation.

"Are we going to look for your genes in everyone in the top ten percent?" Avril demanded. "Just so you know, I have things to do this morning."

Grace turned the pages to the announcement of the Rhodes Scholarship and pointed to Abel Finney. Avril gave it a dismissive wave. "No. I've never seen him."

Grace had intended to show her all the pictures of Julia, but she could tell that Avril wouldn't give any of them fair consideration. She flipped to the page with the only photograph of Julia and all three men.

"Do you know his middle name?" Avril asked softly. She pointed to the assistant professor.

Grace sat back, stunned. "Marcus Valenti?"

Avril reached out and brushed the young professor's image with her fingertips. "Julia called him Jonathan."

Grace stepped outside to call Lily and caught her on her way into the office.

When she'd explained what she wanted, Lily said, "Shouldn't take long. I'll text you." No questions, no chatting, only a hint of sympathy as an acknowledgment of the importance of the task.

Grace felt her anxiety ease a little until she returned to Avril's kitchen and saw her with the yearbook. She looked up when Grace cleared her throat.

"I don't think Julia lied about his name," Avril said. "If you find a Marcus Jonathan Valenti, or Jonathan Marcus, I believe you'll have your father. She said he resembled Dustin Hoffman."

"With aviator glasses?"

"That's what she told me." Avril leaned in closer to the book. "If this young man is the right one, and if he's still alive, he'll be tall and about seventy. He was a good bit older than your mother. I doubt he'll have those same glasses, and his nose will look larger. One the curses of old age, you know. But those eyes of his are the kind that age well." She stopped and took a deep breath, then said, "Julia didn't tell me his last name."

Grace wanted to be angry, and she knew the hurt from Avril's deception would hit her later, but she set all of it aside. "What else did she tell you?" she asked. "I know there's more." The "more" was painfully clear in Avril's solemn expression.

"When he learned Julia was pregnant, he confessed that he was married."

Grace nodded. In a way, she felt better. Her mother's actions were making more sense. And if Marcus's middle name was Jonathan, then Julia hadn't lied about everything.

She studied Valenti's photograph and tried to imagine the conversation between her parents, but nothing materialized. Her father was still a stranger and, at least in this situation, so was her mother.

Avril finally broke the silence. "Julia had a weak moment and told me what I've just told you. To my knowledge, I was the only one who knew about Jonathan. And before you get snippy again and point out that I'm betraying her confidence right now, I claim the death exception."

As upset as she was, Grace fell for it. "What's that?"

"In forty years, if you've gone on to your questionable reward on the other side of the veil, and I'm left here with Fiona and she's demanding answers about, oh, any of the many things you may—understandably—want to keep from her, I'll use the death exception and tell her your secrets, but only if she needs to know."

"This isn't funny, Avril."

"No, it isn't. But it is the first time I've had any reason to tell you anything your mother asked me not to."

"How did it come about?" Grace asked. "I mean, why did she tell you and no one else?"

"A fair question," Avril said. "I'm afraid I took advantage of her. I was at Delaney House one afternoon right before Julia left with you for good. She was out in the rose garden, and she was in a bad way. She started rambling, and once the first words were out, she couldn't stop. Emma was making her crazy because she wouldn't reveal your father's identity. It was all they talked about. Plus, the reality of motherhood was setting in, I think, and Julia couldn't stand fighting with Emma and Stark. She wouldn't tell them anything because she didn't want them going after your father. She said it would be humiliating, and you deserved better."

"What did she mean by that?" Grace asked.

Avril shrugged. "We talked for a long time, but it was all about her inability to deal with her circumstances. Then I asked her something no one else had. I asked her what made her fall in love with him. She hadn't been able to talk about him in so long, I think she couldn't help herself. It sounded like a teenage movie, of course. He was sensitive, and kind, and really handsome, all the usual fluff, but no specifics. Finally, she admitted he was older, and he was married, and that he hadn't told her when they got involved. They had a terrible argument when it all came out, but eventually they came to an understanding. He wouldn't leave his wife, but he'd support Julia if she decided to have the baby. You."

"Big of him," Grace snapped.

Avril said, "When I was younger, I believed Julia let him off too easy. He didn't have to take any responsibility for his actions. He got to play outside the sandbox and go home to his wife with no consequences. Now that I'm older, and I see what he's missed . . . he may never know it, Grace, but he was the loser all the way around. Your mother did what she thought was best for you, and that's all we can ask of anyone, isn't it?"

Grace remembered her own struggle to allow Fiona's father to be an active part of their life. She was in no position to judge anyone, least of all her mother. Or Avril.

Standing, she said, "I'll call you when I know something," and opened her arms for a hug. She had her family, she told herself as they walked to the front door. Knowing her father's identity would bring closure, she didn't need to connect with him.

She'd always trusted Julia's instincts, and she still did.

CHAPTER THIRTY-SIX

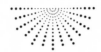

I nstead of leaving right away, Grace locked her tote and briefcase in her car and cut across Avril's backyard to pick up a trail into the small woods behind her house. A short way in, she passed the crumbling brick wall and stepped onto Delaney property. She seldom walked this path anymore, but today, she needed to reconnect with her family's land. And with her cousin.

Niki was one of the few people who would understand how she felt right now.

As she left the woods and crossed the rear lawn of Delaney House, she wished she had driven around the block and used the front door. Who knew what she'd see this time if she barged into the kitchen unannounced? She decided to use the back porch entrance to the main hall. If Niki and Dylan were having a private moment there, they'd just have to deal with the embarrassment. There were twenty other rooms without outside entrances.

Her door key worked, but to her surprise, both the exterior and interior alarms were set. She quickly disabled them and called Niki's name, only to hear her words echo down the long hallway. The kitchen was empty as was the butler's pantry, the dining room, and both parlors. There was no one on the first floor and no sounds coming from the second, but she saw a shadow on one of the glass panels that flanked the front door, and once outside, she found a notice taped next to the doorbell.

On a Tuesday morning in tourist season, The Inn at Delaney House was closed and a telephone number Grace didn't recognize was listed as an emergency contact.

"She promoted the housekeeper to innkeeper in charge of both inns, gave her the keys, a set of instructions, the reservation list, and then left town with Dylan!" Grace was race-walking back through the woods, venting to Mac over a patchy cell phone connection. "Our new innkeeper closes up shop when she has errands or checks on the Victory Manor. What kind of way is that to run a business?"

"Look, honey, I'm late for a meeting—"

"Niki said she and Dylan had plans on Saturday, but she's supposed to be working with me this week on the new operating plan for the inns, and I haven't heard from her. What do we know about Dylan, anyway?"

"Are you sure she's with him?"

"That's what the innkeeper said."

"Then she's fine," Mac paused to tell someone he was on his way. Then, sounding harried, he said, "I made some calls last week. Dylan's background is stellar. Yes, she's being thoughtless and rude, but I have to go."

As Grace disconnected, she realized she hadn't told him what Avril had said about Marcus Valenti. *Later*, she decided. One nerve wracking, energy-sucking crisis at a time.

Not that Niki disappearing seemed to qualify as a crisis for anyone other than Grace. The new innkeeper had assured her that everything was under control, both inns would be full tonight and two new part-time housekeepers worked afternoon/early evening shifts.

Niki had recruited, hired, and trained the new staff more than a week ago and promoted the innkeeper last Wednesday, putting her plan to leave in place days before she consulted Grace. And now she'd left town with a man who was practically a stranger. What if . . .

"Oh, for heaven's sake, stop it," she yelled at herself.

She had clients who *wanted* her to worry about them and paid her to do it. That's where her thoughts should be right now. Not on a father she didn't really want, and not on her mercurial cousin and their wobbly business venture, or even on the murder investigation where she just barely ranked in the lawyer column instead of with the list of suspects.

She needed to go work.

And she didn't have a choice, anyway. Lily greeted her with a cup of coffee, a stack of messages from clients, and the news that Marcus Valenti's middle initial was 'J.'

Grace told her not to rush to find the details. In her heart, she knew his name was Jonathan, and she'd deal with him later.

Two hours passed before she remembered that she'd shut her phone off after talking to the innkeeper. As soon as she turned it on, she saw a string of missed calls and two voicemail messages.

The first was from Niki, who breathlessly apologized for disappearing without telling her and promised everything would work out fine. She and Dylan were on an impromptu whirlwind mini-vacation in New York. "We're having so much fun. Can't wait to tell you about the fabulous restaurants, and the apartment he has here is amazing." Her voice lost its girlish tinkle as she wrapped up the message with, "I need this. Love you."

Grace hadn't recovered from her earlier snit over this inconsiderate behavior, but she couldn't help smiling. Niki, who claimed to have never been in love, seemed to be falling hard. "I guess that means you won't be joining us at the beach," she said into the dead phone, then jumped when she realized she wasn't alone.

"Got a minute?" Lily asked. She was standing in the doorway as if waiting for an invitation. They'd passed that formality long ago. "I have some news."

"Let me guess. Jonathan, right?" Grace waited to feel something, but it was too little, too late. "Well, that's settled," she said, and tried to look like she meant it.

"There's more." Lily took a breath. "You understand, this person I used isn't, uhm, well, he isn't bound by the same legal constraints that we are. Or rather, he does what he does without regard to privacy laws. You'll need to be careful how you use this next part, okay?"

Grace nodded.

"Marcus Valenti is in a nursing home. He's in hospice and he has dementia. It isn't clear what type he has, whether it's hereditary or because of lifestyle risk factors, or any of the other ways and combination of ways—"

"I get it, Lily."

"I also can't tell you his prognosis, other than to say if he's in hospice—"

Grace didn't want to hear another word. "I know what hospice means," she snapped, then immediately felt ashamed. *Get a grip. Don't kill the messenger.* "I'm sorry." She hesitated as the information sank in, then said, "I wanted a medical history for the kids and for myself, and I guess I really need it now."

Lily looked even more uncomfortable. "It's not that my friend wouldn't do it, but it could get messy if you want him to look further."

Grace read between the lines. Would it be so wrong, morally, if she got her father's medical records? It was certainly the very least he could give her—if Valenti was her father. But lots of men were named Jonathan, and Avril's conversation with Grace's mother had taken place forty years ago. What if Julia had been pointing to someone else in the photograph? Perhaps one of the students standing next to the stage?

"And one more thing," Lily said. "I don't want to overwhelm you, but you should also know that Valenti has a child. Another one, I mean. A daughter. She is two years older than you and she has his power of attorney. It was all there in the records my friend accessed this morning. He didn't copy anything, just gathered the basic admission details and next of kin."

Marcus Jonathan Valenti had a wife and a baby when he seduced her mother. If he had seduced her mother.

"Thank you," Grace said quietly. "Tell your friend he can stand down. I don't need him to do anything else."

CHAPTER THIRTY-SEVEN

I f left to her own devices, she might have wallowed in the aftermath of Lily's news for the rest of the day, but a call from Bernadette Xavier ended her brief stint of self-indulgence. The detective's greeting was short and somber. Grace took notes furiously as the detective said that while they were still waiting on reports, they were proceeding as if Stark had died as a result of a blow to his chest.

"The State's Attorney is talking first degree murder, if the results are what he expects," Xavier said. "But how it shakes out is anyone's guess. If someone who fought with Mr. Delaney on the evening of his death came forward and explained the circumstances, I think accidental death—possibly even self-defense—might be argued." When Grace didn't respond, she added, "Especially if Mr. Delaney started the argument and the person he struggled with has proof of injuries."

The fingerprints on Connie's arm. The police had photographs. They thought Connie had killed her husband.

"Do you understand what I'm saying?" Xavier asked.

Grace remembered Connie's chilling words on the morning after their first meeting with the OCPD. *If I killed him, we wouldn't be even.*

"Still with me?" Xavier asked. "You know I've tried to help you before, and I'll try to help you now if you let me."

"I understand," Grace said. "Not that I don't appreciate the update, I do. But to whom should I be passing this advice? You're not warning me on Niki's behalf, are you? Or my own? What are we talking about?"

"You don't represent Connie Delaney?"

"No. Oscar Breedlove does."

Xavier thanked her, sent regards to Mac, and disconnected.

Food, Grace decided. She needed lunch and more caffeine and a brainstorming session with Lily and Aidan. Then she remembered Lily was buried under work, Aidan was fired and gone, and a long-ignored carton of yogurt was waiting in the office fridge to give her ptomaine.

"Lily! Did Aidan take his snack stash with him?"

A pack of crackers sailed through the door and landed on her desk. "Eat fast, boss. The security camera shows an angry lawyer on his way up here."

A corresponding beep from the first-floor outer door alarm confirmed their visitor was bypassing the main office downstairs.

Oscar Breedlove appeared a few moments later and he was, indeed, angry.

"I'm not used to being fired by pro bono clients who are murder suspects." Breedlove glared at Grace. "I want to get a few things straight, and I'd prefer to speak privately."

"An appointment would have been nice," Grace said, then gestured to the vacant chair across from her desk. "I'm happy to talk to you, but I have lunch plans, so please make it quick."

Breedlove flushed. "Look, Ms. Delaney fired me and said you're her attorney. I need to speak to you, confidentially."

"I can leave," Lily said, giving the angry man a "watch it, Buster" look as she left.

"This won't take long," Grace said. "I am not Connie's attorney. If what you have to say can't be said to the police, then you shouldn't tell me, either."

For the first time, Breedlove looked uncertain. "Ms. Delaney called me a couple of days ago, saying she wanted different representation. You. I said fine, and asked her to put it in writing. She hung up on me. I sent her a certified letter confirming our conversation and verifying that I was no longer her attorney. I also notified the court."

"And?" Grace asked. She was hungry and the crackers were calling to her.

"Apparently, Detective Xavier wasn't notified of the change. She called me earlier and asked me to have Ms. Delaney present herself at the State police Barracks in Easton for questioning. I told her you were Connie's attorney. I apologize if that isn't the case."

Grace sighed. That explained Bernadette's call. The detective must think they were all crazy.

"I know how it can be when family members insist you represent them," Breedlove said. "It's never a good idea, and having worked with Ms. Delaney, even for a short time, let's just say that if only on a superficial level, I feel your pain."

"But?" Grace prompted. Breedlove had laid the groundwork and was winding up for the punch that would send Connie right back into Reagan and Mosley's wheelhouse.

"I realize I'm overstepping here, but I think you should reconsider whatever issues the two of you have and look out for your aunt. I have concerns about her safety."

"In what regard?" First Xavier and now Breedlove, both seemingly concerned about Connie's welfare. It was an odd turn of events, to say the least.

Breedlove said, "In my early conversations with her, Ms. Delaney made it clear that she was afraid of her son, but this morning, Detective Xavier said she thought Connie and Winston Delaney were together. I've read up on Winston, and I have to say he sounds as bent as they come."

Grace assured him nobody was going to argue that point. "Did Connie ever tell you about her peeping tom?"

"She did," Breedlove said. "Frankly her accounting sounded

bizarre, but she said a friend had helped her, but she was worried about her son."

"And that was when?"

"Last week. Wednesday, mid-day. She called me and said she needed advice."

"I'll bet she did," Grace said. Connie would have been in overdrive that day after Aidan had tackled the peeper.

"That's where I'm stuck," Breedlove continued. "She fired me the next day. I'm sorry she didn't retain you. I've been trying to reach her since I heard the police are looking for her. I just wanted to make sure she was okay. Her phone isn't accepting calls, and I didn't feel right taking any other steps without going through you. What she does is none of my business anymore, but I don't think she's safe. You may not be her attorney, either, but since you're her family, I'm going to leave the matter in your hands."

Grace walked him to the door, where he turned back and said, "Your aunt is an adult, and I'm sure you know her better than I do." He hesitated, then sighed. "If she needs help and I can be of assistance, let me know. For what it's worth, when she let her guard down, she seemed distraught over her husband's death and worried about her daughter. But mostly, I think she's very scared. If you believe she has any reason to be, please talk to Detective Xavier. I sense she and her partner don't share my concern."

"Why, Oscar?" Grace asked. "Why did you represent her in the first place? Why do you want to represent her now? You know she's dead broke and can't pay you."

Breedlove smiled. "I was told to say she was a pro bono client."

Grace considered his odd wording. "By whom?"

"A friend of mine, a man I admire very much, told me about an interesting client in need of representation. I apologize again for being rude when I arrived. I don't like disappointing my friend, and, frankly, I really was embarrassed to be fired."

Grace felt an eye roll coming on. Mosley's fingerprints were all over this. "I'm sure your good friend understands the no-win situation

Connie's lawyers all fall into at some time or another. She's fired me more often than I've fired her."

Oscar grinned and held out his hand. "Comrades, then."

When he was gone, Lily said, "There's a chicken Caesar salad in the fridge for you. And don't forget, the office is closed the rest of the week, so give me anything you have that's time sensitive."

"I didn't forget my own vacation." Grace, who had totally forgotten the beach trip, tried and failed to sound indignant. "But seriously, you're amazing, and I appreciate the reminder."

"Yeah," Lily agreed. "I was trained by Mr. Mosley. We're always working in the background. He wants to give you and Mac a special dinner for your anniversary, and I'm supposed to arrange it. Any requests?"

"I love you both," Grace said. "But I don't think even you can arrange a romantic dinner that includes two babies, their nanny, Avril, and Fourth of July fireworks. We'll take Cy up on it later, okay? Now, I hope you've already had your lunch because I need you to track Aidan down. I have to sweet-talk him into taking on a side job."

"For us?" Lily looked skeptical.

"Yep. We need a Connie magnet, one who would enjoy crossing paths with Winnie. I can't think of anyone else who fits the bill."

CHAPTER THIRTY-EIGHT

Aidan Banks was three hours into a *Breaking Bad* marathon when Grace's office number appeared on the screen of his silenced phone. He ignored the call until a commercial break, then returned it on the off chance she wanted to apologize.

She didn't.

And when she told him what she wanted, he could have kicked himself. Then she made things worse by talking hourly rates, as if he'd take her money for doing a favor. He let the silence stretch—a nifty trick he'd learned from the Chief back in the day. Grace did it too, he remembered.

"Aidan? *Aidan!*"

He smiled despite his irritation. He did enjoy pulling her strings. "No. I won't work for you, but I will cancel everything I had planned today," he paused to click off the television, "and go look for Connie. And if I run into Winnie, then, bonus. I owe him a few punches for old times' sake. Now, do you want me to tell her to come home, or go to hell? What are my boundaries here?"

"Never mind," Grace snapped. "I'm sorry I bothered you."

He imagined her eyes squeezed into angry slits and had to admit this might be more fun than another three hours of living vicariously through Walter White. "Oh, breathe already, lady. I'll do it. She's my friend, too."

Grace relayed the recent developments in the Connie-Winnie reunion, including Connie's professed fear of her son. She was also clear that Connie was officially a suspect in Stark's death and should be considered dangerous.

Aidan snorted at that. He also refused to agree that he was working for her.

"You're working for me, or you aren't going," she insisted. "If Breedlove isn't over-reacting, you may need some coverage, legally, and I may need to claim whatever you find as attorney work product. You're getting paid your old hourly rate, including travel time, and you have to sign a receipt."

He was going no matter what she said, but he heard the worry in her voice and agreed without giving her any more attitude. Much.

He put her on speaker and started getting ready as she finished up her instructions, warnings, and threats. He was only supposed to find Connie and report back on her circumstances. He wasn't to interfere with the police or their investigation into Stark's death. She also said he had to leave Winnie alone, but they both laughed at that, then he had to listen to her insist that she'd meant it. If there was concrete evidence that Winnie was violating the terms of his parole, Aidan was to call Grace. As if. By the time she stopped talking, he was at the door, his jeans jacket concealing the Glock 22 in the shoulder holster under his arm.

"Do you hear me, Aidan?" she demanded as he switched the call over to Bluetooth Air Pods and locked up the apartment.

"Yeah. Go to Salisbury, find Connie, give her a ride home if she wants one, don't engage law enforcement, don't hurt Winnie. Got it."

He disconnected, hoping she really wasn't expecting him to comply with that last part.

Soon, he was on Route 50 headed south. A large McDonald's coffee, sausage biscuit, and FM107.1 *The Duck* blasting 70s classics made him happy. It was good to be at work again, and the best part of all was the possibility of knocking the crap out of Winnie Delaney.

Also, being able to eat fast food, speed, and listen to the oldies without Desi giving him grief.

Somehow, he needed to figure out a way to make days like this into a well-paying job.

———————

Finding Winnie's apartment was no problem, but he had trouble imagining Connie agreeing to stay in the rundown building on the outskirts of Salisbury. The Montgomery Arms looked like what it was, a place for people with no credit and no job, and who were desperate enough to take a handout from a loan shark named Frankie Elmer. Once the large cinderblock structure might have been a humble but respectable address. Today, it was held together with liberal amounts of low-grade stucco and mismatched paint. Winnie's unit was a shade that had once been blue. Earlier coats of clashing colors bled through the worn and cracked top layer, giving the building the look of a paint ball target.

As soon as he knocked on the front door, it flew open and Connie yelled, "Winnie's gone!"

"Well, I—"

"Shut *up*. I don't care. Wait here and don't you dare leave!" She stepped around a battered half wall that separated the main room from what might be a kitchen, or possibly a landfill, and grabbed two suitcases, which she shoved at him. Yanking the chain of a quilted bag over her shoulder, she yelled, "move it!"

He stepped off the cement slab stoop and she followed him, slamming the door behind her and then kicking it for good measure. When she saw he wasn't moving, she said, "Frankie's guys are after Winnie and me. Do you want to be here when they show up?"

Yes, he really did, but he was afraid she might kill him for his car keys.

Connie climbed into the back seat of his Bronco, locked the doors, and wiggled down to the floor, not seeming to care about the food wrappers and soda cans he'd been meaning to clear out for a month.

"Great," he muttered. "Looks like I'm transporting a dead body."

Without lifting her head, Connie said, "That's exactly what I will be if you don't get us out of here. I don't have the answers those people want. Winnie said they won't hurt me, but I don't believe him."

The Montgomery Arms was at the end of a street of rundown homes, some with plywood over the windows. A chained pit bull that had charged his car on his way in gave him the same treatment as they drove out.

"When we're safe," Connie said, her muffled words coming up between the front seats, "call the animal welfare people down here. That poor dog barks day and night, and I don't think anyone lives there anymore. Winnie wouldn't let me feed him, but we can't leave him like that."

Aidan smiled. This was the side of Connie he'd come to appreciate. She was rude, crass, and selfish, but from time to time, she showed a spark of humanity.

He knew Desi described him in much the same terms.

Three black SUVs with heavily tinted windows took the turn at the corner up ahead of them, then rolled past, taking the lion's share of the badly eroded street. He tried to look like an ordinary guy who was only irritated by the rudeness and forced himself not to step on the gas.

He took a left, heading deeper into the neighborhood instead of right toward the highway. "You expecting friends driving black Escalades?" he asked without looking back at Connie.

The only answer he got was a low moan.

The map on his GPS showed a tangle of residential streets up ahead and he wound his way through them. He continued taking illogical turns, several down alleys, one through a parking lot, until the seemingly erratic route had reversed their direction and dumped them out on Route 50, headed north.

When they'd gone several miles with no sign of the SUVs, he said, "You can sit up, Con."

"Believe me, now?" she said shakily.

He didn't answer, but hit the hands-free phone icon and called Mac, who answered on the first ring and said, "Grace filled me in. What's going on?"

"Got a thing happening, Chief," Aidan said. "Better call Salisbury PD." He recited Winnie's address. "Tell them five individuals, minimum, in three black Escalades are there now. I've got Con, but it looks as if Frankie Elmer has branched out and gotten himself some help, and Winnie's on the run."

CHAPTER THIRTY-NINE

When Mac called, he was sparse on details, telling Grace only that Aidan and Connie would be in Mallard Bay within the hour and he would keep Connie at the department until the Salisbury PD could question her, or until the Ocean City detectives arrived to take her into custody. Both agencies wanted to talk to Winston Delaney's mother.

"Are you arresting her?" Grace asked. She'd been Aidan's second call and was very irritated. She understood his priorities and Mac's professional stance, but still.

"No," Mac said.

"Then Aidan's bringing her to me and I'll produce her for the police when a warrant is issued."

He knew better than to argue the point, but he did it anyway. "It isn't safe to keep her at your office. Plus, you can't stop her from leaving."

"And neither can you." Grace's mind was racing. What if Bernadette Xavier's theory was right, and Elmer thought Connie had the money Stark had stolen? How far would he go to get it back? It was a big leap from the peeper to the SWAT-style team that Aidan and Connie had barely avoided.

"Talk to me." Mac sounded suspicious but curious.

"Who says those were Frankie's guys that Aidan saw?"

"You don't think they are?" His tone told her he didn't think so either.

"In absolutely none of the movies that I watch, do criminal king-pins announce their presence with a fleet of matching black vehicles. But you know who does?"

He sighed. "I never learn."

"Politicians, royalty, and certain lucky police departments who have a federal grant and a sweet deal from a rental company to purchase multiple off lease vehicles."

"That's the last time I gossip with you over cocktails," he said. "It was a Salisbury PD team that's assisting the OC task force. They want to talk to Connie."

"Aidan's going to be so disappointed," she said. "So, does any agency have a warrant for Connie's arrest?"

"Grace—"

"She's coming here. Please let Bernadette know she can bring a warrant when she comes, or Connie stays with me. They can interview her in my office.

"Grace—"

"Mac, Winnie knew the police were coming to talk to her. How? And why would he tell her Frankie's guys were after her? I think he wanted her too afraid to talk to the police."

"So now you're her attorney again?"

"According to Oscar Breedlove, I am, but don't worry, sweetie, she'll fire me before long." She disconnected and called Aidan, who for once agreed to do exactly what she asked him to.

Her next call was to Niki. It went straight to voice mail. Frustrating, but not unexpected. She left a message saying Connie's situation had escalated, she wasn't safe with Winnie and needed a place to stay. Then she called Delaney House, where a recording advised her that the staff was assisting other guests and would be with her momentarily. After three cheery assurances that her call was very important, the newly promoted Innkeeper gave her a chirpy, "Delaney Inns, this is Margo, how may I help you?"

Grace didn't waste time with pleasantries as she identified herself and asked if Niki had left an emergency contact number.

There was a brief hesitation, then, "I'm sorry, I can't give out that information, ma'am, but I'm sure I can help you."

She was going to kill Niki. "This is Grace *Reagan*. We talked this morning. You remember? When I found the inn locked up and a note on the door?"

Silence again.

It was too much. "I own the building you're standing in and this is an emergency. I need any number my cousin left with you, and I need it now." It was an unreasonable reaction, and she half-heartedly apologized, but Margo rattled off the number. Dylan's cell phone.

She left a message in his voice mail and disconnected, thinking that if she were Niki, she not only wouldn't return the call, she'd never come home.

———

Mac picked up Aidan's Bronco as soon as they came off the Mallard Bay exit on Route 50. He followed them to Grace's office, waiting until they were inside before continuing on to the police station.

Connie was impressed with the escort and perked up for the first time since she'd buried herself in a pile of cheeseburger wrappers an hour earlier. As soon as they reached Grace's office, she made a bee-line for the restroom while Aidan described their harrowing escape and Grace burst his bubble by telling him who they'd been running from.

"I didn't ask you to go armed," she said. "Do you have a carry permit for that pistol under your jacket?" When he grinned, she added, "It's just that the police officers who'll be arriving here soon might want to see it, so feel free to leave if you need to. If we need protection before they get here, Lily can provide it."

"I have the damned permit," he called after her as she led a slightly less disheveled Connie to her office. "But don't you think an armed secretary is overkill?"

She mimicked his smirk and said, "Thanks for everything. I really appreciate the help."

Deciding to stick around anyway, he took a seat on the uncomfortable bench that Grace insisted made the place look classy. He didn't like the casual air the women had toward the danger they could be in. Maybe it had only been the police in the Escalades. That didn't mean Elmer's guys weren't right behind them.

"Executive Assistant," Lily said.

"What?"

"I've been promoted. *And* I had a permit for concealed carry before you ever qualified to fire that big boy gun of yours."

He'd missed this. "Hey, now, don't you go sweet talking me, I'm taken."

"By a woman with bigger guns, right?" Lily turned to her computer monitor, ignoring his embarrassed sputtering. "Seriously, I've got this if you want to go."

He started to protest, then stopped. They didn't need him. The sarcastic banter aside, both women had made that clear. Grace might call him if they had an odd job they couldn't handle, but otherwise . . . He noticed the empty corner at the far end of the room. The desk he'd used was gone.

"If you're sure," he said and stood up. "I'm starved. Tell Grace I'll email her an invoice."

"Thanks, Aidan," Lily said. "We were worried about Connie and I'm not sure she'd have cooperated with anyone else but you."

He was saved from ending the awkward exchange when her attention was caught by the security camera. "Incoming," she said, alerting Grace through the intercom.

The police had arrived.

CHAPTER FORTY

Detective Sergeants Xavier and Greenley had an MDSP corporal with them, and all three looked out of sorts. Grace got a whiff of interagency tug of war when Xavier made introductions and Corporal Hoover's first words were to ask where he could interview Connie. Privately.

Grace gave Xavier a look that said, *Is this guy for real?*

The verbal scuffle was short and ended with everyone crowded around the conference table. Grace recorded the session, as did Xavier and Hoover. The trust level was less than zero.

Connie, semi-docile for once, kept her mouth shut except when Grace directed her to answer a question. Even though she cooperated, she was frightened and her voice shook as she described how she'd begged Winnie not to leave her alone in the apartment.

"Why?" Hoover interrupted. "What were you afraid of?"

"Winnie said the police would want to question me soon, and Frankie wanted to get to me first. Winnie could get in trouble with his parole officer for being mixed up with any of it and that's why he had to go. He said all I had to do was not tell you anything but to tell Frankie the truth—that I didn't get any money from Stark. I was so scared, and I didn't know what to do. He left and then I realized my phone was dead and Winnie had the only charger with him. I packed my things, but I had no way to leave except to walk out. If Aidan hadn't shown up when he did, I guess I'd still be walking."

Hoover checked his watch and then said to Xavier, "Gotta wrap this up. It might be better to take her in and—"

"No one is taking Ms. Delaney anywhere," Grace snapped. "Do you want the rest of her voluntary statement, or do you want to try to get a warrant for it?"

She saw Xavier's mouth twitch.

Greenley maintained his permanently bored expression, but Hoover appeared ready to arrest all of them. "If I get a warrant, lady, she'll be going to jail."

"Do it." Grace said.

She won the standoff, mainly because Connie started to cry. Not scared whimpering, but head-in-hands sobbing that took even Grace and Lily—who'd seen it before—by surprise.

"Nooooo," she wailed. "There's a pervert stalking me, I have nowhere to live and no money. My daughter's disowned me, and my son left me alone at the mercy of a gangster who thinks I have his money. Go ahead. Take me to a judge. I need to be in witness protection."

Grace kicked her under the table and the hysterics faded into hiccups. She handed Connie a box of tissues and looked at Hoover. "Well?"

This time Xavier smiled for real as she leaned toward the recorder and said, "Ms. Delaney, when you can, please tell us who this gangster is and why he thinks you have his money." The look she sent Hoover clearly said, *That's how you do it.*

Sniffling her way along, Connie explained that between the bragging that Stark had done the last time she saw him, and the bragging Winnie had done about the bank account his father had set up for him, she had pieced together enough information to guess that Stark had stolen about twenty thousand dollars from Frankie Elmer, maybe more. "That's the money he gave to Winnie."

Hoover said, "So, if your husband stole the money from Frankie Elmer and gave it to your son, why does Elmer think you have it?"

Connie's eyes filled again, and her voice was so soft, it was hard to hear her say, "Because that's what Winnie told him. He said he only did it to buy himself time to get away before Frankie figured it all out. He said Frankie would never hurt me, but I didn't believe him."

Hoover shook his head. "Your son did that to you? Bet that makes you mad, huh?"

"That's enough," Grace said.

"Then I guess we're done," Hoover said. "Francis Elmer may walk a fine line with us, but until somebody more credible than you and your lying family tells me otherwise, he's just a guy with a pawn business and part ownership of a bar."

"No," Connie insisted, talking over Grace's objections. "I need protection."

"Sorry, you don't qualify," Greenley said as he stood and tucked his notebook into his jacket pocket. "Unless, of course, you'd like to confess to something?"

"Well, her story actually makes sense, doesn't it?" Mac said. Grace had given him a recap of Connie's statement and promised to email the transcript to him. "At least you probably stopped her from lying. Again."

Grace picked at the cold dinner she'd given up on a half hour earlier. Talking through the day's events had killed her appetite. Everything was at a standstill and doing nothing was making her crazy.

Even the news about her breakthrough with Avril and finding Marcus Jonathan Valenti was depressing, although Mac didn't agree with her on that. He urged her to look Valenti up, saying that when he died, she might not be able to get any of his DNA.

"And if I barge in with my questions now, and he isn't my father, after all? Or, even if he is a DNA match, I can't go to a dying man with holes in his memory and ask if he had an affair with my mother while he was married. It would be cruel. Let's change the subject."

As if on cue, her phone buzzed and Niki's name appeared on the screen.

"How mad is she?" Mac asked as Grace disconnected from the call she'd been on for a half hour.

"Just about as mad as I am. It's not my fault that any of this has happened, but she's furious that I put Connie at the Victory Manor. Margo the innkeeper got to her before I did and complained about how mean I was, so Niki was already wound up before she learned about Connie."

Mac had been cleaning up the kitchen as Grace paced and talked to Niki. He gave the counters a final swipe and said, "I noticed you didn't tell her about Marcus Valenti."

"Did you also notice I could hardly get a word in edge-wise? But to be honest, I probably wouldn't have told her if she hadn't been mad at me. She's focused on her own issues, not that I can blame her. But still."

Mac didn't respond. He set the dishwasher and turned off the light over the oven before turning to watch her flipping through messages on her phone as she paced. "It's getting late," he said. "Let all that go for tonight and let's get some sleep."

She stopped halfway through her loop from the kitchen area to the far end of the family room and looked at him in surprise. It was eight-twenty.

"Are you mad?" she asked, finally picking up on his mood.

"Tomorrow, Grace," he said. "I'm beat and you've walked miles since dinner. We can't do anything more tonight and tomorrow is a big day. Have you packed anything?"

"What?"

"Not the reaction I was hoping for," Mac said. "We're going to

Ocean City, so don't suggest otherwise. Hallie packed clothes for the kids, but we'll have a lot to do in the morning."

"You can't seriously think I forgot our trip, or that I would suggest canceling it." Even as she said the words, she was desperately trying to remember where she'd put the St. Michael medallion she'd bought months before as a first anniversary gift.

She stood still for a moment after he left the room, and let her thoughts settle. He was out of sorts, and she hadn't even noticed. She was as self-absorbed as Niki, and he'd been too kind to say so.

Over the next three hours, she organized and packed until she was satisfied they could leave in the morning with a minimum of last-minute crises. Then she locked up and turned out the lights, checked on the children, and went to bed with her husband, who, she decided, had been right all along. Tomorrow was soon enough for the problems with no solutions.

Stark's murder was still unsolved, Piper was still missing, Winnie was in the wind, and Frankie Elmer was walking around free. Meanwhile Connie cowered in her room at the Victory Manor Inn, and somewhere in New Jersey, a sick old man with dementia was dying and Grace would never know if she was his child.

She couldn't change any of it, but it was all so wrong.

CHAPTER FORTY-ONE

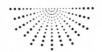

I t was an odd feeling to be running away from her responsibilities, and Grace fretted about it as she finished packing what seemed like everything they owned for the four-day anniversary trip to Ocean City. But her guilt faded as the day passed, and by the time the children were asleep and room service delivered grilled ribeye and tuna steaks to the dining table on the balcony, she'd stopped checking her phone compulsively.

The corner suite, with its expansive view of the Atlantic Ocean, was perfect. Avril and Hallie shared three bedrooms with the children, while Grace and Mac had a luxurious master bedroom on the opposite side of the living area. The possibility of four nights of uninterrupted sleep overrode their guilt at abandoning their offspring and torturing their friends. Also, it would have been impossible to get past the united front of the self-designated Nanny Squad.

"Isn't this great?" Hallie said as she cut into her steak. "Now, I have something to tell you. I know how you two hate surprises—"

"I don't," Grace insisted.

"Me either," Mac said. "Unless your surprise is I have to get up with Sonny at three a.m."

"No, no." Hallie's eyes sparkled with excitement. "Mr. Mosley told

Lily to set up a special surprise dinner for your anniversary, but Grace said no, so instead, how about we all take the kids to that restaurant where they play the *1812 Overture* and the cannons go off as the sun disappears behind the water?"

"Let me see." Grace pretended to take the suggestion seriously. "Fiona, Sonny, and cannon fire. Uhm, no. But you and Avril should go. We're trading off the next three nights, remember?"

"But not your anniversary," Avril said. "When Lily couldn't get you to agree to a special dinner, and Hallie came up with cannons and babies, Cy and I took matters into our own hands. You have dinner reservations at The Hobbit for tomorrow evening at seven. Whatever you decide to do after that is your call."

"We shouldn't be surprised," Mac said, smiling and throwing an arm around his wife. "We cheated her out of planning our wedding, so I guess the least we can do is go along with whatever she tells us to do for the rest of our lives."

"Exactly," Avril agreed. "I suppose I'll forgive you, Lee, at some point. After all, you are just a man. But, really, a judge and two strangers on the courthouse steps in Easton? You could have at least walked over to Christ Church."

"I'm sorry you didn't get the wedding you wanted," Grace said gently. "We had a photographer, and you have a full set of the pictures. My dress was lovely, and the tourists who were there were very nice." She leaned closer to Mac and said, "Do something. You know she's just winding up."

"Okay." Mac kissed her, then told Avril he'd keep doing it if the complaining didn't stop.

Much teasing later, the conversation turned to the vacation itinerary. Plans were made, and no one mentioned murder, betrayal, or the hard decisions that waited for them back in Mallard Bay.

Life was good for two whole days.

"You're older and should be more sensible," Grace grumbled as they neared the Inlet. "Who in their right mind goes to the boardwalk on the Fourth of July weekend? We could have had a lovely lunch at one of the restaurants up near Fenwick."

"Hate to disappoint, but they celebrate Independence Day up there, too," Mac said. "Besides, someone has to broaden your horizons. You're getting a tad provincial in your thinking, Mrs. McNamara. What you need is a walk on the wild side, exposure to different people and cultures. An afternoon with the crazies and left over fireworks ought to put you right."

"The last time I was here on a holiday weekend, the only exposure I got was a sunburn and a look at some naked bodies that never should have been uncovered. And you're not fooling me. What you want is Thrashers fries and Bull on the Beach pit beef."

"And a beer at The Purple Moose," he agreed. "I'm reliving my glory days and showing off my trophy wife. I wish I'd rented a convertible, though. Next time."

The southern tip of Ocean City, known as the Inlet, was packed with carnival-type rides, restaurants, bars, shops, and arcades that attracted heavy crowds. On the Fourth of July, the partying always hit a fever pitch. The official fireworks were over, but July 5th was enough of an excuse for some people, all of whom, it seemed, were on their way to the boardwalk.

Everyone was mashed together in a throng that spilled off the side-walks and into the streets. By the time they'd parked half a mile away and joined the melee, she was laughing at the warring emotions on Mac's face. His teenage memories were rapidly losing ground to his cop's instincts.

At Talbot Street, they entered the stream of humanity on the wide boardwalk and walked south until they joined the long line at Thrash-er's. Grace's phone sounded a text notification when there were only two people in front of them.

"Turn that off if it isn't about the kids," Mac warned.

The message said, "Turn around."

Niki and Dylan were ten feet away.

"This is crazy," Niki said for the tenth time.

They were sharing one end of a picnic table and were lucky to have snatched that small space from a departing family of four. Mac and Dylan were in heaven with their pit beef and fries, and even Grace had to admit the food was worth the trouble. Niki refused to taste anything and the men had graciously offered to dispose of her portion for her. She watched them all eat, shaking her head.

"When I told Dylan where you were, he insisted on coming. I was happy in New York, but he thought we needed a break from too much fun. I see the reasoning behind his madness now."

Dylan's mouth was full, but he gave her a thumbs up.

"Also, I wanted to apologize in person to you both for getting so mad the other night. I'm sorry. I appreciate the help with Mom, and I know you did the best you could."

Grace handed her own still half full cup of fries to Mac and said, "You guys enjoy. I'm taking Miss Healthier than Thou down to Dumser's for ice cream."

"I don't want—" Niki started, then stopped when she saw the looks aimed in her direction. "Do they have pistachio?"

"Dumser's has everything," said Grace, who actually had no idea if the iconic ice cream shop had pistachio. She just wanted to put as much distance as possible between her lack of control and the rest of the fries. Plus, she was hoping coconut chocolate chip was still on the menu, and she wanted to keep Niki talking. As they walked, she said, "Have you heard from Connie?"

"I blocked her, remember? Guess I should take that off until all of this is over."

Grace pulled out her phone, checked and said, "Nothing for me. The office calls are rolling over to Lily's phone and she promised to let me know if anything happened. Plus, Mac would hear about any developments. He's meeting with the OC detectives on Sunday before we go home, and I'll tag along."

Niki said, "Want to hear something weird? Margo says Mom's

actually been a help at the Victory Manor, if you don't count the lost room rate. She's pitching in with the cleaning and is working in the yard. Aidan's been by to check on her. I swear if I didn't know better, I'd think they had something going on."

Grace winced. "Am I too old to say *Ewww*?"

"Yeah, yeah. I know it's just Aidan's protective nature, but still. I hope he doesn't think it's impressing me."

Dumser's did indeed have pistachio ice cream and coconut choco-late chip. The sugar rush quickly put them back in holiday mode. They looked in the windows of jewelry shops that popped up between the t-shirt and beach gear stalls, and Niki asked if she should take Mac for a walk later so he could surprise Grace with the gold hoops she was admiring.

"We've already exchanged anniversary gifts." Grace pulled her hair back to show off the delicate ruby earrings.

But Niki was looking over her shoulder. "I've been all turned around! The Blow Back In is right down there."

Grace didn't like the look on her cousin's face. "I didn't realize how far we've walked. Let's get back, the guys are waiting."

"Give me a minute, okay? I'm gonna pop in there and see if anyone turned in my bracelet."

"That was nearly two weeks ago. Angie has your number, and she'd have called you if they found it. We don't know where Winnie is, remember? You don't want to get mixed up in anything to do with that place."

But the stubborn look on Niki's face was firm. "I want to check for my bracelet, and I won't be intimidated by Winnie or anyone else. Those days are over, Gracie. You can wait here. I won't be a minute."

"No, wait!" Grace called after her. But Niki was gone and all she could do was try to catch up to her cousin and keep her out of trouble.

CHAPTER FORTY-TWO

The Blow Back In was packed. Four bartenders worked behind the circular counter, filling glasses from taps and blending icy cocktails in a deafening roar from the daiquiri bar.

"No Angie," Niki said as she stood on tip toe to scan the crowd. "But there's the bouncer guy." She hesitated, then snapped her fingers. "Billy! That's his name, right? I'm gonna go see if he knows anything."

"The guy who picked Winnie up? This isn't a good idea," Grace said, hurrying after her.

Niki stopped and said, "Let me do this alone, okay? This guy liked me and the faster I get my bracelet, the sooner we're out of here."

"You have to listen to me. We aren't safe in here." Grace stopped. Yelling over the noise was a bad idea, and Niki's expression told her she was wasting her breath. "Just come outside with me and I'll explain what I mean."

"You really are a compulsive worrier," Niki groused. "Just stand here where you can see me and I'll go have a quick word with Bobby—"

"Billy," Grace said, knowing she'd lost the argument.

"Whatever. I'll ask him about the bracelet, and I'll come right back. You can watch me the whole time."

Feeling foolish, Grace stood like a hall monitor, watching Niki, who true to her word returned quickly.

"He took my number and said he'll call me if the bracelet turns up. And I was right, he likes me. He said to let him know if Winnie bothered me."

"Oh, great," Grace said. "Let's get out of here."

"After I go to the Ladies." Niki left Grace to follow in her wake as she pushed through the crowd toward a red neon sign at the rear of the building.

They were separated when a bartender holding a full tray over his head cut between them. The gap widened again as a table full of women got up to take a group trip to the toilets. When Grace finally reached the hallway that led to the restrooms, Niki was gone and four women were ahead of her in line outside the Ladies. She started to join them, but her attention was caught by a closed door at the end of the hall. *Office* was stenciled on the frosted glass window.

Oh, no, she thought, and changed directions. She imagined Niki marching into Angie's office and asking if her bracelet had been turned in. Her concern grew as she neared the door. She could hear angry voices, but the words were indistinct until her hand was raised to knock.

That was when she heard Stark's name.

"He was your friend," a woman was saying. "And you vouched for him. And now you've dragged his moronic son in here to pick up where his father left off. The thefts are on you, not me."

It was Angie Glass. Grace was sure of it. But who was the bar owner arguing with? She could see two indistinct forms through the opaque glass, the larger one standing still, the other moving erratically around the room.

"Oh, yeah," a man said. "You think I'm buying that crap? This operation is so sloppy I'm wondering if you've been skimming all along. No wonder Stark thought he could just help himself. We're done, Angie. You got that? No way am I mixed up in whatever you're doing. I'm out and you *will* pay me back, and not in jewelry."

Frankie Elmer, Grace thought. It had to be. Bernadette Xavier had said he was Angie's business partner. She needed to call the detective and fill her in, but as she turned to leave, the door was yanked open. Too late, she realized that if she could see shapes through the glass, so could Angie and Frankie. Both of them were glaring at Grace.

"The Ladies is behind you," Angie said and started to close the door, then stopped. "Wait. You're Stark Delaney's daughter, right? Or are you the niece?"

"Niece," Grace said, smiling and trying to look as if she hadn't just heard everything they'd said.

Angie said, "You want to ask her what she knows, Frankie?"

Grace took a step backward. Elmer's face had gone white at the mention of his name, and she didn't want to know why. Not now anyway. "I didn't mean to bother you," she said, wincing at the tremor in her voice. This was the man who'd sent Dennis Mays to terrorize Connie and who may have caused Stark's death. She needed to call Bernadette.

"Oh, don't run off," Angie said. "It's Ms. Reagan, right?" Looking at her partner again, she added, "You were talking about Stark's family just yesterday, weren't you, Frankie?"

Several more laughing women came into the hallway from the bar and joined the line for the toilets. Grace's nerves eased up a bit—surely nothing would happen in front of this many witnesses? She looked past Angie to see Elmer's reaction, but it was what she saw on the desk just inside the door that caught her attention.

"Reagan?" Frankie Elmer said quietly.

"Yeah." Angie's voice was sharp with sarcasm. "Stark's niece. You remember I told you his whole damn family has been in here? And you told me I was overreacting. Well, what do you think now, *partner*?"

Grace checked the hallway behind her again. Still crowded. "I was wondering if you'd found the bracelet my cousin dropped the last time we came in?" she said loudly. "I see you found Stark's rings. We've been looking for those, too."

"I know you," Elmer said, his voice cold.

Angie stepped over to the desk and picked the rings up.

Grace held out her hand and said, "If I could have those, I'll see to it Stark's daughter gets them." She tried to appear impatient instead of scared. There was a bad vibe in the room, and even the chatter from the hallway wasn't as reassuring as it had been.

Angie laughed. "You'll take them? I don't think so. These were given to me to settle a debt. They're mine."

"Winnie had them last," Grace said. "How much did he owe you? I'll reimburse you—in cash."

"No need," Elmer said. "You know who this is, Angie? She's the wife of the chief of police in Mallard Bay. She's a McNamara. Give the lady her family's jewelry."

"No!" Angie shouted. "She said she'd pay for them." Jerking back to face Grace, she said, "How much? Stark stole twenty-five thousand from us. You willing to pay that much?"

"Shut up!" Elmer snapped. "Give her the damn rings now!"

"Go to hell." Angie's face was an alarming shade of red and she was breathing heavily. "Maybe we should get her husband in here. How does that sound, Frankie? You good with calling the cops? No? I didn't think so." Her rant ended in a gasp as Elmer stepped forward and grabbed her arm, twisting it until she let the rings fall to the floor, where they rolled under the desk.

Breaking free from Elmer's grasp, Angie scrambled after them, screaming, "Touch me again, and I'll tell everything!"

Grace didn't wait to see who ended up with the rings. She turned to run, only to be blocked by Niki, who barreled past her into the office, demanding to know what was happening.

A wail from Angie drowned her out, then a soft popping noise froze everything for a second. When Angie called out again, it was a weak, "Oh, my God!" as she tried to stand, moaning, and clutching her abdomen.

Grace couldn't see around Niki, who moved forward to help Angie, then jumped back as the taller woman fell to her knees.

"You shot her!" Niki said, looking up at Elmer. "You *shot—*"

"Look out!" Frankie yelled. "She has a gun!"

He moved to Angie, and Grace grabbed Niki, dragging her toward the door in a slow motion sequence that seemed endless until a gun fired and a bullet thudded into the wall behind them.

Shouts, then screams rang out from the hallway. *He's killing them! Somebody call 911 . . . Run!*

Grace shoved Niki into the hallway, stumbling as another shot rang out and slammed into a file cabinet they'd just passed. Another shot and more screams, one from Niki, who fell, tripping Grace.

Shooter! He's killing people! Help! The hysterical shouts came from all directions, but Grace only heard the scream that came from the office behind her. Covering Niki's head with her hands, she looked back to see Angie push herself up and shoot Frankie Elmer right between the eyes.

CHAPTER FORTY-THREE

"Elmer's lawyer had the nerve to say that his client was totally innocent. An upstanding citizen!" Grace's outrage brought a fierce cry from Sonny, who preferred that his mother not yell while feeding him.

"I'll take that child," Avril said. She handed Sonny and his bottle over to Hallie and told her to take the children to their bedroom. "I'll fill you in later, but their mother will give them nightmares."

Grace got reproachful looks from Hallie and Fiona as they left, but she was relieved to have them out of earshot. Avril was right. What kind of mother was she to be dissecting a murder, and an attempted murder, during her baby's dinner?

"I'm never having children," Niki said, giving Dylan a meaningful look. "Just so you know."

"I'm impressed with your takeaway from that little scene," he said. "A guy might think you're being a bit overconfident, but then you are medicated."

Niki cradled her wounded arm and said, "Am not. I refused pain meds. It isn't much of a flesh wound and I was able to handle fifteen stitches without anesthetic, thank you."

Dylan smiled at Grace. "I keep telling her saline wasn't all they put in her drip bag, but she thinks she knows everything."

"Get used to it," Grace said. "Could we get back to the murder we witnessed? Now that Frankie Elmer's dead, we may never know who killed Stark."

She immediately wished she hadn't said it. The four hours that had passed since the police released them had seen both Grace and Niki careening between horror and incredulity. Mac had stayed on with the Ocean City officers while Dylan, Avril and Hallie had taken on the thankless job of trying to keep the cousins reasonably calm.

Niki looked sick again. "What did Mac say when he called?" she asked. "I mean, what about Angie? Is she being charged with murder? Frankie shot her first, and we don't really know which one of them was shooting at us, do we?" She gasped and sat up straighter. "Oh, Gracie, I just thought of something—if Angie pulled her gun before Frankie shot her, maybe she was going to shoot *you*. Do you think he tried to save your life?"

"Don't know," Grace said, picking up her glass of iced tea and wishing it was something stronger. When all of this was over, it would be, she promised herself. "He wanted Angie to shut up, and she wanted me to pay for the rings. Those are the only things I'm sure of. I told the police he shot her first, then one or both of them shot at us, and then Angie shot Frankie. That's really clear in my memory. The rest, not so much." The shock was wearing off, but waiting for details was making her jumpier by the minute.

Mac was tied up with Xavier and Greenley and the hunt for Winnie, who had fled the state, apparently not caring about covering his tracks. The MSP expected to have him in custody by morning.

No one had heard from Piper, but Greenley seemed confident that they'd find her with Winnie. "Dumb and Dumber go on a joyride," was the way he'd described them.

Niki was still talking and bouncing a foot furiously since she only had the use of one hand to punctuate her words. "I can't believe we let the EMTs rush us out of there without getting Dad's rings!"

"Yeah," Dylan said. "Those paramedics sure get excited when their patients are bleeding profusely. I'm telling you, cupcake, when the sedatives and painkillers wear off, I think you'll have answers to a lot of things that seem puzzling right now."

"Saline," Niki snapped. "I'm tough, remember? But Dad's rings! Who knows where they are now? Gracie, are you sure you saw them roll under the desk? What if the police find Winnie and he says they're his? Or Piper says they belong to her because they're part of Dad's estate?"

"Calm down, hon," Dylan said, gently. "This isn't helping."

"You don't understand," Niki said. "They have to stay in the family. They *have* to. Winnie and Piper will sell them."

This was another topic Grace wished she hadn't raised earlier when she was worrying about all the unresolved angles of the horrible afternoon. She'd thought Niki would be relieved to know that the rings were safe in police custody, but when she called Bernadette, she learned they hadn't turned up.

"The techs aren't finished with the scene, yet. I'll call you if we find them," the detective promised.

It wasn't enough to appease Niki, and no matter what they talked about, she turned it to the lost rings. "First, my bracelet. Now Dad's rings. I haven't got anything of his except a ratty old jacket." Her lower lip trembled, and it was clear she was reaching the end of her rope.

"That's not true," Avril said, weighing in for the first time. "You have a pair of very special earrings that your father had made for you. Not for your mother, for you. And before you say he was only trying to cover up his theft of the real diamonds and sapphires, think about this. Did he ever go to that much trouble for anyone else?" She looked at each of them, then answered her own question. "No, he did not. He didn't give a rat's ass what anyone thought, except you, Niki. He didn't want you to be disappointed. And even if he didn't stand up to Connie, he saw to it that you eventually got the earrings. He also gave you the only nice words anyone in the family got in his will. It was the only time I ever heard Stark Delaney apologize, and he said he wanted to change. For you. Your mother was right. Your father loved you best."

There wasn't much to say after that. Niki looked equal parts relieved and shellshocked and Grace thought they both might fall asleep before they could get to a bed. Her head throbbed from the antiseptic wash and cleaning of a small graze wound on her scalp.

"Time for us to get out of your hair," Dylan said, staring pointedly at Grace's small bandage until the rest of them got the bad pun. He stood, pulling Niki up with him. "You'll call us when there's news?"

Grace said she would, and walked them down to the elevator, where she hugged Niki, whispering, "It'll be okay. I promise. I'll figure out a way to get the rings."

Three hours later, she wished she'd kept her mouth shut.

"You're going down to that bar to snoop around." Avril was furious and forbid her to leave. "It's nearly nine! Lee will have a fit if he gets back and you're not here."

That was exactly what Grace had said a few minutes earlier when Niki called to say the bouncer at the Blow Back In had found her bracelet.

"Even if I could get past Dylan, he was right," Niki had wailed. "They must have given me some serious drugs at the hospital, because they're wearing off and I feel like I'm gonna die. Mac's married to you. If he gets mad, he'll get over it, but one of us has to go meet Billy."

It had been easier just to agree to go. Until Avril caught her leaving.

"I'm going to the store—" Grace started.

"You're going to that bar."

Grace gritted her teeth, wishing she were a better liar. "I've rested, I feel fine and I'm only running by the bar to get Niki's bracelet. You heard her tale of woe. Would you say no to her?"

It was the wrong question to ask.

"I'd certainly have better sense than to do what Niki told me to! Who has it?"

"I don't know the man's last name, but I've met him and he's nice.

He works at the bar and he's the one Niki left her number with." This
was all true. She didn't know Billy's last name, but she'd thought he
was great when he'd dangled Winnie like a broken doll. "He just called
her and said he found the bracelet. He's waiting to give it to me."

"And what else?"

Grace sighed. It was true that she hoped she'd get some information from the bouncer, but she'd rather be doing it tomorrow. Still,
she'd only taken Tylenol for the scrape on her head, and a long nap had
refreshed her a little. When Niki insisted Billy might give the bracelet
to the police if Grace didn't get it right away, it had been impossible to
say no. She kept seeing her cousin jerk sideways from the bullet that
creased her upper arm.

Pausing at the front door of the suite, she said, "I'll have my phone
if you need me and I'll check in. The man I'm going to see is Billy, and
I'm meeting him on the boardwalk in front of the bar. There'll be a
bazillion people around, and I won't be alone with him. I'll get the
bracelet and leave. Please don't worry."

"Oh, sure," Avril said, still looking unhappy, but resigned. Shaking
her head, she added, "Since you're going to the store, I have a list."

Five minutes later, Grace was on her way to collect jewelry from a
murder scene, and to buy diapers and a teething ring to replace the one
Fiona had thrown in the ocean that morning.

"This can't be normal," she said to herself as she drove. Then she
wondered what the other nursery school mothers were going to think of
her. It was a petty concern, but a real one, and thinking about mean-
girl-mommies was less stressful than worrying about what Mac would
say when he saw her later.

CHAPTER FORTY-FOUR

S he got the diapers and pacifiers first. Somehow that made meeting up with the bouncer more of a sidestep in her evening.

Traffic grew heavier as she neared the Inlet and became a slow roll around 21st Street. A few blocks later on, she snagged the last spot in a parking lot, paying twenty dollars for the dubious privilege of wedging the BMW into a narrow opening that looked suspiciously like part of an exit aisle.

"I won't be long," she said as she handed a ten to a teenage boy who didn't look old enough to drive. "I won't be blocked in, right?"

He didn't answer but kept his hand out. She added another five.

He seemed disgusted at her paltry effort, but said, "I'll get you out when you're ready to go."

She wanted to snatch the money back and leave, but he was already jogging across the small lot to yell at the next unwary customer. Wishing she'd worn her sneakers instead of sandals, she joined the throng moving toward the boardwalk. Five long blocks later, she was in front of the Blow Back In. The rolling metal doors were down and padlocked and looked odd in the middle of all the other brightly lit shops and food bars.

Video arcade bells and whistles competed with music blasting from a t-shirt shop. It took Grace a minute to realize someone was calling Niki's name. Billy glowered when she told him Niki had sent her.

She had seen him that afternoon as the police had gathered the bar's customers for questioning. He'd been crying as they watched the paramedics carry Angie out. The big man looked even worse now, and she smelled alcohol.

"You got any news about Angie?" Billy wobbled a bit as he said her name.

She glanced around and spotted a couple getting up from a nearby bench. "Come over here with me," she said, moving to claim the seats ahead of a group of teens who quickly changed direction at the sight of the huge, emotional man.

Billy sank down and put his head in his hands.

Grace patted one of his boulder-like shoulders. "She's alive, but she's in the hospital. I haven't heard anything new since this afternoon, so let's keep positive, okay? She was talking when the paramedics arrived, and that's a good thing."

"Maybe," Billy said, lifting his head. His leathery cheeks were wet. "Maybe not. You told them she shot Frankie."

"In self-defense," Grace said quickly. "Angie saved Niki and me. She's a hero." It could be true, she told herself, and she wanted to keep him calm. As calm as a drunk and weepy man could be, anyway.

"That Frankie guy," Billy said, then wiped his face with the bottom of his t-shirt. "He was no good. Angie said he was her business partner, but I told her she didn't need him. I know his kind and she shoulda stayed away from him." He sighed a cloud of alcohol fumes that nearly knocked Grace over, then said, "I love her, y'know?"

"Yeah," Grace said. "I guessed that. She seemed really fond of you, too."

"If she makes it, she's marryin' me whether she wants to or not. I'm taking care of that woman for the rest of her life." He gave Grace a hard look. "She's always said we was just friends, and I know I have problems, but I can see to it that she's safe. Nobody's hurting her again. You hear what I'm saying?"

Grace nodded, hoping he wasn't warning her off. She decided it wouldn't be wise to ask and settled for, "I hope it all works out for you both."

He looked at her for a long moment, then nodded. "I like that girl, Niki. How do I know she sent you?"

"Call her. She's pretty banged up and couldn't come. She was shot too, you know."

"Yeah. Thas' what I heard." He gave her another hard stare. "I'm real tired of people lying to me."

Her hope of questioning him about Stark, Frankie, and Winnie was fading fast. He was too drunk, and she didn't like the belligerent turn in the conversation. "I wouldn't know about any of that," she said, "and I've got no reason to lie to you. I'm an attorney, I'm not allowed to do that."

He let out another noxious breath. "Right. You guys lie all the time."

Maybe it was nerves, or the absurdity of the situation, but Grace burst out laughing. "All right. If you have the bracelet, I can give it to Niki." Then she had another thought. "And if you know anything about the rings Winnie gave Angie, I'd like to hear that, too."

Billy stared at her. "You ain't that Winnie's lawyer, are you?"

The urge to laugh died. She said, "Not in a million years. He tried to kill me."

As she expected, this impressed Billy, who said, "I thought he was inside for dealing."

"That, too."

She waited while he processed what she'd told him. Or zoned out. It was hard to tell, and she thought more might be going on with him than just the effects of shock and alcohol. The blank expression on his face was disconcerting, but when he spoke again, his words were clearer. "The bracelet is kinda beat up."

"It's okay. Can I have it?"

He had to stand to fish it out of his jeans pocket. "Beat up" was an understatement, but she took the twisted strand of metal and thanked him. He didn't answer but looked away again.

"Did you see—" she started, but he turned back to her abruptly.

"Angie said that loser, Winnie, gave some rings to her cause his dad owed her money."

"Do you know where they are now? The rings, I mean. They mean a lot to Niki. They've been in our family for a long time, and we'd like to buy them back from Angie." Grace hoped she wouldn't be the one actually paying the bill, but she'd deal with that when, or if, the time came.

Billy seemed relieved. "I bet Angie'll be happy about that. I'll tell her as soon as they let me see her."

Grace knew Angie had a gunshot wound to her lower abdomen, but she wasn't going to be the one to tell this poor man. She wasn't going to lie to him, either. He was looking at her steadily now, and she knew he was waiting to see if she would say the woman he idolized wasn't coming back.

"She'll be gone a long time, Billy. If she recovers, it'll be weeks before she's well enough to work."

"Yeah. I know," he said slowly. "But she'll need the money if she does, and if she doesn't, I guess Niki should have her father's rings."

"The thing is, right before they shot each other, Frankie and Angie were fighting over the rings and we don't know what happened to them." Grace paused, but he seemed like he was interested, so she said, "We just want to know they're safe where Winnie can't get them. Would you be comfortable searching for them when they let you go inside the bar?"

He stood, still a bit shaky, and said, "I gotta key to the back door. Angie let me lock up for her on nights when there weren't no special games going on. You know 'bout them games, right?"

She nodded.

"Yeah, the cops did, too. I told Angie she could get busted. I told her it was gonna be trouble if she got in with that Frankie guy." He smiled. "I just didn't think he'd be the one who came out the worse for it. She's a hell of a woman, my Angie." The smile disappeared, and he held himself a bit straighter. "There's no tape across the back door if you want to come with me. I'll go look, now."

"No!" she said, but he was already on the move, and she ran after him. The police wouldn't hesitate to arrest him for disturbing the scene and she was the one who'd asked him to do it.

There were a few lights in the alley behind the Blow Back In, but it was still dark and shadowy compared to the boardwalk. Trash cans and a large rectangular box were lined up next to the steps leading to the back door. As Billy had said, there was no caution tape, and the door opened easily with his key.

There was only a faint light coming from inside the building, and the big man blocked most of it. "You coming? There's rats in the alley, you know."

Grace looked down at her sandals and over at the shadows stretching past the steps. "You can't go in there, Billy. It's a crime scene. You could be arrested."

"Maybe you'd get arrested, but not me. That lady officer told me I could get in tomorrow and clean up. Tomorrow's just a coupla hours away and I won't touch nothing except the rings if they're there." He held the door open wider. "I'm going in whether you come or not. I'm going to stay a while after you leave, too. I need to be in Angie's place. You know what I mean?"

She told him again not to go inside.

"Yell if you need me," he said, and let the door close behind him.

She trotted up the steps to the landing outside the back door, sliding her tote off her shoulder as she went. It had enough weight to be used as a weapon if rats came up here for her bare toes.

A light appeared in a window to her right and illuminated a bit more of the alley. As she scanned for rodents, she saw that the large box beside the steps was actually a freezer. As the minutes ticked by and lights came on and went off inside the building, her thoughts drifted to the incongruity of storing food in an alley where anybody could get to it. It was an old-fashioned chest freezer with no visible locks. Then she saw the chain that stretched out from under it. An open padlock lay off to one side.

Her first thought was that the police had been thorough in their search. But why leave it unlocked? Any food would disappear or spoil long before anyone reopened the bar.

She tapped the screen of her phone. Ten forty-five. She dashed off a text to Avril, saying she had been to the store and was on her way home. The door opened as she sent the message.

"No rings," Billy said. "But I'll look again in the morning when I clean up."

"Thanks, I'm sure they'll turn up." Grace pointed over the railing to the freezer. "I guess the police searched out here, too, but maybe you should lock that freezer up again. Hope the food hasn't been stolen."

Billy frowned. "No food in that thing. Only old equipment Angie don't wanna get rid of, but they shouldn't have left it like that. It ain't safe." He went down the steps, muttering about how dangerous unsecured freezers were.

Grace thought he was sobering up a bit—a situation that would probably be rectified in the dark bar as soon as she left.

"And nobody better not have taken nothing, neither," he said as he reached for the handle on the lid and gave it a yank.

For a moment nothing happened, then Billy screamed and stumbled backward, frantic to get away. Losing his balance he fell hard, then lay motionless on the pavement.

Grace saw it all, but didn't go to help him. She was focused on the view from the top of the stairs, and what she saw in the freezer was all she could process.

Piper wasn't missing anymore.

CHAPTER FORTY-FIVE

Any rats that may have been in the alley disappeared when the police cars, crime scene techs, and coroner's ambulance showed up. Grace and Billy were separated and escorted to the Ocean City Police Department, where Grace came face to face with the wrath of Bernadette Xavier. The story of Niki's bracelet and the rings sounded ridiculous when told under the bright lights of Interview Room 1.

"Calling me wasn't an option?" Xavier said. "I thought we had a rapport going."

Grace wondered how Billy was getting along with Greenley. She imagined him saying, "And then that attorney asked me to look for the rings, but she knows they belong to Angie."

She wouldn't blame him.

"Hey!" Xavier slapped both hands down on the scratched metal table between them. "Still over here. Still waiting for an explanation."

"What I did was stupid," Grace said. "That's all I have. If a client of mine did it, I'd be right where you are. It was careless, and ill-advised, and all I have by way of an explanation is that I thought it was all over."

"What was over?" Xavier asked. She wasn't yelling anymore, but she wasn't friendly either.

"Niki is huge on our family's history, and those rings mean a lot to her. But Piper got them and gave them to Winnie, who gave them to Angie to cover a debt. That's what Angie and Frankie were arguing about this afternoon. She didn't want the rings, she wanted money, and she said she'd give them to whoever paid her twenty-five thousand dollars."

"I've already heard this," Xavier snapped.

"I thought it was all over because I knew eventually the rings would be returned to Angie Glass or her estate, and we could buy them from her. Then you told me they hadn't been collected as part of the evidence—"

"*Yet.*" Xavier's face flushed. "The last thing I said to you this afternoon was that I'd check all the collected evidence and get back to you."

"I know, but I thought it couldn't hurt to ask Billy to look, too, and then I couldn't stop him from going inside."

"So you say. You should have waited, though. The final sweep of the scene turned up two rings that matched your description. They're locked in the evidence room."

Imagining how happy Niki would be almost made Grace smile, but the look on Xavier's face said it would be a bad idea. She settled for, "Thank you. That means a lot."

"Someone above my pay grade will have to decide who gets them," Xavier said. "And it'll be a while before they're released. Now if we can get back to the reason we're here? At what point this evening did you decide to ask Mr. Keating to break into the bar?"

"Now, wait a minute." A shot of adrenalin snatched Grace's thoughts back to the trouble she was in, and she straightened up. "I didn't even know that was Billy's last name. My cousin told you in her statement this afternoon that she talked to him about looking for her bracelet. I told you he's inebriated and grieving and you need to get medical attention for him. You did that, right?"

"He's fine," Xavier said. "Why did you tell him to go into the bar?"

"I didn't!" Grace stopped, closing her eyes. What was she doing? *I need a good lawyer*, she thought and tried not to laugh at her nearly hysterical and physically exhausted self. Aidan would never let her live it down if he could see her getting the same treatment she'd given him. Lily would be horrified at her unprofessionalism. Cy—

"Here."

Grace opened her eyes to see Xavier holding out a sealed plastic packet.

"City can't get the damned AC straight in here. You're shaking. Wrap this around you."

Her instinct was to refuse. She needed to show the police she was a competent, clear-headed legal professional they could work with, not a victim, or, God forbid, a perpetrator. The temperature in the interrogation room was fine, but she *was* shaking. She opened the packet, pulled out a small blanket, and pulled it over her shoulders. "Thank you," she said quietly, then straightened up. "Shock. Sneaky, isn't it? Always hits you at an inopportune time."

Xavier nodded, then said. "Let's start over. Tell me again why you went to the Blow Back In and what happened when you got there."

Grace made herself speak slowly at first and felt the tension ease as she regulated her breathing and pushed her emotions aside.

Xavier didn't seem any happier when she finished. "That'll all sound good in court," the detective said. "Especially the part where you wait in a dark alley while Keating breaks in."

"He didn't break in," Grace insisted. "He works there, and he had a key. He said you'd told him he could clean up in the morning and I thought the crime scene had been cleared. I should have called you, and I'm sorry I didn't, but there was no criminal intent on his part, or mine."

"How about when you told Keating to look in the freezer in the alley?"

Grace didn't blame the detective for being skeptical but explaining that she and Billy had thought the police had been negligent didn't seem like a good idea. "I suggested he lock it back up. He hadn't noticed that the chain was off, and expressed concern that the contents might have been stolen."

"So hanging out in an alley, in the dark, only a few hours after a murder, while a man you don't know breaks into the crime scene wasn't enough for you? You had to hang around and direct him to another murder? No, wait. You're connected to *all* of the homicide victims, aren't you?"

"I've explained what happened," Grace said, refusing to respond to the provocation. "I went to the boardwalk to get the bracelet for Niki, and that led to the discovery of a dead body that you guys missed when you searched the property." She was tired and angry, and without considering the repercussions, added, "Which, now that I think about it, is kinda embarrassing for you, isn't it?"

Her face flushed with anger, Xavier stood up and said, "Mr. Keating backs up your statement. You can leave but stay here in Ocean City until we can talk tomorrow." She went to the door and opened it, then turned back and shut it behind her again.

"Look, your husband will have already heard this, so there's no point in not telling you now. Maybe you'll even apologize for your rotten judgement and rude behavior. Piper Tilden's body wasn't found in the earlier search because it wasn't in the freezer this afternoon. Your good friend, Billy, put it there so he could be seen 'discovering' the woman he'd murdered. And who better to act as his witness than a gullible lawyer?"

Grace didn't apologize, and she didn't leave the police station.

"What do you mean, you're his attorney?" Xavier demanded. "You weren't representing him five minutes ago."

"Five minutes ago, I didn't know you'd take the easy way out and charge him. Talk to the man, Bernadette, and you'll know he didn't kill that girl."

"I don't have to talk to him. His prints are on the freezer, and it took someone strong to break her neck and move her body into and out of a vehicle, then into that freezer. Plus, he has a key to the padlock."

Grace didn't back down. "Lots of people connected to this situation are strong." She was thinking about Winnie's pumped up muscles but kept that to herself for the time being. "Billy had the padlock key because he worked at the Blow Back, so it stands to reason lots of other people had one, too. And, of course, his prints are on the freezer, he found her. You don't have anything on him that will hold up in court."

"Is that all?" Xavier asked.

Grace rolled her eyes. "Oh, all right. I can see how you might have come to the wrong conclusions, but you're wasting time."

"Gee, thanks," Xavier said. "I feel all better now."

"I'd like to see Mr. Keating."

Xavier didn't budge. "You can't go client shopping in our holding cells."

She hadn't wanted to lead in with this angle, but Billy's state of mind was the only card she had to play. "You haven't talked with him, have you?" she asked. "Was he checked by a doctor? I'm sure he passed out."

"I have the reports from the arresting officers. Mr. Keating is fine, or as fine as someone in his situation can be."

Grace shook her head. "I'm asking you to please talk with him. About anything. Pick any topic and talk. If you give it a few minutes, I think you'll agree with me he shouldn't be acting in his own defense. And I'm betting he refused counsel, right?"

Ignoring the question, Xavier said, "Are you implying he's mentally incapacitated?"

"I'm not qualified to imply anything of the sort. But at the very least, he's inebriated and in an emotional crisis right now. He loves Angie Glass and is devoted to her. I know the perfect person to work with him, and obviously, I can't represent him much past tonight or we'll have a conflict if I have to testify. I'll just get him through the preliminaries and arrange new counsel for him."

"*When* you have to testify," Xavier corrected. "You're going to be visiting our courthouse regularly for a while. Three murders in one day must be a personal best for you, am I right?"

"Three," Grace repeated dully.

"Yeah. Angela Glass died about an hour ago."

Grace regrouped and focused on Billy. "Let me tell him, please. I want to explain his rights and advise him. I feel strongly he's innocent in Piper's murder and he'll be devastated by the news about Angie."

"How do you know? You talked to him for what, a half hour?"

"It's not what he said," Grace hesitated, then decided to elaborate on her earlier, bare bones statement. It didn't seem as if she could make matters much worse for Billy. "If you'd heard how he screamed when he saw Piper, you'd know he was innocent. He was so shocked, he tried to get away and fell backward. He's got to have a lump on his head, because it hit the pavement. If you won't let me see him, at least get him a doctor."

She got an appraising look from Xavier, who finally said, "He didn't mention an injury." She left the room and when she returned, it was to escort Grace to Billy's cell. "See if you can get him to accept treatment, I'd like to get him to go to the hospital voluntarily. He won't let a medic near him and keeps falling asleep, and if he has a possible head injury, he should stay upright and awake. Right now, he's alert enough to accept your offer of representation, but I don't know how long that will be the case."

"You talked to him," Grace said.

"I'm cooperating with you," Xavier said, irritability creeping back into her voice. "Don't push the incompetency claim tonight. Don't do it at all until you have a medical opinion, got it?"

Their tenuous detente held, Billy officially accepted Grace as his attorney, and allowed her to go to the hospital with him. It was two thirty before she left the emergency room to find Mac waiting in the lobby. Tired to her bones, she couldn't think of anything to say except, "I'm sorry."

He pulled her in for a bear hug and said, "Don't be."

CHAPTER FORTY-SIX

They sat on the balcony off their bedroom and talked until the sky lightened and the surf fishers and early joggers began to appear. Grace insisted she couldn't sleep, but Mac said they shouldn't waste a kid-free morning in bed. They were both snoring five minutes later.

A late breakfast with the children at the Dough Roller put them in reasonable moods as they surrendered Fiona and Sonny to Avril and Hallie.

"Can I go with them?" Grace said as she watched from the balcony as the little foursome crossed the wooden walkway that bridged the dunes between the hotel and the open beach. "I don't think anyone down at the police station likes me. My client may not like me, either, if his thinking has straightened out."

"You broke the news to him as gently as you could," Mac said. "Someone had to do it and it was better coming from you."

"He was pitiful. I'm relieved Oscar Breedlove agreed to take him, but now I have to go talk Billy into accepting the change."

"You think he'll want someone else?"

"I don't know. I'm acting on pure instinct here, and it's telling me that Billy Keating isn't capable of seeing the big picture regarding his own welfare. Not in a situation like the one he's in now, anyway. I think he's a gentle soul with a single-minded devotion to Angie Glass and maybe some other issues. His heart's broken, and he's rudderless, plus he's got a concussion. That'll buy us a little time."

"Us?" Mac said, following her inside.

"I'm still in this until I can get Oscar in place." She checked herself in the mirror, frowning at the skimpiness of her sundress. "Thank goodness Niki brought better clothes than I did, but I wish she'd get here with the jacket she's loaning me."

"Is it going to cover your legs?" Mac asked, giving her an appreciative look. "If not, let's hope the judge appreciates beautiful women."

The conversation ended when Niki arrived, one arm in a sling and a shopping bag in her uninjured hand. "My treat," she said, holding the bag out. "It's the least I could do seeing how much trouble I got you into."

Grace pulled out a dark blue knee length linen skirt and an ivory silk blouse. Beneath them, she found a pair of navy slingback dress sandals. She shot Mac a sideways look that said, *See?* He had expressed a strong opinion about Niki taking advantage of her during their talk on the balcony. "I'll just run to the bedroom and change."

Niki correctly interpreted the undercurrent. "I really am so sorry about all of this. I've been a pill lately and I know it. No excuses. I won't be dumping my problems on you two anymore, I promise. Dylan's gone back to New York, and as soon as I give my statement to the police, I'm returning to Mallard Bay. You don't need to give the inns another thought. We'll work everything out when the time is right, but for now, I'm back and I'll handle Mom. I can't thank you enough . . ." Her voice broke.

"What about Winnie?" Mac asked. "What happens when they find him? I don't want you caught up in whatever he's into."

It was so out of character that both women stared at him.

"What's Winnie got to do with me?" Niki said. "I mean, I can't control him, all I can do is cut him out of my life and I've done that, but Mom—"

"Her, too," Mac snapped. "Look, I'm tired of this crap. I want my family safe and I want Winnie the hell away from all of you." His eyes didn't leave Niki as he spoke, not even when hers filled with tears at the rare rebuke. "You can't help who you were born to, and you aren't responsible for your mother and brother. You can love them because they're a part of you, but you don't have to let them hurt you anymore. We are your family. All the time, not just when it's convenient, understand? Winnie and Connie aren't part of us and if necessary, I'll explain that to both of them in terms that, I promise *you*, they'll understand."

Niki threw her arms around his neck, hugging him until he gently peeled her off, saying, "You didn't ask my opinion about this, either, but for what it's worth, I think Dylan's a great guy. I hope he's not staying in New York permanently."

"Don't worry. He has to work, and New York is his home. We're settling a few things between us." This time, Grace got a hug.

"Say it," she pushed Niki back to look at her face. "You know what I mean. It's happened, hasn't it?"

Mac didn't know what had both of them laughing, and in Niki's case, also crying, but he didn't think he'd caused it.

"I love him, Gracie! Can you believe it? I'm finally in love."

"I need to go to work," Mac said hastily. "I have a meeting with the task force. Plus, I don't want to hear any more."

"Spoken like a real brother-in-law," Niki said, and hugged him again.

Her new clothes fit, and Grace had a reasonably positive meeting with a subdued and monosyllabic Billy who met and approved of Oscar Breedlove. By the time they had been through the arraignment process and Oscar had officially been entered into the court record as Billy's attorney, she was feeling better about life in general.

Her good mood faded when she met with Bernadette Xavier and Gordon Greenley for a rerun of her own interview from the night before. Neither detective was pleased when she tried to turn the tables and question them on the searches for Winnie and Dennis Mays.

"I'm sure we can't tell you anything you don't know," Greenley said. His usual *I'm bored out of my mind* expression momentarily gave way to hostility. "You witnessed the shootings at the Blow Back In, you're related to all the suspects in Delaney's death, and you helped Piper Tilden's killer set up his not-guilty plea. Plus, you're sleeping with a cop involved in the investigations. That's why we're the ones who get to ask you questions. Got it?"

Grace ignored him and spoke directly to Xavier. "I'm off Billy Keating's defense. He's being represented by Oscar Breedlove."

Greenley groaned, but Xavier only nodded.

Grace didn't add that at that moment, Oscar was filing a petition to have Billy examined by a psychologist to determine his ability to assist in his own defense. She had a feeling Xavier already knew, and she didn't care if Greenley did. She asked for an update on the evidence found at the Blow Back In.

"You've been watching television again," Xavier said. "Ballistics and other forensic testing take time. As far as the manhunt, I might have something for you tomorrow on Delaney's whereabouts, and maybe even on Mays. No promises, though. We're a bit busy right now."

"You had more than one body dumped in a freezer?" Grace asked dryly.

"Watch your mouth—" Greenley started, but was quickly interrupted by Xavier.

"I didn't say Ms. Tilden wasn't a priority, just that it'll be tomorrow before I can tell you anything. And, as you know, it can take weeks to get answers from an autopsy in complicated cases, but by tomorrow we should know something."

Tomorrow would be when the press was briefed, Grace realized. She wasn't in the need-to-know group anymore—if she ever had been.

Xavier gave her a transcript of their earlier interview. Grace read and signed it, all the while ignoring Greeley's bad jokes and snide remarks. For a man who'd been silent through most of their other meetings, he was a motor mouth today. She handed the transcript to him and asked for a copy, trying not to smile at his outraged reaction.

"I'll take care of that for you," Xavier said. "Detective Sergeant Greenley has a new assignment and his briefing starts in a few minutes."

Greenley left, but he didn't go quietly.

Grace jumped when he slammed the door behind him. "Guess he's unhappy about the transfer, huh?"

"Not at all," Xavier said. "His skills are needed elsewhere. Greenley's a good officer. One of the best, technically."

"Just not a people person," Grace said.

"He's a terrific *dead* people person, and that's all he needs to be to get this job done." Xavier's tone said she wasn't going to discuss her former partner any further.

"Well, then, I'm sorry you're losing him. Can I ask you a question, though? Who do you believe killed Stark?"

Xavier didn't answer immediately, but stepped over to the copier in the corner of the office and ran the transcript through. She handed the copy to Grace and said, "Your firm will get the medical examiner's report later today. Stark Delaney's official time of death is eleven p.m. with a margin for error of sixty minutes either way. However, his cause of death has changed. While he was in an altercation of some kind before he died, his heart disease was advanced, as was his cancer. The ME lists both conditions as the cause of death. He couldn't believe your uncle was on his feet, let alone smashing up his apartment and leaving bruises on his ex-wife within an hour of drawing his last breath."

"So, no one murdered him, after all?"

"We're closing the investigation. Any halfway decent attorney could get Connie Delaney off, and if anyone killed him, it was her." Xavier smiled, but Grace thought it was more unnerving than the scowl she'd been wearing. "Can you understand my former partner's frustration now?"

This didn't sit well on Grace's conscience, but she couldn't change the circumstances. Connie had an alibi, and a medical examiner had provided an irrefutable cause of death. "Not my problem, then," she said to Xavier.

"Well, any ideas about who strangled Piper Tilden?"

Grace nodded. "Strictly going on the process of elimination of bad guys in our cast of characters, I'd say it was Winston Delaney, but I'm having a hard time seeing him acting alone. Or killing the girl he wanted to run away with."

Xavier nodded. "I agree. I don't think he did. And that brings us back to Dennis Mays. We may have to deal with the peeper after all. Unless, of course, Billy Keating killed her. Interesting situation, isn't it?"

CHAPTER FORTY-SEVEN

When Grace couldn't provide any information that Xavier didn't already have, the conversation was over. The detective would not be moved and Grace left the station frustrated. She was really on the outside now, and she wouldn't be surprised to return to the hotel and find Mac suddenly free to enjoy their vacation, too. The murders had all occurred in Ocean City. Mallard Bay cops and lawyers were welcome to offer assistance, but shouldn't expect to join the investigation.

She went to her hot car in the parking lot, opened the front doors to let the heat out, and called Oscar Breedlove. The connection was staticky. "How'd you like a co-counsel?" she asked, speaking louder as the noise level at his end increased. "I'll help with the grunt work."

"Which one of OC's finest kicked you out?" he asked. "My money's on Greenley. That dude does not like me. Hang on."

She waited while he ordered a double cheeseburger, fries, and a chocolate shake. Seagull squawking drowned out his next words and she could envision his car in a fast-food takeout line, being dive bombed by hungry scavengers. "You'll cement your arteries," she said when she could hear him again.

"Probably," he mumbled, then the connection cleared. "But until then, I'm William Keating's attorney and you're not. But hey, if you want to help me with my new pro bono client, I can use a paralegal."

"Done," she said. "Make a note you hired me at two thirteen. And when you finish that greasy feast, look up a guy named Dennis Mays."

"Ms. Delaney's peeper?"

"The very one. I'll be with my kids until about seven, but if you want to join Mac and me for a drink after that, we can brainstorm. Mays is going to end up behind bars for something, and the charge might be for Piper's murder. Assuming, of course, that he's guilty."

"Which you think I can prove."

"With the help of an over qualified paralegal, a chief of police, and a detective sergeant named Bernadette Xavier, yes, I think you can prove it."

She arrived at the hotel suite to find Mac rinsing a sandy baby off in the kitchen sink.

"He's not lettuce, you know," she said, bundling Sonny up in a towel.

"I do know that. But his dear old dad would prefer not to kneel on ceramic tile in the bathroom."

"Feeling our age, are we, Poppy?"

"Yep. But that's okay, because I can nap with him."

Grace checked the time and realized she'd missed all but an hour of Fiona's playtime on the beach.

Mac reached for Sonny, saying, "I promised the Nanny Squad I'd be very careful with my child, and they decided to trust me to give him a nap."

Grace was about to say that sounded wonderful when he threw her under the baby bus.

"I had to agree to send you down to take over with Fiona so they could get some swimming in before they leave for their night out. It was you or me, honey, and Little Man and I are bushed. I'll nap in the kids' room with him, in case he wakes up before I do. Right now, I think I could sleep through to tomorrow."

He looked haggard, and Sonny's eyes were already closed. She decided not to mention her invitation to Oscar until later and went to change into her swimsuit. As she was leaving the bedroom, she saw her laptop and realized she hadn't checked her emails since yesterday morning. Knowing there wouldn't be an opportunity once she had Fiona, she crossed to the small table she'd appropriated as a desk and powered up her MacBook.

One email message header stood out. Find My Roots, the DNA test she'd sent in, had results. *Close family connection discovered!* seemed to pulsate on the screen. How was that possible? The DNA sequencing was supposed to take up to four weeks for the full health results to come back.

Then she remembered the second component of the test, the one she'd convinced herself she didn't care about. The option to connect with any relatives who were also in the Find My Roots database. Those notices were sent as the connections were found. She hadn't expected to hear from anyone, but here she was, alone with a message that could change her life.

This had been her problem all along.

Grace didn't want her life to change. Not one bit of it. She didn't want Niki to leave, or Mac's knees to hurt, or her children to grow up and leave her. She didn't want a world without Avril and Cyrus, or with Delaney House in a stranger's hands.

And she felt like all of it could happen in an instant if she opened the email.

Keep moving. It had been her perpetually active mother's motto, and Grace felt Julia by her side. She opened the message and began to read.

The next hour passed in a haze of unreality as she and her daughter played in the sand and splashed in the shallow waves. The beach day left Fiona hungry and nodding off ahead of schedule, just like her brother. Grace went through all the routines while telling herself nothing was different, nothing had changed. She'd known Marcus Valenti was her father as soon as Avril had pointed to his photograph. She hadn't needed a mail-order test to connect them, but it had, and she had seriously underestimated the effect of a definitive answer to the question of her parentage.

It was complicated, of course. Valenti wasn't registered with Find My Roots, but his daughter was. StephiV1978 wanted to connect with her family, and by now, she would have gotten her own email and learned about Julia1980. At least Grace had known all along that she had a father somewhere. Marcus' daughter had probably been searching for long-lost branches of the family she knew, not her father's illegitimate child. Which, Grace realized, made her own decision easier. This test would produce the health history she needed. She also had the information Lily's friend had turned up with his ethically questionable search.

Once again, she decided to trust her mother. She knew enough about her father.

Change might come, but she didn't have to let it run over her. If the Valenti family initiated a connection, she would decide how to handle it. Until then, there was no point in wasting energy on "what ifs." She already had everything, and everyone, she needed.

CHAPTER FORTY-EIGHT

Drinks with Oscar Breedlove turned into a late dinner. He and Mac had many friends in common, and they seemed to sense that Grace's mind was drifting to other things. When she finally returned to the subject of Dennis Mays, both men looked surprised.

"Ready to share your thoughts on *our* case?" Oscar asked. "I was wondering if you'd only invited me for my charming personality and expansive contact list." His grin faded when she didn't smile at his teasing.

Grace said, "Does Mays work for anyone other than Frankie Elmer?"

Oscar said, "Not to my knowledge."

Mac agreed.

"Are you saying that because it's common knowledge, or do you have any other proof?" she asked Oscar.

"He might take an odd job on the side, or go after someone for his own reasons. He's been popped in the past for stalking women—including looking in their windows—but, no offense to Ms. Delaney, she's nowhere near Mays' type. As in, she's about four decades away. Anyway, now he's tied pretty tightly to Elmer. Or he was."

Mac said, "I knew him in the early days when I was on patrol with the MSP. I arrested him two, maybe three times, but back then, looking in uncovered windows only got you a ride home and a lecture."

Oscar said, "Still does with a good attorney."

Grace shook her head. "Surely in all these years he's been arrested for something else? Menacing? Voyeurism? Stalking?"

"Yes, yes, and yes," Mac said. "And he is always released on his own recognizance because it doesn't happen regularly—that they can prove, anyway. It's how he makes his living. He's a professional intimidator and deliverer of bad news, mostly to the late-paying customers of shady bookies and pawnbrokers like Frankie Elmer. As Frankie's business grew, so did Mays' role in it."

"They say if you love your job, you'll never work a day in your life," Oscar said. "And Dennis Mays always has a smile on his face. When he's not scaring the hell out of people, that is."

"So," Grace said slowly, her thoughts racing. "Frankie pulled him out of Mallard Bay suddenly and couldn't use him anywhere else until the investigation into Stark's death wrapped up. Stands to reason Mays had time on his hands and would be happy to take on a little job for someone else."

"Well, since Stark died before Connie and her friend tangled with the peeper, and Angela Glass and Frankie Elmer killed each other, you must be talking about Piper Tilden's murder." Oscar said.

"Who was threatened by Piper?" Mac said, and got a smile from his wife. "Who needed to stop her from talking about unlicensed gambling operating out of the back rooms at the bar?"

"Piper aligned herself with Winnie," Grace said. "Her friend, the generous and kind Mr. Delaney, told her about his handsome son and what bad breaks he'd gotten. He may have also talked about his good friend, Frankie Elmer. I'm sure Winnie and Frankie sounded better to Piper than Angie, who made her work hard and was constantly haranguing the employees about the missing money."

"You think Angie Glass sent Dennis after Piper," Oscar said.

Grace smiled. "Bingo. But first, she sent him after Winnie. She was frantic to get the twenty-five thousand back, because—regardless of how it came to be—Stark was her employee and she was responsible for the money."

"You're guessing at all of this!" Oscar protested.

But Grace wasn't finished. "I think Dennis Mays got Starks' rings from Winnie because that was about all he had left that was of any value. Dennis handed them over to Angie. And it's easy to assume Winnie also told Mays, who then told Angie, that Piper had Stark's car and cash."

Oscar looked skeptical. "And how did Dennis Mays get paid if Angie was short on money?"

Grace shrugged. "You said it yourself. He likes pretty young girls. I doubt he would have charged Angie much to visit Winnie, and Piper was probably a freebie. Remember, Mays was only supposed to get her money and maybe the car, not kill her. While he did that, Frankie was at the Blow Back In with Angie, who was trying to get him to take the rings as part of his repayment."

Mac said, "That's what they were arguing about when my overly curious wife and her hard-headed cousin showed up."

Grace ignored him. It was still a sore spot between them. "Frankie shot Angie to shut her up before she said too much in front of me. But she was armed, too. Which isn't hard to believe, given the nature of the business she was running. She didn't pull her gun until after he shot her."

Oscar said, "I may need another beer."

"Scotch?" Mac asked. "My wife has that effect on people sometimes."

But Oscar was still working out Grace's crooked trail. After a moment, he said, "Again, you can't prove any of this, can you?"

"I'm only a volunteer paralegal," she said primly. "You're the attorney of record. All you have to do is help the police arrest Mays and Winnie, then pit them against each other to see which one breaks first with verifiable information. Oh, and you only have to deal with Bernadette. Gordon's been transferred, and he's already off the case."

Oscar blinked, but didn't let her change the subject. "Well, it all fits, but if neither Delaney nor Mays back your theories, the police are going to stick with the killer they have in custody."

Grace said, "You have to start somewhere, Oscar. And once Mays and Winnie are picked up and all the forensics are completed, there's bound to be physical evidence tying Mays to Piper, and when that happens, Winnie will talk as loud and as fast as his mother does."

"I'll take that Scotch now, thanks," Oscar said, giving Mac a sympathetic look. "Man, you must buy that stuff by the case."

CHAPTER FORTY-NINE

When Bernadette Xavier stopped in to see Grace late on Tuesday, the detective was in a cooperative mood. Piper Tilden's murder had been solved on Sunday afternoon when Dennis Mays tried to sell Stark's Toyota to a used car dealer in a small town near Cincinnati. Sadly for Mays, he chose a dealership run by a retired police sergeant. The car's trunk still held a faint, but distinctive smell of bodily fluids and Mays had missed a length of rope that had been pushed behind the seat backs. The peeper was in handcuffs before he realized he was in trouble.

But it was news of another arrest that Xavier delivered to Grace with a huge smile. Winston Delaney was going to prison. He'd been stopped that morning in Miami while trying to board a non-stop flight to Venezuela. His fake passport was good but not that good, and the $75,000 the TSA agents found sewn into the lining of his carryon bag didn't help him, either. He was being returned to Maryland, and upon learning that everyone who might want to kill him was dead or awaiting trial on murder charges, he was talking as fast as he could. According to Xavier, it would take quite a while to run down all the details he'd given them on Frankie Elmer's operations, Stark Delaney's thefts, and assorted, unrelated but juicy tidbits he'd heard from Dennis Mays.

Xavier said, "According to Oscar Breedlove, you figured out most of the hows and whys on Saturday night. I wanted to be the one to tell you that you and your family are safe—at least from Winston—and the charges have been dropped against William Keating for the murder of Piper Tilden."

"Are you sure Winnie will be charged with aiding Mays in Piper's murder?" Grace asked. "If he testifies for the prosecution, he might get a pass." She didn't add that it had happened in her case three years earlier.

Xavier said, "If you'd seen him during his interrogation, you wouldn't be worried. Your cousin went through his intake procedures like he was a star witness and hadn't been brought in wearing hand-cuffs. The arresting officer said it was quite a performance. Especially when Winston asked what they were having for lunch. The guys in Miami got a chuckle out of that."

"Well, it sounds like Winnie."

"Listen," Xavier said, looking Grace squarely in the eyes. "I'm not trying to make you feel better. Winston Delaney is an arrogant fool who's already run his mouth to the point that if I follow up on every-thing he told me, I'd close half the open investigations on my desk. I'm not saying they'd stay closed, understand. Truthfulness seems to be a foreign concept to him."

Winnie's tell-all statement was just icing on the Worcester County state's attorney's case against Dennis Mays. Oscar Breedlove's persis-tence and Detective Sergeant Xavier's searches of Frankie Elmer's home and pawn shops had turned up a goldmine of evidence. In a plea deal, Mays had told all he knew about the unlicensed gambling and a money laundering business operating out of the Blow Back In.

Her smile gone, Grace asked for details.

"Frankie Elmer was sure that Connie Delaney was holding a large amount of money for her husband. He told Winston he wouldn't have sent Mays to intimidate her otherwise. The twenty-five thousand Stark Delaney skimmed off the illegal games at the Blow Back In was the perfect excuse for Frankie to come down hard on Angela, who was about to lose her share of the business to him, by the way. But what Elmer was really looking for was the half million that disappeared from his home last year during an unreported robbery. Winston told Elmer that his father had bragged about the nest egg he had and how gullible Elmer was in keeping him around. Stark was dead by then, but there was Ms. Delaney yelling for all she was worth that her husband had money and had given it to Piper Tilden."

"Unbelievable," Grace said, even though it really wasn't. They were talking about Stark, Winnie, and Connie, after all. "What do you think happened to the five hundred thousand?"

"We're working on tracing the $75,000 your cousin had. If there was really a theft from Elmer's home, and if Stark Delaney was the thief, then the money he left his son was more than we were originally told."

"A lot of *ifs*," Grace said.

"And most of them won't be resolved. But my point is, Winston Delaney will be back in Jessup for the rest of his original sentence, and he could get another stretch for his part in Piper Tilden's death. He's insisting Mays strangled her and then forced him to help dispose of her body, but it'll take a murder trial to sort that out. Mays says Winston killed her and used her car to transport the body to the freezer in the alley behind the Blow Back In."

"Will you look for whatever is left of Elmer's money?"

Xavier said, "So far, we can't prove there ever was any stolen money. Not from the Blow Back In and not from Elmer's home. Elmer's wife said there was no theft. Angela Glass handled the finances at the bar, and she's dead. Someone in the state attorney's office might decide it's worth pursuing, but at what cost? An investigation would be expensive."

"But you think the money was stolen, right?" Grace asked.

"Maybe, if your cousin and your aunt were telling the truth."

"I wish you'd quit calling them that," Grace said.

Xavier laughed. "We've all got them, you know. Family. You can't live with them, and it's messy if you kill them."

Grace remembered those words when Connie arrived a few minutes later, without an appointment and insisting she had to have a restraining order to protect her from Winnie. Grace broke the news about Winnie, and for once, there were no tears from his mother.

"I don't want to be relieved," Connie said. "But I am. It will all hit me one day and I'll fall apart then, but right now, I have to be strong and make myself a priority. I want to do what's right. It's just . . ."

"No money," Grace said wearily. "I'm sorry about what happened to you, but—"

"Oh, I don't need money." Connie stopped, seemed to reconsider, and started over. "I'll be fine. I have an aunt in Wyoming who's gotten in touch. She wants me to stay with her for a while and I've decided to accept her offer. I'm actually leaving today."

"Okay." Grace drew it out. She'd never heard about any family of Connie's.

"But I need to take action against Winnie. He called me last night. He was crying and begging me for help, but the things he's done can't be reversed. He said I have to get him a good lawyer and fight the charges. And he said I had to give him money because he couldn't be in prison without it and he'd spent everything Stark had given him."

"Where did he get the $75,000 he had on him when he was arrested?"

"I don't know," Connie snapped. "And I don't want to know. I'm afraid of him, Grace. He was always his father's child, and I've never understood him. Stark used to visit him in prison and they talked. I never went. I just couldn't bear it and Stark always said to let him handle Winnie. It was the only thing we agreed on at the end. The money came from Stark, somehow, and now that it's been confiscated by the police, Winnie says it's my turn to take care of him. A restraining order will make him stop."

"How?" Grace asked. "It won't be valid in Wyoming."

"No. But it will get him in trouble with the prison authorities. I've called everyone I can think of and reported that he's threatening me, and no one seems to care. Maybe they'll pay attention to you and a court order."

DNA, Grace thought. DNA was on full display right in front of her. Mother and son were two sides of the same coin. "No," she said. "And don't bother Cy, either."

Unfazed, Connie looked at her watch and stood up. "So, you won't help me. I'm not surprised. I'll handle it on my own, like always. Tell Niki I'm sorry about the damage to the garage apartment at Queen's Brooke. I hope that doesn't mess up her sale of the place. That's final today, right?"

The statement was too casual, and too late to give Niki time to make repairs. "Is this how you make yourself a priority?" Grace asked, then had to endure a stream of outraged squawking. Wearily, she said, "What kind of damage?"

"Oh, it's really nothing." Connie said with a sniff. "Things got out of hand when Winnie was there. He got antsy that afternoon before you two arrived, and put a few holes in the kitchen wall, and dismantled the ice maker in the freezer. Oh, and he ripped up the carpet in a couple of places. Just a wild child, he never changes. I'm sure Niki's insurance will cover the damages."

Grace remembered how easily Winnie accepted Niki's order to leave the night they'd met at Queen's Brooke. Had he grown tired of looking for the money Stark had stolen from Frankie's home and the Blow Back In? Or had he found the money?

Had Connie?

She wished she could do Avril's stink eye glare. "So, you have enough cash to get you settled in your new life? How'd you get it?"

Connie said, "You're sweet, but don't worry about me. You watch things here like Cy always has, and I'll take care of myself. And Grace? The only reason I can leave Niki with a clear conscience is because she has you and a good life. I hope she remembers her father wasn't always a bad person. We loved each other, once upon a time, and even at the end, he loved me, it just took me a while to find the proof."

"Where was it?" Grace asked, for once hoping Connie would keep talking and boast about having Frankie Elmer's money.

"He still loved me, and that's what's important. I burned the envelope with all of those bills—they can't get money I don't have, right? So, I'll file for bankruptcy when I'm settled in Wyoming. Niki is selling our house, and Stark sold everything else I had that was important to me. I'm free." She paused at the door, blew Grace a kiss, and was gone.

Grace considered her options. Should she call Bernadette? And tell her what? Connie hadn't said anything they could act on.

And she was leaving town.

Mac. She'd talk to Mac, and they'd work it all out. But for now, Connie and her antics weren't her problem.

Bigger things were on the horizon.

CHAPTER FIFTY

To Grace's surprise, Mac agreed with Bernadette's assessment that there was nothing to investigate regarding Stark's alleged thefts. He was equally unexcited about Connie's announcement that Stark had left proof of his love for her.

"The woman lies like a rug," he said. "If Stark stole money from Frankie, it wasn't the kind that could be deposited in a bank, or the kind Connie can flash around if she wants to stay alive. Frankie had a lot of enemies and all of them would love a chance to get some of their lost bets back. Now, let it go. If there was ever an NMP, this is it."

Grace hadn't been sure what to expect when she told Niki about Connie's move to Wyoming, but a shrug and a smile hadn't been her first guess.

"It's the poem, don't you see?" Niki said. "I can't believe I've figured it out and you haven't. It reads as if Dad was taking the things we wanted most away from us, but some of us benefitted from his odd gifts."

Niki had been busy with the inns and a side trip to New York, and this was the first chance they'd had to catch up since Ocean City. They were in the front parlor of Delaney House, having cocktails under their grandmother's bemused gaze. Mac brought in a second round of drinks, handing a glass of Pinot Grigio to Grace and a martini with olives to Niki. He was still on his first beer and paying close attention to the conversation.

Grace recognized his expression. The cop was on duty.

"How so?" he asked Niki. "Connie's credit is ruined, she's being threatened by Winnie, and she's reduced to living on the other side of the country with her aunt. Winnie's in prison, and Piper's dead. You have earrings with fake stones, instead of the real ones Emma left you." He stopped short.

"Go on," Grace said. "Say it. I've driven you crazy over the yearbook."

"Not so much lately."

If Niki noticed the change in tone in their conversation, she ignored it. "You're looking at all of it in a negative light," she said earnestly. "Dad showed his love for me by duplicating the earrings when he could have just blamed everything on Mom. He loved Winnie and took care of him the only way he knew how. Dad never admitted how ruthless Winnie is, and he never imagined his son would be a spy for the police, or that he would double cross Frankie, and turn on Mom. My brother is back in prison because he belongs there, not because Dad tried to help him."

"Interesting," Mac said. "Gin really improves your mood, doesn't it?"

"Even Mom's okay," Niki said. "She's starting over and I, for one, don't think past due bills were the only thing Dad left her. She can finally live out her dreams and leave me alone."

Grace decided not to ask what those dreams might be. "What about Piper?" she asked.

"I think Dad really enjoyed giving a pretty young girl money, and the car, and setting her up with his son. But Winnie and Piper squandered the favors he tried to do for them. Winnie because he was greedy, and Piper because she was dumb enough to believe everything Winnie said."

"Go on," Grace said. "Tell me what you think about my gift from Stark."

Niki's face fell. "I can't see that you got anything good from that yearbook, but you're still happy. Dad wasn't able to hurt you, and I'm so grateful for that."

Grace looked at Mac, who nodded.

"What?" Niki asked, perking up a bit.

"Actually," Grace said. "Your father gave me a wonderful gift."

She'd told Mac about StephiV1978 while they were still at the beach. He'd been surprised, then worried, but after much debate, he stopped throwing advice around and waited for her to decide what she wanted to do. Grace remained steadfast in her decision not to contact Marcus Valenti's daughter.

Then, as they'd been about to leave to meet with Niki that afternoon, Grace checked her email and saw another message from Find My Roots. She read it then passed her laptop to Mac, whose only response had been to hug her and whisper, "Whatever you decide, honey."

Avril might never have told Grace the little, but vital, bit of information she knew about Jonathan if she hadn't been questioned about the yearbook. And Grace wouldn't have taken a DNA test if she had been able to put the yearbook out of her mind. Leaving the long story for another day, she told Niki about the test and the results.

"Jonathan's real and he's in the yearbook?" Niki said, shaking her head in amazement. "Our parents were just full of surprises, weren't they?"

"Only one thing left to do," Grace said when they got home.

"Now?" Mac asked. "You don't have to rush, you know."

"I think I do. She's waiting for an answer, and I know how that feels."

In her little office off the kitchen, she opened her laptop and reread the Find My Roots message from StephieV1978.

My name is Stephanie Valenti Rogers and I've been on this website for six months hoping to find the answer to a mystery. I checked in today and saw our link. Your user name, Julia1980, was a huge shock. You have to be the person I've been looking for, but the link says we're half-sisters, so Julia might be your mother? And if she is, I hope that means your name is Grace. If it is, your father—our father—would very much like to see you. So would I.

Grace closed her eyes and listened to her children's voices in the next room, mixed with ambient noises from the Orioles game Mac was watching. This was the safest place she knew, and she'd waited long enough. She clicked 'reply' and began to type.

Hello, Stephanie.

My name is Grace Reagan McNamara and I am your sister.

THE END

AUTHOR'S NOTE

Many kind and generous people assisted me in bringing this book to life. I took advantage of them shamelessly, and their talents and patience are sincerely appreciated.

First readers Vicki Ellingson, Cindy Haddaway, and Judith Hohman provided excellent feedback, as always. They remained cheerful and enthusiastic in the face of garbled drafts and last-minute copy errors. They are all talented editors who are generous with their time and I am so grateful to have their help.

Elaine Hyatt of Clarity Editing Services saved me from my comma addiction and dozens of other grammatical errors. She also saved Grace and Mac when I had them bouncing around the storyline like drunk time travelers. Thank you, Elaine, for keeping up with four plots and for making me look good, but you know I changed a few things after I said it was a wrap, right?

All errors in this book are mine.

As always, thank you to my family: Ron, Patrick, Kate, James, Jack, and Miss Ellie Grace, the Wonder Spaniel. Each of you is a blessing in my life.

Finally, to my sister, Clara Ellingson (Vicki). It's only fitting that this is your book. May Grace's sister turn out to be half as wonderful as mine.

May 1, 2023
Easton, Maryland

And the Winners Are . . .

A special thank you to the winners of the "Name the Characters" contest that ran in the November edition of **The Eastern Shore Mysteries Newsletter.** The following good natured (and talented!) readers helped name four new characters who make their debut in this book.

Shout outs to:
Myrna B. for Detective Sergeant "**Gordon**" Greenley
Terry Sue G. for "**Regina**" Waller
Lisa S. for Detective Sergeant "**Bernadette**" Xavier
and
Mary T. for "**Stephanie**" Valenti

If you aren't a member of the monthly newsletter gang, what are you waiting for? You can sign up on my website and get a free short story.

https://www.CherilThomas.com

Thank You!

I have the most wonderful readers any author could ask for. Your reviews, notes, and kind words are such blessings and I am so grateful for each one of you. I hope you'll keep in touch with me—and of course, keep reading! Book 7 will be out early 2024.

You can reach me through my website, on Facebook, or my Amazon Author Page. I hope to hear from you!

www.CherilThomas.com for series info and newsletter sign up, including back issues. You'll also receive a **FREE short story**!

The Eastern Shore Mysteries Facebook Page. "Follow" my page for (almost) daily updates from the Eastern Shore, as well as related topics, photographs, and things that make me smile.

Cheril Thomas Amazon Author Page. "Follow" me here and you'll be notified when I release a new book, or when there's a sales promotion.

Until next time, happy reading!
Cheril

ABOUT THE AUTHOR

Cheril Thomas is the author of the Eastern Shore Mysteries series, numerous short stories, and articles. When she's not writing at home in Easton, Maryland, she's traveling with her long-suffering husband, an otherwise brilliant soul who for some reason doesn't mind being married to a woman who researches methods of murder. Their lives are directed by a sassy little spaniel named Ellie Grace.

Connect with Cheril on her website and sign up to get the latest news from the Eastern Shore Mysteries. You'll receive a FREE short story as a thank you gift! **www.cherilthomas.com**